Praise for Shirley Wells's previous book
Presumed Dead

"I almost felt as though I was right there witnessing some of these conversations, leaning forward in my chair to see what witnesses would say.… The interrelationships between the people in the town are almost as intriguing as the mystery itself and the author lets readers piece together images of Dawson's Clough in bits and snatches. The setting is most definitely not a generic one, and it gave the story a brooding mood, which matched Dylan Scott's character well indeed."
—*All About Books*

"The characters' lives are all interwoven, and as you read along, you wonder just who hated Anita Champion, a happy-go-lucky woman, enough to want to harm her. There's no end of suspects, several guilty parties and no real hope for a happy ending when the mystery is solved. Ms. Wells keeps you turning those pages, though! I look forward to reading more of Shirley Wells' work."
—*Journey of a Bookseller*

"Excellent read, worthy of a five-star rating. Shirley Wells does an incredible job of writing a fast-paced thriller that will have you guessing until the end.… The quick pace of this book will keep you up at night, wanting to find out what the next page holds."
—John O. Raab, editor of *Suspense Magazine*

SHIRLEY WELLS

was born and raised in the Cotswolds, where her headmaster wrote on her school report, "Shirley is content to dream her life away."

Years later—as an adult living in Cyprus—it dawned on her that this wasn't necessarily a bad thing and that fellow dreamers, in the guise of fiction writers, had been getting away with it for centuries.

A move to the Orkney island of Hoy followed and, during the twelve years she spent there, she wrote short stories as well as full-length romantic fiction for U.K. women's magazines.

She's now settled in Lancashire, where the Pennines provide the inspiration and setting for her popular mystery novels. She and her husband share their home with an ever-changing selection of deranged pets, who often insist on cameo roles in Shirley's novels.

When she isn't writing, Shirley loves reading (anything and everything), listening to live music, watching TV, eating chocolate and drinking whiskey—though not necessarily at the same time. She's also a season ticket holder at Burnley Football Club and can often be seen in the biting wind and pouring rain cheering on her favorite team.

And she's still content to dream her life away.

Dead Silent

SHIRLEY WELLS

CARINA
PRESS™

To my partners in crime.
(You know who you are.)

CARINA PRESS™

ISBN-13: 978-0-373-06263-8

DEAD SILENT

Recycling programs
for this product may
not exist in your area.

Dead Silent

Many people helped make this book possible.

Thanks must go to family and friends for their unfailing
support, and to the amazing team at Carina Press,
especially my awesome editor, Deborah Nemeth,
for taking this story and making it so much better.

The biggest acknowledgment of all goes to my husband,
who is my sounding board, critic, first reader, best friend
and bringer of chocolate and whiskey. Thank you!

ONE

DYLAN didn't believe in spirits, vampires or zombies, but if the undead *were* stalking the planet, they couldn't feel any worse than he did right now. He'd only managed a couple of hours' sleep and his eyes felt like gravel pits. The motorways had been stop-start because of roadworks, and later a collision, so he'd spent six hours in his car.

He was awake enough to know that a black Jeep had been tailing him for the last ten miles though.

He left the motorway and drove down into Rawtenstall, where a Tesco superstore loomed on his right. He turned in to the car park and checked his rearview mirror. Sure enough, the Jeep followed.

Dylan parked his Morgan as near to the store's entrance as he could. It was bliss to get out and stretch his stiff muscles.

God knows what was happening with the weather. An ominously dark sky glowered at him. The air was heavy with moisture and it was as hot as hell.

He ambled slowly toward the store's entrance and stood for a moment to gaze at the window, where he saw the reflection of a tall, well-muscled man wearing a white T-shirt and ill-fitting black jeans.

Dylan strolled into the store and stopped to look at

the newspapers' front pages. He walked on, past the café where the smell of roast beef made him salivate, and to the door marked Customer Toilets.

No one else was in the Gents, and he stood behind the door, muscles tensed. God, he could do without this.

Moments later, the door opened to give him a brief glimpse of black jeans and white T-shirt. It was enough. He lunged at the figure and slammed him against the white tiles. "Right, Sunshine, what's your game?"

"Hey, steady on. I don't know what you're talking about." He spoke with a local accent.

"I'm sure you do. Out with it."

Dylan released his grip slightly. Big mistake. The lump of muscle landed a punch that had blood spurting from Dylan's mouth.

"I've got a message for you, mate. Stay away from Dawson's Clough. Stay. Away. Got that?"

Dylan spat out some blood. "Says who?"

"Says me. Crawl back to where you came from, okay? If you're seen round here again, you won't be walking away."

Dylan was about to argue when a fist flew into his face. A punch in the ribs had him dropping to his knees. A kick in the stomach followed.

He managed to twist away from the boot that was aiming for his teeth by falling back and hitting his skull on the hard tiled floor. His head screamed in pain before the silent blackness wrapped around him like a blanket. He welcomed it. Sank into it willingly.

TWO

"CHRIST, you look like crap, mate."

"As good as that, eh?" Dylan shared an awkward embrace with Frank, ex-D.C.I. Willoughby, the man who had once been his boss and who had since become a good friend. "You reckon I'll survive then?"

"What happened?"

Dylan nodded at the pub. "Let's go inside, shall we? And I'm sorry I'm late."

"What happened?" Frank asked again as they crossed the car park to the pub.

"I ran into a spot of bother on the way here."

"What sort of bother?"

Dylan pushed open the door and headed for the nearest table and chairs. Sitting was slightly less painful than standing, he'd discovered. "Some bastard tailed me along the M66. We met up at Tesco's and had a bit of a disagreement."

"About what?"

Dylan wasn't entirely sure. He'd been warned away from the area, but not from any specific person. "He said I was to keep away from Dawson's Clough. Threatened me with broken kneecaps if I went poking my nose where it wasn't wanted."

"Bloody hell, Dylan."

That about summed it up.

When he'd regained consciousness, he'd been lying beneath the washbasins. He'd struggled to his feet and leaned against the cool tiles for a good five minutes until the dizziness subsided.

It was impossible to tell if any ribs were broken, but a quick and very gentle exploration with his tongue reassured him that no teeth were missing. His lip was bleeding badly though and he had to wash his face in cold water several times.

Did he have the registration plate of that Jeep? Did he—hell. RW. He was sure there was a RW in the registration.

He left the supermarket with his hair sticking up everywhere—not that he could entirely blame that on the lump of muscle—his lip swelling to the size of a small country, his ribs screaming in agony, and his shirt spattered with blood.

He'd had better days.

After checking in at his hotel, he'd washed his mouth yet again and changed his blood-stained shirt. He knew he still looked a mess.

"So what are you going to do?" Frank asked.

"Avoid big ugly brutes in black Jeeps." Dylan was going to do what he'd come to Lancashire for, and that was look into the disappearance of a young woman, one Samantha Hunt. "Perhaps he got the wrong bloke. Why the hell would anyone want me warned off? More to the point, how would anyone know I was here?"

"Search me." Frank scratched his head. "Unless

Rob's told people. I know he's grown friendly with one of the local reporters. You can't blame him for that as he wants people to know Sam's still missing."

"Christ, Frank." When they'd spoken on the phone, Dylan had specifically asked Rob Hunt not to announce his involvement. "If he's told some bloody reporter, I won't be going anywhere incognito, will I? It won't make the job easy."

Dylan would think better on a full stomach. "Let's get something to eat. I'm starving."

They'd chosen to meet at the Mill, a pub on the outskirts of Dawson's Clough that offered a menu of traditional English food. Dylan's breakfast had been a mug of strong coffee, and the aroma coming from the dining room was delicious. If his mouth hadn't been throbbing like something from a Tom and Jerry cartoon, it might even have watered.

Their table overlooked a lake at the rear of the pub. A chevron of ducks flew in to land with a splash. The sun peeped out from heavy dark clouds to glint on the water as the ducks splashed.

The hills swept down to the valley and the town. From above, Dawson's Clough looked to be a haphazard sprinkling of old townhouses and tall chimneys that served as a reminder of the town's once-thriving cotton industry. The mills had long been silent. Some had been abandoned to the elements, others had been redeveloped to offer luxury accommodation.

Several people had chosen to sit at tables outside and were being mobbed by greedy, squawking ducks. It was as noisy inside until a mother grabbed her two shrieking children and ushered them out to the small play area.

"Never mind my problems," Dylan said. "How are you, Frank? You look pretty good."

Frank looked in great shape. No one would have guessed that, since his heart attack, he spent half his life attending hospital appointments and the other half concentrating on his diet.

"I'm fighting fit."

Fit but lonely, Dylan guessed. Frank had divorced three wives and was then forced to retire from the job he loved because of ill health. He had too much time on his hands.

Dylan knew what that was like. After a spell in prison, he too had spent months being totally aimless. He'd felt like a waste of space.

He pushed the thought aside and studied the menu. He needed a decent-sized steak and chips. By the time Frank had decided on a chicken salad, the waitress was there to take their order.

"So how does it feel to be back in Lancashire?" Frank asked when they were alone again.

"Bloody painful." Dylan dabbed at his lip to check that it wasn't bleeding. "And it feels a long way from home." Strangely, it had been good to see landmarks that had become familiar to him. Dawson's Clough was a typical northern town that would struggle to find its way into a tourist brochure, yet, thanks to the sweeping Pennines that surrounded it, it had a beauty of its own. "It's good really."

It was thanks to Frank that he was in the county.

Frank had given his contact details to his friend, Rob Hunt, and Dylan, reluctant at first, had agreed to look into the disappearance of Hunt's daughter.

He'd thought getting registered as a private investigator was a good idea, but he had no real enthusiasm for the job. Other than some matrimonial work, which had to be the dullest pastime ever, he'd had one missing-person case. Thanks to his success—or luck—with that, he now had a second case.

On hearing it meant returning to Lancashire, he would have turned it down, not because he had anything against the place, but because it was over two hundred miles from his home, his wife and his son. Hunt had opted for the emotional blackmail card, though. He'd told Dylan he'd been diagnosed with terminal lung cancer and Dylan, probably foolishly, had let his heart rule his head and accepted the job.

"I don't go much on the weather, though," Dylan said. "It's like a bloody sauna out there."

"Too true. It's too hot to sleep. Too hot to do anything. Still, a good thunderstorm will sort it."

"Let's hope so."

"How's Bev, by the way?" Frank asked.

"Fine." Dylan expelled his breath. "Well, as fine as she ever is."

"You're still in that flat then?"

Give Bev her due, when she threw a tantrum, it was a damned impressive one. Most women would sulk for a couple of days. Bev had thrown him out, found him the smallest flat in the land. "She's making noises about us living together again, just to see how it goes, and I know it's only a matter of time before I'm back home, but yeah, I'm still in that sodding flat."

That was another reason he'd felt obliged to look into the disappearance of Hunt's daughter. He was paying the mortgage on the marital home, rent on the pocket-sized broom cupboard his bastard of a landlord insisted on calling a studio apartment, as well as maintenance on two cars. He had no idea where Bev's salary was going, but he was broke.

"Can't you just apologise to her?" Frank asked.

"Apologise for what? Being a drunkard and a loser? That's why she threw me out. A drunkard and a bloody loser, she called me."

Frank tried to hide his smile. And failed. "I expect it was difficult for her. You ending up on an assault charge, I mean."

"It wasn't a picnic for me."

"True. But at least you understand the politics behind it all. Today, you'd be hailed a hero for taking a known thug off the streets."

Infuriating to know that Frank was right. The force had been having one of its cleanup sessions to show the public that complaints about their officers were taken seriously. There was no use worrying about it now though. Dylan had served his sentence and lost his job, and Bev had thrown her strop.

"If you ask me, Bev reads too many magazines filled with articles about women intent on finding themselves. Whatever that means. Or she spends too much time with my crank of a mother." He smiled as much as his lip would allow. "Bev flits from one—

idea to another and she's busy applying for jobs at the moment. The headmaster where she teaches is quite young so his job won't be coming vacant for a while. She wants a head's job so says she'll move out of London if necessary. It's just a funny phase she's going through, that's all. She'll soon come round."

Women, and Bev in particular, were a mystery to Dylan and he refused to dwell on his marital problems.

"I hope you're right," Frank said.

Of course he was right. "It'll serve her right if they offer her a job in the Outer bloody Hebrides."

Their food was brought to the table and Dylan tucked in. His steak, medium rare, was exquisite, but it was difficult eating with a lip that hit the fork ten seconds before the rest of his mouth.

"What about this bloke who split your lip?" Frank asked. "Would you recognise him again?"

"Too right I would. About six feet two. Tall. All muscle. Ex-copper or army perhaps. About my age. Dark hair. Yes, I'd recognise him."

"And you reckon he was trying to stop you digging into Sam's disappearance?" Frank was frowning. He clearly found it as surprising as Dylan did.

"I don't know. All I know is that he wanted me away from Dawson's Clough."

"Seems a bit bloody odd."

"Tell me about it."

Only a person who knew there was something sinister surrounding Samantha Hunt's disappearance would want him out of the way. Unless it was a case of mistaken identity.

"Did you manage to find anything out from our friends at Lancashire CID?"

"Not a lot." Frank chewed on a lettuce leaf. "Sam's disappearance was taken very seriously but, other than lots of possible sightings that led nowhere, nothing turned up. Oh, except a scarf. They found a scarf that everyone—everyone except Rob that is—said was hers."

"What made him think it wasn't?"

"Denial, I think."

"But why? A scarf doesn't mean she's dead."

"No, but it makes the idea more feasible. It hints at a struggle of sorts."

Dylan wasn't so sure that it did. It simply said that she'd been there. "So what's Rob like? Apart from being a blasted liar."

"Dylan, he's not."

"He's exactly that. When we first spoke, he said his daughter had been missing for two years. Two years, Frank."

"Well, yes, but he's explained that. He thought you specialised in cold cases." Frank filled their glasses with water. "Like it or not, you're something of a celebrity in these parts. People think you can work miracles, so they'll say anything to get you to listen."

"They must think I'm a pretty stupid celebrity. Surely he knew I'd look it up?"

"Of course he did." Frank took a long drink of

water. "He believed that if he could just get you here and talk to you, you'd take the case. He simply—"

"Lied."

"No. He exaggerated a little to get you here, that's all."

Dylan didn't appreciate being taken for a fool, but he was here now. And he needed the money. "So what's he like?"

Frank moved some salad around his plate with his fork. "It's difficult to say really. I haven't seen him for a while."

"What? But I thought he was a friend."

"He is. Was." Frank gave a self-conscious shrug. "We exchange Christmas cards but that's about all these days. His ex-wife, Marion, and my ex-wife used to be friends. Probably still are for all I know. I phoned him when I first heard about Sam, of course. I told him to give me a shout if there was anything I could do, and I tried to reassure him that some of the best officers were looking for her." He speared another lettuce leaf. "I didn't hear from him again until he asked for your phone number. It was Marion's idea to use you. She'd seen your name in the paper—Mr. Miracle Worker—and there was a reference to me. As soon as they realised I knew you, Rob phoned."

So they weren't the close buddies Hunt had led Dylan to believe. Still, he wasn't taking the job because of their friendship. Even if he hadn't needed the money, he would have agreed to look into Samantha's disappearance in the hope that he could give Hunt some peace in his final months. Hunt's daughter had set off for work one morning, ten months ago, and had never been seen again. It was every parent's nightmare.

Frank put down his knife and fork and took a sip of his mineral water. "He's seen a medium."

"A medium what?" Realisation dawned. "Oh, Christ, not a bloody clairvoyant?"

"This one definitely calls herself a medium. I suppose Rob's desperate enough to try anything. He visited this medium—she's highly rated and has been on the telly apparently—to see if she could let him know if Sam was dead. That's what they do, isn't it? Get messages from the spirit world?"

"Con people out of their money more like."

"Yeah, well, apparently this medium told him his daughter is still alive. She said she'd seen her."

"Great."

"In the same situation as Rob, we'd probably all go a bit mad," Frank said.

He was right. If anything like that happened to Luke, Dylan would be beside himself. All the same, Dylan knew he wouldn't waste his breath talking to mediums, clairvoyants or whatever else they chose to call themselves.

"Samantha's case didn't get much national coverage," he said. "Why was that?"

"Come on, Dylan, you know as well as I do that a lot of missing-person cases go unreported. It depends on age, resources, other crimes at the time, even photographs."

As crazy as it sounded, Frank was right. Dylan

remembered his days on the police force when some
missing persons, usually cute, blond-haired blue-eyed
children, filled all available media slots and some, especially those over eighteen, barely warranted a mention.

"Did you know Samantha?" Dylan asked.

"Not really, no. Rob's a member of the golf club,
or was, and I only really saw him there. Our wives—
ex-wives—sometimes arranged things so I'd see him
then and sometimes Sam too. I'd recognise her, but
that's about all."

Frank's plate was empty. It was taking Dylan twice
as long to eat because of his battered lip, so he concentrated on his food and wondered why anyone
would go to the trouble of warning him off. It didn't
make any sense. Perhaps, after all, it had been a case
of mistaken identity.

They chatted about old times over coffee and then
it was time for Dylan to make himself known to Hunt.

"It's a bit out in the sticks," Frank said. "Do you
want directions?"

"No, I'm fine, thanks. I've got the sat nav."

THREE

Sods Law or Murphy's? Dylan didn't know. He did know, however, that since investing in a disgustingly expensive satellite navigation system, he'd spent half his life getting lost. The smug voice's "Complete a U-turn when possible" drove him crazy.

He parked his car in front of a row of shops, mainly fast-food outlets, and dashed inside the newsagent's. It had probably featured in a Charles Dickens novel, with the overall-clad man behind the counter stealing the scene.

Dylan inched his way to the counter, avoiding stands full of greetings cards, plastic toys and tins of cat food. "Excuse me, but I'm looking for Hayden's Row. I wonder if you could give me directions."

"Of course." The man behind the counter had been sorting out huge piles of magazines. "You go to the end of this road and—" He broke off, tore a small white paper bag from a string behind him and groped in the pocket of his overall. What he found was a two-inch pencil. "I'll draw you a map."

It wasn't necessary. Dylan was quite capable of following directions, even wrong directions that his sat nav insisted on giving him, but he was grateful for the help.

The man licked his thumb and forefinger to wet the pencil's lead. Why did people do that?

With the paper on top of the magazines—hiding naked brunettes destined for the top shelf—he began to draw.

"Anywhere in particular?" he asked.

"Yes, Wickham House. Do you know it?"

"Oh, yes. It's a big place. Huge." He drew a small square on his map, put a cross through it, held it at arm's length to check for errors and handed it to Dylan. "There you go. You can't miss it."

Dylan had been driving round the area for at least an hour before stopping to ask for directions, so he probably had missed it. Half a dozen times.

"Thanks for your help," he said. "I appreciate it."

"That's not your car, is it, mate?"

Dylan's car, a 1956 Morgan in Daytona Yellow, always attracted attention. He glanced outside, ready to bask in the reflected glory of those oh-so-fine lines—and saw a traffic warden writing out a ticket.

"Hell's teeth. Thanks for this. Must dash." Dylan kept his elbows tight in as he escaped the shop and managed not to bring the entire stock with him.

The traffic warden—a vast bulk of what would loosely be described as female—was putting the ticket under the windscreen wiper. Dylan grabbed her arm. "Hey, no. Wait. You can't do that. I only nipped in the newsagent's to get directions."

She looked from his face to the hand on her arm. "That's what they all say." She shook herself free.

"Pay the fine within seven days and it'll cost you less."

"But I've been parked here for two minutes. Literally. Two. Minutes."

She wasn't particularly tall but she was as wide as she was high. She was more pit bull terrier than woman.

"Then it was an expensive two minutes, wasn't it?" She nodded at the No Parking sign. "You'd have to be blind to miss that, dear. As I said, pay it within seven days."

She was walking away.

"Are you married?" Dylan called after her.

She turned to look at him as if he were mad. Which he was. Absolutely furious. "No."

"Now why am I not surprised?"

Something approaching a smile touched her gruesome features. "Ah, but I'm not the one with the parking ticket, am I? Have a nice day, sir."

"I've certainly made yours, haven't I?"

She strutted along the street, paying Dylan and his insults no heed whatsoever.

"Welcome to bloody Lancashire." Clutching the parking ticket and his map, Dylan got in his car.

People—well, Bev really—accused him of being a misogynist. It wasn't him. It was women. They were the bane of his blasted existence. It was getting to the stage when Dylan wouldn't much care if he never saw another.

Bev couldn't seem to grasp that it was expensive as well as inconvenient for him to squat in the smallest flat in the land while she rattled about in the marital home.

The dope-smoking, leaf-eating irritation he was forced to call Mother refused to return to her own home. For some reason that he'd never been able to fathom, he loved the woman dearly, but try as he might—and God he'd tried—he couldn't get rid of her. Dylan's hopes had rocketed when her new man, Richard, had taken her to Greece. It hadn't worked out, though. Richard, she'd claimed, was "too stuck in his ways." The bloke was heading toward seventy, for God's sake. He was entitled to be stuck in his ways.

Dylan fired the engine and set off, giving the traffic warden a suitably rude gesture as he passed her.

After driving the length of Barley Road, something he'd already done three times, he glanced at the map and, as instructed, took a left. That was something he hadn't done, mainly because it looked like a dead end. He drove cautiously and it narrowed still further so the hedges were in danger of scratching the Morgan's paintwork. After a sharp bend, it widened again, allowing two vehicles to pass each other if the drivers were careful. Knowing his luck, he'd meet a female driver who was busy applying mascara or reading a blasted magazine as she drove. They should be banned from the road.

If the map was correct, and Dylan had to assume it was, there should be a right turn at the end of this road. Sure enough—

The heat was becoming even more oppressive, if that were possible. It was unbearable. Heat was fine.

Humidity was the killer. That leaden sky still threatened thunder.

Despite feeling as if he'd stepped into Dante's inferno, Dylan could appreciate his surroundings. The sweeping hills that circled Dawson's Clough were spectacular. Apart from the long drive and the split lip, he was happy enough to be in Lancashire. While Bev was "getting her head sorted," whatever that meant, and while he had to share a pokey flat with his mother, being two hundred and fifty miles away from home wasn't a huge disadvantage.

He whistled as he spotted it. There, right at the end, peering down at the road from its lofty perch, was Wickham House.

It was rare for him to be impressed by people's homes. After all, bricks and mortar could be presented in thousands of different shapes and sizes. Wickham House was something special though, and it certainly boasted one hell of a lot of bricks—or in this case, local stone. The building was vast, square with arched windows. Probably a listed building, it had a stately-home air to it. Half a dozen other properties, mostly bungalows, were scattered along the road, but Wickham House looked down on them all.

A four-car garage sat to one side. Neatly trimmed lawns sloped down to the pavement. Two bay trees stood sentrylike beside the wide oak door. To the left of the property, Dylan could see the corner of a tennis court.

He supposed he shouldn't have been surprised by the house. Its owner was an architect, someone who appreciated fine buildings. Dylan had also been assured, by said owner, that money was no object when it came to his fee. Somewhat sceptical of such claims, he'd looked up Hunt on the internet. He'd designed a huge, modern hotel in Manchester that had won him several awards. Hunt wasn't just an architect, he was a very successful architect.

Dylan drove onto the steep driveway and hoped the Morgan's handbrake wouldn't let him down. Parking anywhere else, like the road, wasn't an option. The way his luck was going, his car would end up on the wrong side of a cattle stampede.

He grabbed his briefcase—there was very little of use in it but it gave him a businesslike air—looked at the ominous black clouds and put the Morgan's hood up. Then he strode across to that oak door and prodded a finger at a brass push.

The door was opened immediately as if the man looking at him had been standing behind it waiting for him.

"Dylan Scott? Rob Hunt. Good to meet you."

"You too." They shook hands. "Sorry I'm late, but I had a bit of trouble finding you."

"No problem. Are you all right? Your face—"

"What? Oh, yes, I'm fine." Dylan ran a finger across his lip. "I had a spot of bother on the way here."

"I'm sorry to hear that." Hunt was still for a moment as he gazed at Dylan's car. The expression on his face was difficult to fathom. Not envy or admiration. It was more—sad. "That's yours, I take it?"

"It is, yes."

Hunt nodded but didn't comment.

He was late forties, thin and gaunt, dark-haired and, against all odds, managed to look cool. His clothes were quality, but either he'd lost weight since he'd bought them or, like Dylan, couldn't be bothered to try them on for size before buying. Given his state of health, he'd probably lost weight. A slim gold Rolex watch peeked out from a shirt cuff, and the bracelet needed a link or two removing.

"Come inside." He stepped back, allowing Dylan to enter. "I'm sorry. My ex-wife should be here to meet you, but she couldn't make it."

"That's okay. I'll catch up with her later."

"We'll go into the study, shall we? It'll be more comfortable there."

Dylan glanced through a couple of open doors along the wide hallway and thought the whole house looked comfortable. Acres of polished hardwood floor were adorned with expensive rugs.

"Here." Hunt pushed open a door and stood back. "Take a seat. Now, can I get you something to eat or drink? You must want something after your long journey." He spoke quickly, as if he didn't have time for the social niceties.

"I'm fine, thanks. I met up with Frank for a meal."

"Ah, Frank. I keep meaning to invite him over. Time just flies though, doesn't it? A drink then? Coffee? Tea? Something stronger? Beer? Whisky?"

Dylan liked persuasive people. "A beer would be welcome, thanks."

"I'll have one with you. Won't be a minute. Make yourself comfortable."

Dylan chose a large black leather armchair, one of two in front of an attractive stone fireplace. Logs nestled in the grate waiting for the chilly evenings but wouldn't be needed tonight.

The room was almost as big as that confounded flat Bev had found him. Tall French windows overlooked a rear garden stocked with shrubs and small fruit trees, two stone statues and the tennis court. Furniture consisted of the two armchairs, a large glass-topped desk, black ash bookcases and dressers. Here, again, a large rug covered most of the floor. The walls were decorated with black-framed monochrome photographs of buildings—houses and offices—perhaps designed by Hunt.

Dylan stood up, intending to inspect them more closely, but he didn't get that far. An open padded envelope on the desk caught his attention. He peered inside. The sight of so much cash, all big-denomination notes, took his breath away. There had to be a thousand pounds there. Maybe two thousand.

He took a closer look at the envelope. It was brand new, still had the seal intact. There was no address.

Hearing his host's footsteps, Dylan returned to his seat.

"There we go." Hunt put a tray holding two pint glasses of cold beer on the low black ash table.

The study was in better shape than the man. The room looked relaxed and comfortable. Hunt looked neither of those things. Dark circles surrounded eyes that were a very pale grey. But the man was ill. What did Dylan expect?

"Thank you." He wasn't quite sure how to put this. "The spot of bother I ran into—"

"Yes?"

"I was warned away from Dawson's Clough," Dylan said. "Of course, it may have been a case of mistaken identity, but I was wondering if you'd had any problems?"

Hunt looked blank.

"I gather," Dylan said, "that you're friendly with a reporter. Have you mentioned my coming here to them?"

"No. No, of course not. You told me not to. Are you saying someone beat you up because of Sam?"

"Not necessarily. As I said, it could be a case of mistaken identity. Have you mentioned it to anyone?"

"No. Well, Marion knows, of course. My ex-wife. Sam's mother."

Dylan nodded. The girl's mother was unlikely to want him warned off.

"Oh, and Alice, my cleaner," Hunt added. "She's no gossip and I told her not to speak to anyone about it."

"Then perhaps he got the wrong bloke." Dylan hoped so. He didn't fancy running into him again. "So tell me how—and why—you think I can help, Rob. May I call you Rob?

"Yes, of course. I don't suppose you can. But I have to try everything, don't I? You've earned a name for yourself." Hunt took a gulp of beer. "Your picture was

in the local paper for weeks and Marion, that's my
wife—ex-wife now of course—said you'd be the man
to help us. As soon as she realised you were friends
with Frank, she wanted you here."

"I see." He saw that Hunt was going along with
his wife's wishes and, despite Dylan having earned a
name for himself, didn't have any faith in him whatsoever. "Did Frank tell you how me and him came to
be friends?"

"He said you were in the police force together."

"That's true." Dylan waited for more but nothing was forthcoming. "Did he tell you I was kicked
off the force?" It was clear that Frank had kept that
gem to himself. "A man I was arresting—an habitual
offender—claimed I used unreasonable force on him.
I spent five months in prison."

"I see. Well, I'm sorry to hear that, but what does
it have to do with me?"

"Nothing. Nothing at all." Dylan wished he hadn't
bothered. "I thought you should know, that's all.
People seem to think I can work miracles. The reality is that I couldn't even keep my job."

"Miracle was the exact word Marion used when
she said we should employ you."

"I got lucky once, that's all."

Like a lot of others—thanks mainly to exaggerated
stories that sold newspapers—Marion Hunt believed
Dylan had a magic touch.

Dylan only hoped she wouldn't be too disappointed. "I, um, gather you visited a clairvoyant?"

"I did." Hunt didn't flinch, didn't seem embarrassed. "People have been telling me I must prepare myself for the worst. Marion's new husband said we needed to get on with our lives and Marion half agreed with him. I couldn't believe it. Not from Marion. That's why I went to see the medium."

For as long as Sam's whereabouts were a mystery, they never would be able to get on with their lives. The truth, good or bad, would bring closure. Until then, they would continue to exist in a sort of limbo.

"I only went for Marion's benefit," Hunt said. "I've always known Sam's alive. I needed to convince Marion."

What could Dylan say to that? He, too, believed he would know if something bad had happened to his own son.

"What did this clairvoyant tell you?" He found himself speaking slowly, as if Hunt was mad. Dylan couldn't be sure that he wasn't.

"She said Sam was still in this world. Often, she's not able to tell. In this case, she knew for sure. She'd seen Sam, you see, and she knew she was still alive."

"Seen her?"

"Yes. She'd had—well, a vision, she called it. She'd seen Sam dancing in a field of sunflowers."

"I see. Did she happen to know where this field was?" Dylan might as well play along.

"That wasn't clear."

There was a surprise.

Dylan was in the wrong business. How much could you charge for inventing the sort of heart-warming rubbish people wanted to hear? Anyone could dream up stuff like that. If this medium had told Hunt his daughter was dead, that would most likely have been his last visit to her. To tell him she'd seen her in a vision was a stroke of genius. Hunt would go back time and time again, living in hope that his daughter had "appeared" again. All the while, the medium would be laughing all the way to her Swiss bank account.

"Tell me about your daughter," Dylan said. "Sam, is it? Or Samantha?"

"Sam. No one's called her Samantha for years." He took another swallow of beer and looked to be struggling to sit still. "I told you, she set off for work one Friday morning and no one saw her again. It was ten months ago. The thirteenth of August, 2010. Friday the thirteenth."

The medium would have loved the date of her disappearance.

"How old is she?"

"Twenty-two. It was a few weeks after her birthday that she vanished."

Dylan settled back in his extremely comfortable chair ready for a long chat. "Where did she work?"

"Carlton's Classics. A small company that specialises in buying, selling and restoring classic cars."

"As what?"

"A mechanic."

"Really?" Dylan had expected him to say secretary, receptionist or salesgirl. At least it explained the odd expression he'd seen on Hunt's face when he'd arrived.

His daughter would have known all about the Morgan. "Did she enjoy her work?"

"She loved it." Hunt stood, looked out the window for a moment, then spun round to face Dylan. "Obviously, it's not the job you want for your daughter, but what can you do?"

"Not a lot. What about the police? What have they come up with?"

"They're doing all they can." Hunt sat down again. "I can't fault them really. They still get possible sightings and they check them out but—"

"I see." After ten months, the police wouldn't be devoting a great deal of time or resources to the case. "She lived here with you, did she?"

"Yes. I can show you her room if you like?"

Hunt was already at the door as if he welcomed— needed—the activity. Dylan followed him up a long, curving staircase and onto a wide balcony. At the end of this, Hunt, struggling for breath after the climb, pushed open a door.

"Are you all right?" Dylan asked.

"Yes. I get breathless, that's all. Oh, and the only people I've told are you and Frank. I'd be grateful if you could keep news of my illness to yourself."

"Of course."

If Dylan had a terminal illness, he would tell Bev. He might, if pushed, tell his mother. He wouldn't, as Hunt had, choose to tell someone he exchanged Christmas cards with and a private investigator who was a stranger. Then again, if Hunt hadn't mentioned his illness, Dylan would be in London with his face and ribs still intact.

"I haven't even told Marion. I don't want her coming back to me because of that."

"I won't breathe a word."

"Thank you. The doctors don't know much anyway. When they diagnosed me, they said I might have a year or five left. They've no real idea though, so it's not worth mentioning." Having dismissed the entire medical profession, he stepped into the room. "It's just how Sam left it. All ready for when she comes home."

Dylan didn't ask where she was supposed to come home from. Instead, he took in the details of the large room. What drew his eye were the posters. There were no long-haired, slinky-hipped singers or actors here. Only cars. A gleaming Lamborghini took up most of the wall behind her bed. He couldn't fault her taste.

The rest of the room was tidy but not particularly feminine. A pair of jeans, tossed over the back of a chair, had a paint stain on them. A pair of black boots that owed more to comfort than fashion sat neatly in front of the wardrobe.

Perhaps what struck him most was the feel of the room. Vastly different to the rest of the house, it was almost old-fashioned. A leather chair, complete with tapestry cushions, had been designed, decades ago, for lounging in rather than as a visual statement. An antique desk and captain's chair sat in the corner of the room.

"That was her grandfather's," Hunt said. "She was

close to him and couldn't bear to see his things thrown out when he died."

"How long ago was that?"

"Four years. Sam was eighteen."

Floor-to-ceiling shelving on one wall held books, CDs and various trinkets. The CDs were by bands Dylan hadn't heard of. The books were all mysteries. A couple of Agatha Christies, three by Ruth Rendell, several by Ian Rankin and Lee Child.

Two framed photos stood by the books and Dylan peered closely. One showed a laughing young woman with a pint of beer in her hand and a dark-haired man's arm draped round her shoulders. Another showed the same young woman with two young girls.

"That's Sam," Hunt said. "The man with her is Jack Fleming and the girls are her half sisters."

Sam's long chestnut hair cascaded down her back in huge curls. Not a practical style, especially for someone who enjoyed working on cars, but certainly eye-catching. Around her neck was a small heart-shaped gold locket. Freckles dotted her laughing face.

Hunt paced from one end of the room to the other and his constant activity was wearing Dylan out. No, it wasn't the activity, it was the knowledge that Hunt needed to be still. His breathing was too laboured for comfort. Dylan needed to sit him down and ask him questions. A lot of questions.

"There's her computer." Hunt pointed to the laptop sitting on a small, low table near the window. "The police took that to check for—well, anything. There was nothing on it though. There wouldn't have been.

She wasn't really interested in computers and was too busy to bother with social networking or whatever it is they call it."

"I see. Right—let's go downstairs and get down to business. I need to ask you a lot of questions, Rob."

"Yes, of course. I'll get us another beer and you can ask all the questions you need."

Dylan returned to the study while Hunt got the drinks. He was pleased to see that no books on the occult or mysticism adorned the bookshelves. Most were to do with art and design.

Finally, the drinks were in front of them and Hunt sat, reluctantly it seemed to Dylan.

"Now then," Dylan said, "perhaps you could tell me about Sam's home life. She lived here with you, you say? What about her mother?"

"Marion and I divorced twelve years ago." His hands shook as he spoke and Dylan guessed this was more desperation than nerves. "Sam was ten at the time and lived with her mother until she was fourteen. Marion had—well, she'd met someone else. Married him even. Sam didn't like him and wanted to live here. I was more than happy to have her, and Marion thought she was old enough to decide for herself."

"Was the split amicable?" Dylan asked.

"Of course. I'm always here for Marion. They have two daughters now—one's eight, the other's six."

The relationship had been over for a long time yet Hunt still wore a wide gold wedding ring. That wasn't normal, was it?

He'd said he didn't want Marion coming back because she felt sorry for him. Dylan was no expert but, after twelve years, surely there was no way she was coming back.

"I'm sorry to ask such personal questions, but I do need to know. Before you divorced, was the atmosphere difficult for Sam?"

"No. Not at all. There were no arguments, fights, anything like that. Marion found herself besotted with—with Alan. It was all quite sudden. No, there was no unpleasant atmosphere."

"I see. And what about Sam? Does she get on well with Alan?"

"She doesn't like him—who would? He's a lorry driver. Goes abroad a lot. But there's been no trouble. She gets on well with the girls, her half sisters. She sees quite a lot of them. Or used to."

Which must mean she saw a lot of her mother too. Was there anything more complicated than a family?

"What was her life like?" Dylan asked. "What did she like to do? What was a typical week for her?"

Hunt looked impatient, as if he'd rather Dylan went tramping the streets in search of his daughter. "She'd work five or six days a week. In the evenings, she'd either stay in or go to the pub—"

"The man in the photo, Jack Fleming, that's her boyfriend?"

"Yes. She'd usually go to the pub with him. Sometimes to the cinema. On Sundays, they'd take the dog for a good walk."

"Sam's dog or Jack's?"

"Sam's. I've still got him. He's at the grooming parlour this evening but he should be back soon."

"You got along well, did you? You and Sam, I mean?"

"Very. Oh, yes, we're very close. I used to do a bit of fishing and, sometimes, Sam would come and spend the day with me. She liked that. She was more than happy to sit on the riverbank with a paperback. She loved to read."

Had she been happy? Dylan would imagine a twenty-two-year-old girl wanting to spend time with her boyfriend, or her girlfriends. At twenty-two— well, it was impossible to make a comparison. Dylan had never known his father so he couldn't comment on whether he would have liked spending time in the bloke's company. If forced to tolerate sitting on a riverbank with his mother though, he would have reached for the nearest brick, tied it to his feet and jumped.

"What about her boyfriend? Do you like him?"

"No." The word came with all the force of a bullet. "He's a bad one. Bad right through to the core. What she saw in him, I'll never know."

Dylan was taken aback by such animosity. Appearances could be deceptive but the photo in Sam's room showed a happy, laughing, harmless-looking man.

"What makes you say that, Rob?"

"He has a police record. And do you know what for? He locked his girlfriend—ex-girlfriend I should say—in her flat. He terrified the life out of the poor

girl. He's common, uncouth and downright danger-
ous."

Dylan wasn't sure what to make of that. "So when
Sam went missing—"

"He was taken in for questioning. Obviously. Why
she had to get involved with a lowlife like him—"
He broke off as a coughing fit seized him and it was
several moments before he was able to continue. "Of
course, I tried to keep my feelings to myself. God
knows, I didn't want to alienate Sam. I longed for the
day she got him out of her system though."

Sam was twenty-two, old enough to make her own
mistakes, but Jack sounded interesting. The police
must have had something to warrant questioning him.

"You say she liked going to the pub? Which one?"

"The Old Weaver—just down the road. You probably passed it on your way here."

"Ah, yes." He'd spotted it and thought it looked like
one of those old-fashioned places that didn't rely on
karaoke or Elvis lookalikes to bring in the trade. A
sign outside had mentioned guest ales too.

"Sometimes they went into the town centre, but not
often. The pubs there get a bit rowdy."

The girl got her hands dirty working on classic
cars. She drank pints. Her boyfriend had a criminal
record. She didn't sound the sort to worry about a
rowdy pub.

"Did she drink much?" Dylan asked, already guessing the answer.

"Oh, no. A couple of pints maybe. No more than
that."

That was the answer he'd expected. Hunt was drawing a picture of the perfect daughter, and Dylan wasn't convinced such a thing existed.

"I gather a scarf was found that some people thought belonged to her."

"She had one like it, that's all. But I suspect thousands of other girls did too."

Perhaps he had a point. "Where was it found?"

"In the field at the back of the house." He nodded in the general direction.

"How did she go to work? Walk? Bus? Drive?"

"She usually drove but, that morning, she was walking. She'd left her car at the garage—Carlton's Classics—because she was doing some work on it."

"And would she have gone via the field? The one where the scarf was found?"

"Possibly." Hunt seemed reluctant to admit it. "It depends. Sometimes, if she walked to work, she'd call on her half sisters and take them to school. If she did that, she'd usually cut through the field."

Hunt wanted Dylan's help but couldn't seem to grasp that it went both ways. He seemed reluctant to tell Dylan anything that might help.

"Was she planning to call on her sisters that morning?"

"Yes."

Dylan would pay them a visit. Their mother at least. Perhaps she would be more willing to talk. "What sort of car did Sam drive?"

"A Porsche."

The girl worked as a mechanic and yet she could afford a Porsche? "Very nice."

"Yes. Oh, it wasn't new. She got it cheap, through the garage. I gave her the money."

That was feasible.

"What about Sam's work colleagues?" Dylan asked. "How did she get along with them?"

"Very well."

Naturally. Even if they'd fought day and night, Hunt would never have admitted to it. He had the perfect daughter and woe betide anyone who so much as hinted otherwise.

"How did she come to get the job—or even want it?"

"Sam was never going to be a Samantha." A smile tried to tug Rob's lips into an upward curve. And failed. "She was always a tomboy. Even as a young child, she hated wearing dresses and playing with dolls. Marion and I thought she'd grow out of it, but she never did. She loved toy cars and trains. She went to night school, then got a job at a small garage. When the vacancy at Carlton's Classics came up, she walked straight into it."

"She didn't go to university then?"

"No. I tried to make her see sense, as did Marion, but she wouldn't listen. Her heart was set on working with cars."

So she was also wilful.

"Are her colleagues male or female?"

"Male. Yes, apart from the girl who answers the phone, they're all male."

Dylan wasn't going to get a full picture of Samantha Hunt from her father. No one could be as angelic and as perfect as the daughter he was describing.

"You said you'd prepare some information for me," he said. "Photographs, names and addresses, stuff like that."

"Yes, and I have." Hunt went to the nearest black set of drawers, opened the top one and pulled out an A4 envelope. "There are lots of photos. Copies of four payslips. Oh, and the letter from Carlton's Classics offering her the job."

Amazingly, that was the lot. "You mentioned addresses. For her friends."

"Yes." Hunt caressed a black leather notebook. "You can borrow this, but I'd like it back."

"Of course." Dylan flicked through the pages of what he realised was Sam's address book and put it in the folder before Hunt could change his mind. "This is great, thanks." It wasn't. It was barely adequate. "I'll go through it tonight and see where I go from here. I expect I'll soon be back asking a lot more questions."

Just as he stood, a door in the hall opened and closed and, within moments, a small brown dog raced into the room. It took no notice of Dylan or Hunt, but ran round the room three times.

"You see?" Hunt said. "Rusty still looks for her."

The dog smelled of cheap perfume, as if he'd returned from a brothel. He was followed by a grey-haired woman in her mid-sixties wearing a grey skirt and white blouse. Her face was scarlet from heat or exertion.

"Ah, you're there," she said, speaking to Hunt but nodding at Dylan. "He's had a good walk so you won't have to bother tonight, Rob."

"Thank you, Alice."

It didn't look as if any introductions were going to be made so Dylan stepped forward and offered his hand. "Dylan Scott."

"Sorry." Hunt took the hint. "This is Alice. She's been cleaning for me for years now. Alice, this is the gentleman I told you about. He's going to see if he can find Sam for us."

She didn't seem too optimistic. If anything, her expression was filled with sympathy for Dylan's plight. "I wish you luck."

Perhaps the housekeeper would be able to provide a more accurate picture of the oh-so-perfect Samantha Hunt.

"Right, I'll leave you both to it," Alice said. "I'll be here at nine in the morning, Rob."

"Fine. Thank you, Alice."

"I'm just leaving," Dylan said. "Can I offer you a lift anywhere?"

"Well…" She hesitated. "If it's no trouble. I'm taking the bedroom curtains with me, you see. I want them at the dry cleaner's tomorrow and they'll weigh a bit heavy. I only live at the bottom of the road so it won't be out of your way."

"It'll be my pleasure."

Dylan wasn't sorry to bid Rob Hunt goodbye and rejoin the real world.

FOUR

ALICE TURNBULL wished she'd walked the few hundred yards to her bungalow. Dylan Scott's car was a pretty yellow, like a canary, but cramped, noisy and uncomfortable didn't begin to describe it. She was relieved when he was helping her out—she couldn't have managed the task alone.

"Let me carry these for you." He reached for the curtains.

"You're all right, love. I can manage from here."

"It's no bother. Besides, I'd like a word about Samantha, if it's convenient."

"You want to talk to me? Oh, right." She hadn't thought of that. "You'd better come in then. I'll make us a nice cuppa and we'll have a chat."

Alice hadn't met a real private investigator before and she was disappointed. Perhaps she'd seen too many gun-toting American PIs on TV. Dylan Scott looked too ordinary. Walking round with a swollen, bloodied lip didn't look particularly ordinary, and his car wouldn't go unnoticed, but she couldn't imagine him bringing down hardened criminals.

She'd put him at late thirties. Probably unmarried if the crumpled, stained shirt was anything to go by.

Rob had said he was driving up from London, though, so perhaps he was simply travel-creased.

As they walked through her hallway, she made a mental note to have a good sort-out. Her bungalow was small and, with Dylan Scott inside, it seemed to shrink still further. It was certainly too small for the amount of clutter she'd accumulated over the years. There were a few items she couldn't bear to part with but, mostly, it was dust-attracting clutter. China owls gazed wisely from various shelves. Alice liked owls, of course, but this was getting out of hand. It had all started twenty years ago when Sean had bought her a porcelain owl. It had been a beautiful piece and, naturally, she'd given it pride of place. Since then though, every birthday and Christmas had found her unwrapping something else with an owl theme and she had to keep the items on show so as not to offend the giver. The truth was, she'd gone right off owls.

"Ooh, look at that!" screeched a voice from the sitting room.

"That's Snowy," she explained, embarrassed. "My parrot."

Snowy only had two phrases and Alice very much hoped he'd keep his other one to himself.

She took Dylan straight to the kitchen, where he put the curtains on the table.

"Thank you." She'd move them later. "Now then, let me put the kettle on. Milk and sugar?"

"Two, please. Thank you."

She knew he'd had beer at Rob's house and, given the unbearable heat, he'd probably like another, but she had none to offer him. She didn't drink, never had, and since Sean had died, there was rarely any alcohol in the house. Perhaps Dylan was happy with tea though, as he was driving.

While it was brewing, she opened a tin and put an assortment of biscuits on a plate. Then she opened another tin and added four larges slices of cherry cake to the selection.

She poured the tea into bone china mugs that were decorated with owls. A present from her nieces.

"Let me." He took the tray from her and carried it into the sitting room. He was certainly a gentleman.

"I'll open the window," she said. "I hate this sort of weather. It's so—stuffy. You can't get your breath, can you? Well, perhaps you can, being younger an' all, but I can't. We need a good thunderstorm, if you ask me."

"It looks like we'll get one soon."

"Ooh, look at that!"

"Snowy, quiet!"

"Ooh, look at that!"

Dylan Scott wandered to the cage and peered in at Snowy. "Hello, Snowy, you're a handsome chap."

"Ooh, look at that!"

"Does he say anything else?" Dylan asked.

"Not really." She hoped he wouldn't anyway. "Now, you help yourself, love. If I'd known you were coming I would have baked. As it is, I'm afraid I only have cherry cake."

"That's more than generous. Thank you."

Another of Snowy's habits was pecking strangers'

fingers so she was relieved when Dylan sat down and helped himself to a slice of her cherry cake.

Baking was a passion but it never seemed worth it for one. When her sister or her nieces visited she did a lot as she liked to give them cakes, biscuits or pies to take home.

"Can I ask you, Alice, if you told anyone that I was coming to Dawson's Clough to investigate Sam's disappearance?"

The question surprised her. "Not a soul. Rob said I shouldn't."

"It's best," he said. "It helps me no end. Now then, about Samantha. How well do you know her?"

"Very well." Of course she did. "I've been cleaning for Rob for the last eight years, you see. He's an architect—not that he does much work of any description these days. I suppose if you have enough money to get by, you don't need to work, do you?"

"I certainly wouldn't." He took another bite of cake. "It's a big house. It must take some cleaning."

"Not really. It's big, yes. Six bedrooms, three bathrooms, two cloakrooms. Most of it's not used though. And Rob's a tidy person."

"Are they close, Sam and her father?"

"Oh, yes. Very." She couldn't help smiling at her memories. "He's pretty hopeless round the house. Can't change a plug or anything like that. It was always left to Sam."

It was Sam who'd helped Alice get to grips with her new television and DVD recorder. The man in the shop had convinced Alice to buy it. He'd installed it for her, and given her a quick run through the controls, but it had been Sam who Alice had phoned when she couldn't set it to record *Coronation Street*.

"He's really gone downhill since she went missing," she said. "And he's got a bad cough now. I keep telling him he should see a doctor, but he won't hear of it."

"Do you know her boyfriend?" he asked.

"Jack, you mean?"

"How many did she have?"

He was teasing her, but she couldn't help wondering if he could read her mind.

"Just the one. Jack's fine. I know people say he's a bit wild, but I've never known him cause trouble. I suppose you'd say he's high-spirited."

"Did they have plans to live together or anything like that?"

"Oh, I shouldn't think so." Alice had never thought about it. "Well, maybe one day. I don't know."

"What would Rob have thought of that, do you think?"

He wouldn't have liked it. Few fathers liked seeing their little girls lavishing affection on another man.

"Sam always got her own way. Rob would have missed her company, of course, but I don't think he would have stood in her way." Alice felt disloyal. She couldn't say anything bad about Rob. He'd been good to her over the years. In any case, there was nothing bad to say. It just felt as if she were talking behind his back, like a sneak in the night.

"So Rob got on well with the boyfriend, did he?"

"As far as I know, yes."

"I gather the police found a scarf that they believe belonged to Sam?" he said.

"Well, yes. I recognised it immediately." Again, she felt disloyal. "At least, I thought so at the time. As Rob said, it could have been anyone's. The police couldn't prove it was hers. They thought they might be able to, but it had rained overnight by the time they found it and people had trampled it into the mud. Who knows?"

"I see. So what's your theory, Alice?" Dylan Scott helped himself to another slice of cake.

"I don't really have one. Well, all sorts of things go through your mind, don't they, but you never know what might have happened." Nothing she ever thought of was good though. No wonder poor Rob was in such a state. She picked up her cup and drank her tea. "There are so many evil people about these days."

She would give anything to know. Sometimes, when she was dusting at Rob's, she would imagine Sam breezing into the house, throwing her bag down on the table, tugging off those big boots she wore.

"I wouldn't say as much to Rob, of course, but I worry that someone might have mugged her. She wouldn't have had much money on her, but these young thugs don't seem to bother about that, do they? They'll do anything for a couple of pounds. And then, just before she vanished, a young girl went missing. They found her, thank God. She'd met up with some-one bad, someone she'd met through her computer. Not that Sam was silly like that." Her bottom lip began to tremble and she had to reach into her pocket for a tissue. Just thinking about it upset her. "I hope I'm wrong, but I can only think that something very bad happened to her. People don't just vanish, do they, Mr. Scott?"

"Dylan. And no, I'm afraid they don't, Alice."

"All I know," she said, trying to pull herself together, "is that she left home and began walking toward her mum's house. According to her mum, she'd promised to call and take the children to school. She never turned up."

Alice wanted to show him the mug. She never used it but— She went to the kitchen, took it from the top shelf and carried it into the sitting room to show him.

"Sam bought me this." On the mug, the words *A Balanced Diet is a Piece of Cake in Each Hand* were printed in red. "We used to joke, you see. She had such a good appetite and she loved my cakes. It was just a joke, a reminder that I should bake a cake for her. I was right touched when she gave it me."

She felt the sting of tears in her eyes again and had to blink them back. More than anything, she hoped Rob was right and that Sam was alive and well.

"Ooh, look at that!"

"Snowy, shush." If he wasn't quiet, she'd cover him with his blanket. That usually sorted him out.

"Do you know Sam's mother?" Dylan asked, seemingly unperturbed by the bird's interruptions.

"Not really. I met her twice when she called at Rob's house, but we only said hello. I'd be hard pushed to recognise her if we met in the street." Alice had a sudden vision of a tall, elegant woman. "She's in charge of a nursery," she said. "For preschool children, you know?"

He nodded. "In Dawson's Clough?"

"Yes. It's called Tiny Tots. She's got two daughters of her own. Apart from Sam, I mean. They're too old for the nursery, of course."

"And Sam had a good relationship with her mother?"

"I think so." That sounded evasive. "Yes, she did. They sparked a bit sometimes, but all mothers and daughters do, don't they? Sam adored her half sisters, I know that. Absolutely loved those girls. I suppose you wouldn't say she was close to her mum. It was difficult, you see. Sam loved her dad and it was hard for her to see her mum with someone else."

"What about her stepfather? Did Sam like him?"

"Well…" All these probing questions. It didn't seem right discussing such personal matters behind people's backs. Yet if it would help him find Sam— "She used to call him Slob. Once, I gather he called her a snob and she told him she'd rather be a snob than a slob. After that, she always called him Slob. I don't suppose she said it to his face, but that's how she referred to him."

Alice was growing more and more uncomfortable. Rob had employed her because she was reliable and didn't tittle-tattle. Whatever would he think if he could hear her now?

"There's nothing I can tell you really," she said. "All I know is that Sam set off for work one day and vanished. I wish I could help, but I can't. The police asked me all sorts of questions and I couldn't help them either."

She was expecting him to take the hint and leave. He'd polished off the cake, drunk his tea and asked her questions. There was no reason for him to stay. He looked settled for the night though.

"Apart from Jack," he said, "was there anyone else? A girl of twenty-two, a pretty girl of twenty-two, might have other boyfriends."

"No. Not that I know of." She could feel her face burning at the lie. She'd been a hopeless liar sixty years ago and she hadn't grasped the art as an adult. "Really, there's nothing else I can tell you."

Still he didn't move.

"Some people, Alice, don't like talking," he said. "They think of it as gossiping, as something they shouldn't do. In some cases, though, people have to gossip. Anything you know, no matter how insignificant you think it, might be the very thing that helps us find Samantha."

Porcelain owls looked on in silence as Alice debated with herself. Owls were wise, or so they said.

"Ooh, look at that!"

She wished her parrot would take a leaf out of those owls' books.

"Anything at all," he said.

"I saw her with someone." She heard the wobble in her voice. "One night—it was the night before she disappeared—I was coming out of the bingo hall with two of my friends, Jane and Bridget. We'd crossed the road to Jane's car and, for some reason, I glanced inside a parked car. I saw a flash of red hair."

"Sam?"

"Yes. It was dark but the car was parked beneath a streetlight. Sam was kissing the man sitting in the driver's seat."

Alice could still remember the sense of shock when she'd realised it was Sam. Their gazes had collided head-on.

"I didn't get a good look at him, but I saw enough to know it wasn't Jack. This man was late thirties or even early forties. He was wearing a tie with big spots on." It was funny the things you noticed. "I hurried on my way. Well, I didn't know what to think. I was shocked and confused. And yes, I disapproved."

"Did Sam know you'd seen her?" Dylan asked.

"Oh yes. She caught up with me and tugged on my arm. 'Oh, Alice. You won't tell, will you?' she said. Well, of course, I wouldn't have mentioned it. She told me she knew I wouldn't approve because he was married. She said nothing would come of it. Anyway, she made me promise not to tell."

"And you've never told anyone?"

"Not a soul. Until now." She felt thoroughly ashamed of herself.

Sam had thrown her arms tight around her and hugged her. "You're the best, Alice. I do love you," she'd said. Alice hadn't seen her again.

"Not even the police?" Dylan asked.

"No. For one thing, I'd promised. For another, there

didn't seem much point. I couldn't have told them who it was."

"What sort of car was it?"

"I've no idea." She didn't drive and didn't know one car from another. "It was low. One of those sports cars. Dark blue or black, it was a job to tell. It had a badge on the back and that struck me as funny. It was two red squiggles that looked like a funny letter *S*. I wondered if he'd done it for Sam. You know, *S* for Sam."

Alice was beginning to wish she'd never seen Dylan Scott. She didn't like to gossip out of turn, no matter what the circumstances. She wished she'd kept quiet.

"Would you recognise the man if you saw him again?" he asked.

"No. I was too shocked to get a good look at him. Besides, it was dark. Look, you won't mention this to Rob, will you?"

"No, of course not. I won't tell a living soul, promise. You've been very helpful, Alice. Thank you." He stood up and Alice was relieved. "Thank you for the tea, and the cake too. It's much appreciated."

"You're welcome." Alice couldn't get rid of him quickly enough.

"Bugger it!" Snowy cried from his cage. "Bugger it, bugger it, bugger it!"

"Snowy!" Alice didn't know where to look. "I am sorry. Sometimes Sean, that's my late husband, used to say that. I am sorry."

"At least he's expanding his vocabulary, Alice." Dylan Scott was smiling.

"Well, yes, but I do wish he wouldn't."

"Bugger it!"

"Snowy! Stop that at once!"

When they'd said their goodbyes, Alice watched Dylan Scott drive off in that yellow car of his and made herself another cup of tea. She sat at her kitchen table, surrounded by her mute owls, and worried about it all.

She picked up the local newspaper. On the back page was a request for blankets and good quality clothing as well as general bric-a-brac that could be sold to raise funds for a charity that helped two orphanages in Romania. Alice had more bric-a-brac than she knew what to do with. She had blankets in the loft that hadn't been used and probably clothes she wouldn't wear again.

Boxing it up would take her mind off things, and if her donation helped children in Romania have a better life, it would be worth it.

FIVE

OVER a thousand miles away in Bucharest, the heat was no less oppressive. Which was perhaps why, Anca decided, the shopkeeper was in such a filthy temper. He'd turned his back, just for a second, and she thought she'd had time to grab the loaf and make her escape without being seen. She hadn't. He was after her.

"Come back, you no-good thief, or I'll call the police."

Terror spurred her on. She and Crina hadn't eaten a crumb for two days. Surely he could spare one small loaf of bread.

Head down, running as fast as her young legs would carry her, she cannoned straight into a man. Her head flew up as his arms steadied her.

He wasn't a policeman. At least, he wasn't in uniform. He was tall, handsome and foreign-looking. A suit jacket was slung over his shoulder, a blue tie was loose at his neck, and Anca had never seen a shirt so crisp, so white.

The shopkeeper, breathless from his exertions, caught up. "Thank you, sir. I'd seen the little devil hanging around. I should have known she'd steal something."

The man looked down at Anca. "Did you steal from this gentleman?"

What could she say? The proof was in her grubby hands. "My little sister and me—we're hungry."

"Have some compassion, man." Anca's well-dressed saviour fished in his pocket and pulled out a note. "You might be willing to let these street children go hungry, but I'm afraid I can't."

The stranger spoke with an accent Anca hadn't heard before.

"If I let them all eat for nothing, I'd have no business, would I? I wish I could afford to be more generous, but I can't."

"Here." Anca's new friend pushed the note at him.

"Thank you, sir." Happy with his profit, the shopkeeper returned to his business.

"Thank you," Anca said.

"So—" Smiling kindly, the man looked down at her. "What's your name? I'm George."

"Anca."

"Anca is a very pretty name for an exceptionally pretty girl."

Anca blushed. Everyone said she was pretty but she knew Crina, younger than her by two years, was far prettier. With dark, almost black hair touching her waist, Crina could pass for an angel.

"Where do you live, Anca?"

Live? She didn't live anywhere.

"I—we move around," she said. "We're down by the railway station now."

It was supposed to be easy picking with lots of

tourists visiting the city, but it wasn't. The police moved them all on. Tourists visited Bucharest to see the tree-lined boulevards, the Casa Presei or the Arcul de Triumf. They recoiled in horror and pretended they didn't see the bundles of rags begging for coins.

She and Crina had run away from the orphanage in November and were new to life on the street. If they hadn't met Dănut, she dreaded to think what would have happened to them. Dănut was sixteen. He was clever, wily, funny and had proved himself a good friend.

"Who's *we?*" George asked.

"Me and my sister, Crina."

"How old is Crina?"

"Thirteen." She was grateful to him, but she wanted to get away now. Crina would be worrying. Besides, she was hungry.

"And is Crina as beautiful as you?" His voice was teasing.

"She's as pretty as an angel."

"Really?" He took her arm. "Come with me and we'll buy you some real food. What would you like?"

"I have to get back to Crina."

"And so you will, just as soon as we've bought some nourishing food to take to her. Now, what would you like?"

"I don't know."

He laughed at that and they began walking back to the station. Anca clung to her loaf of bread. If he bought her food, he'd want something in return. He'd already paid for the bread and probably thought that entitled him to do as he wished with her. It didn't.

In a street near the station, stalls sold mouthwatering hotdogs, pork kebabs, helpings of goulash and slices of pizza.

"Pizza?" As soon as Anca had it in her hand, she'd make a run for it.

"Pizza?" He laughed at that. "My dear girl, if you want pizza, you shall have pizza." He stopped walking and turned to look down at her. "You have no other family? Just your sister?"

"No one else." Her eyes were on the pizza stall.

"Have you heard of England?"

"Of course." Dănut was always talking and dreaming of travelling to England. Perhaps he was there now. She hadn't seen him for weeks. "I've heard it's very beautiful."

"It is. That's my country, Anca. I was born in England. Would you like to go there?"

"Of course." He was wasting time with his idle chat. If they weren't quick, all the pizzas would have been sold.

"No money, eh?"

Anca had to look down at her trainers to make sure they were the same ones she'd rescued from a bin. Her jeans had worn so thin that they had more holes than denim. The grime, accumulated from months of sleeping rough, still clung to her jacket.

"No money," she agreed.

"If I could get you to England, would you like to go?"

The pizza was forgotten as Anca's mind flooded

with images of England. Reality soon returned though.

"Let me tell you what I do, Anca. I've been working in Romania for many years now. I run a charity, and help as many homeless children as I can. Sometimes, I take them to England where they can find work. It's very expensive, but I might be able to get you and your sister there and find jobs for you both. You'd have to pay me back, of course."

"Why would you do that?" A tiny spark of hope flared. Maybe, just maybe, he was a kind, honest man who really did help people.

"Why? My dear Anca, I have money to eat. You don't. No one on this small planet of ours should starve. I would like to help you. It's as simple as that."

Anca shook her head. "I've heard about what happens to girls who—"

"Anca." He was smiling. "Do you speak English?"

"No."

"Then no one would put you into prostitution, if that's what frightens you. Believe me, there are more than enough English girls willing to make a living that way. Besides, it's far too risky."

Anca didn't know what to think, much less what to say.

"You could earn more as a prostitute admittedly," he said, "but the only jobs I can find are in hotels. English girls don't like cleaning rooms. They feel it's beneath them. But perhaps you prefer to take your chance in Bucharest."

"No!"

There was no future for them here. Ever since Dănut had told her about England, she had longed to go there. "You can earn a fortune," Dănut had said. "People like us can work in bars and hotels. It's big money. Really big money."

If George was telling the truth, they would live in London. Just her and Crina. They would have money for food and clothes.

"Crina's only thirteen," she said. "She couldn't—"

"And no one would expect her to. You're right to be on your guard, Anca, but I promise you I don't have any dealings in the sex trade. I'm afraid you'll just have to trust me on that one. All I may be able to offer is cleaning jobs. The pay wouldn't be very good as too many people are fighting for too few jobs, but it would be a weekly wage." He patted her hand. "Let's get you some food and take it back to Crina."

Anca had lost all appetite. She was too busy dreaming of England. She'd seen pictures of London. Someone had dropped a book about it at the station and, although Anca hadn't been able to read the words, she had spent hours gazing at the pictures.

She was soon holding a bag filled with pizza slices, donuts and Coca-Cola and marching, beside George, to the shelter that was currently their home.

Crina was waiting but, shy of strangers, she backed away when she saw George.

"It's all right," Anca said. "This is George. He's a friend."

"Indeed I am, and it's a pleasure to meet you, Crina." He looked at her sister for long moments, then nodded. "Have a think about what we talked about, Anca. If you decide you want to go to England, meet me outside the station at eight o'clock on Monday morning."

"We'd work as cleaners? We'd have somewhere to sleep?"

"Of course." He smiled warmly. "Eat your pizza before it gets cold. Perhaps I'll see you on Monday."

Anca watched him stride away with a sudden fear in her heart. What if she never saw him again? He'd offered his help and she hadn't trusted him. What if he found someone else to take to England? Someone more grateful?

SIX

EVERYTHING about the hotel was familiar, from the threadbare carpets to the small, creaking lift and missing light bulbs. Dylan had stayed at the Pennine before and, despite the icy temperatures he'd suffered then, the place had grown on him. The food was good and the staff were friendly and helpful. There had to be worse places to stay.

This week he'd been given a different room, a larger one on the fourth floor. If he lay on his double bed, he stared straight at a painting of a voluptuous purple nude. At least, it looked like a nude. Very modern, with sweeping brushstrokes, it was difficult to tell.

He took a couple of painkillers—his lip was still throbbing as a reminder of this morning's unwelcome encounter—and then poured himself a generous helping of brandy from the bottle he'd had the foresight to buy from the nearby off-licence. He'd need a second mortgage to drink from the room's mini-bar.

Sitting comfortably on his bed, with his drink beside him, he opened the envelope Hunt had given him.

The black leather address book that had been parted with so reluctantly was crammed with addresses and phone numbers. Some friends had moved house two or even three times, and each old address had been carefully crossed through before the new one was added. The colour of the ink varied from blue and black through to green but Sam's handwriting was small and neat. These days, most people carried friends' contact details on their phones. Not Sam. Perhaps she'd learned early that phones could fail and swallow data.

Dylan put the address book aside. He would go through every name in that book over the next few days.

He sorted out the photos and looked at each one in turn. It was impossible to see a young woman capable of having an affair with a married man. All Dylan saw was a lively, fun-loving teenager growing into a happy young woman. He also saw someone with a penchant for wearing baseball hats back to front. A snap taken at a wedding, and another at a dinner of some sort, showed Sam wearing a dress with her long, curling red hair cascading over her shoulders. In the other pictures, however, she was in jeans, T-shirt and baseball cap with her hair tied back. Her dog, Rusty, appeared in a few. Some had been taken where she worked, young men with spanners gathered round her, laughing for the camera. Jack stood by her side in several.

Dylan studied those more closely as he tried to work out what sort of man Jack was. It was difficult to tell yet he looked slightly in awe of Sam, as if he couldn't quite believe his good fortune.

A couple of snaps showed Sam with her sisters.

Half sisters, as Hunt had described them. Sam's mother or stepfather didn't feature anywhere.

He put the photos in a pile and read through the letter Sam had received offering her the job at Carlton's Classics. It told him the hours were long and the pay was poor but promised as much overtime as she liked. It also stated that her position would be reviewed after three months. As Sam had worked there for almost two years prior to her disappearance, Dylan assumed she'd been a satisfactory employee. He knew they'd been paying her, and that she'd taken advantage of overtime, because Hunt had provided copies of four payslips.

He poured another measure of brandy for medicinal purposes. If the paracetamol he'd swallowed weren't going to have an effect, the alcohol would have to.

He ought to call his mother. So far today, he'd managed to ignore her seven calls.

Taking a deep, self-righteous breath, he hit the button on his phone. For a moment hope flared, as it always did, that she would be out of earshot, unable to answer, but that was soon dashed.

"Dylan, I was wondering where you'd got to. You arrived all right then?"

Dylan wouldn't have used the term *all right*, but he'd arrived. "Yes. What can I do for you, Mum?"

He could hear her hero, Bob Dylan, singing something about staying forever young. That bloke had a lot to answer for—including Dylan's name. He could picture his mother clad in long skirt with bells and bangles tinkling as she moved, listening to her favourite singer, rolling a joint, filling Dylan's flat with the pungent smell of marijuana and scented candles, looking at holiday brochures that promised adventure—

"Me? Oh, I was just ringing for a chat, love."

No change there then. He wished, just for once, she could find someone else to chat with. "About what?"

"You're sounding decidedly tetchy," she said.

"Am I? I'm sorry. A busy day, that's all. I'm ready for my bed."

"I'll let you go then. Oh, Bev phoned this afternoon. Have you spoken to her?"

"No." Chance would be a fine thing.

"She asked if Luke could stay here Friday and Saturday nights. Apparently she's off somewhere for the weekend. She rang me because she didn't know if you'd be home at the weekend."

"Of course I'll be back. Where's she going?"

"She didn't say. So that'll be nice, won't it? Luke being here when you get back on Friday, I mean."

"Yes." Of course it would. But where— "Didn't you ask her where she was going?"

Dylan's question was greeted by a burst of laughter. "I certainly didn't. Heavens, I'm not Bev's keeper. She's entitled to a bit of fun just as you are."

Fun? Dylan's life could be called a lot of things right now—crock of shit being top of his list—but fun certainly wasn't one of them. Besides, he didn't want fun without Bev. They were married. They should have fun together.

"Are you sure she didn't say where she was going?"

"Dylan! No, she didn't, and I didn't ask. Why would I?"

Presumably for the same reason she insisted on asking him where he was going, who he was going with, how long he would be—

Of course, Dylan had learned long ago that there were different rules for men and women.

"Anyway, I won't keep you, love. I expect you want a good night's sleep after that drive. I put some camomile teabags in your case. They'll help you sleep."

They might have if Dylan hadn't seen them when he'd changed his bloodstained shirt and slung them in the bin.

"Yes. Right, thanks, Mum. I'll see you on Friday."

"Okay, love. Don't forget the camomile."

As if he could.

He wondered if anyone other than a mother could make a man feel so guilty. Dylan felt guilty when he didn't phone her and guilty for being so unsociable when he did. It was a lose-lose situation.

Forgetting her for the moment, he stretched out on his bed and drank his brandy. An angry rumble of thunder rolled around the hills as he mentally planned the following day. First he'd call at Carlton's Classics and chat with Sam's workmates.

Then he'd track down the boyfriend. It would be interesting to know if Jack realised he'd had competition.

SEVEN

CARLTON'S CLASSICS surprised Dylan. He hadn't known what to expect, but certainly something a lot less classy than this.

He parked the Morgan on the forecourt and went inside a long, sleek showroom that was constructed almost entirely of smoked glass. It would have looked more at home in Mayfair than the northern mill town of Dawson's Clough.

Given Samantha's payslips, Dylan had expected old sheds, grime and oil. Here were dust-free glass and chrome tables and blue upholstered chairs where presumably people sat to admire the three Ferraris on show. All red, of course. A 308 GT4 sat alongside a Dino 246. A 328 GTS, its paintwork acting as a mirror, had pride of place.

A young woman smiled a greeting from a long curving reception desk. "Can I help you?"

Dylan recognised her from one of the photos Hunt had given him. She and Sam had been holding cocktails and smiling for the camera.

"I hope so." Dylan gave her his warmest smile and winced as his lip objected. It hurt more than ever this morning so talking was difficult. He felt as if he'd just been released from the dentist's chair having had enough Novocaine to fell an elephant. "I'm Dylan Scott." Perhaps it was a mistake giving his real name. Perhaps not. "I'm looking for Sam Hunt."

"Sam?" Half a dozen paperclips fell from her hand and her face drained of all colour. "She—um, no one's seen her for months."

She was in her mid-to-late twenties. A plain girl, although not unattractive, with shoulder-length dark hair. Nails were bitten to the quick, and the skin around those nails had bled recently.

"She no longer works here?"

"No. She vanished. August it was."

"How do you mean 'vanished'?"

"She didn't turn up for work one morning and no one's seen her since." Her face didn't lose its startled expression but the words sounded rehearsed. Or perhaps she'd simply spoken them too often.

"Good God. You know her, though? Know who I'm talking about?"

"Yes, course I do. I've worked here for almost six years so, yes."

Unless Dylan was mistaken, she looked guarded. She lowered her head slightly and her hair fell around her face. She wasn't looking him in the eye.

"What am I to do then?" Dylan spoke more to himself than to her. "I've got to find her."

"You won't do that. The police couldn't."

"Well, well. This is a shock, I can tell you." He rubbed his chin, pretending to be deep in thought. "Are you a friend of hers?"

"No. We only worked together."

"You didn't go out together? Socially, I mean?"

"No."

She was lying. Dylan had seen the photo.

"Well, a couple of times, maybe," she said. "If it was a work thing. Someone's birthday or something. That's all." As she spoke, she kept looking at a door to her left.

"Good grief. Sorry, but I can't get my head round this. When was the last time you saw her?"

"The same as everyone else. The night before she vanished. When I left work for the day, she was still here. I didn't see her again."

"She had a boyfriend, didn't she? Did you know him?"

"Who's that?"

"Jack, I believe his name is."

"Oh, yes. Yes, I know him."

"Did she have anyone else in her life?" Anyone who might explain the hesitation, or the relief when he'd offered Jack's name. "Anyone who might know where she could be?"

"No."

"Do you know Jack well?"

"Not really, no." She gave a start as the door to her left opened. A man, probably late thirties and wearing a smart suit and silk tie, emerged. "James, this is Dylan—"

"Scott. Dylan Scott. And you'll be—?"

"James Carlton. How can I help?" He looked outside and his gaze rested on the Morgan. "Oh, yes, very nice. Are you selling or is it needing work?"

"Neither." Dylan offered his hand. "I'm looking for one of your employees, Sam Hunt."

Dylan's hand was shaken, but Carlton's smile cooled by several degrees. "Good grief. She's no longer my employee. Hasn't been for months."

"So I gather. This young lady was just explaining. I'm at a complete loss now."

"What did you want with her?"

"I'm a TV producer." It wasn't his best invention, but the receptionist was hiding something, he was sure of it, and a TV producer might fare better than a private investigator at finding out what that was. "I met up with Sam in the summer and we talked about a project I had in mind. I wanted someone young, presentable, knowledgeable—I'm sure you know the sort—for a new motor show. To cut a long story short, Sam was interested and I said I'd get back to her. The programme had to be shelved, though, and it's only just been given the go-ahead. I really need to talk to Sam. I've been trying her mobile for weeks and getting nowhere."

"I see. Sorry." He gestured to the blue chairs arranged around a chrome table a short distance from the reception desk. "Please, sit down, Mr. Scott."

"Thanks. I'm at a complete loss. I mean, what can have happened? She didn't strike me as the type to just up sticks and go."

"Me neither."

"What can you tell me about her? I assume you thought highly of her as an employee?"

"Very." James Carlton was at ease with himself

now. Conceited perhaps? Tall, dark, slim and presumably wealthy, he had plenty to be conceited about. "I didn't really take her seriously when she applied for a job here. Her being female, I mean. But she was persuasive and I agreed to take her on for a three-month trial period. I was very impressed."

"How did she get on with the other mechanics?"

"Very well. They took the mickey at first, of course, but it was water off a duck's back. She could take care of herself."

"Before she disappeared, did she seem okay to you?"

"In what way?"

"I don't know really. Was she behaving strangely in any way?"

"No. She was her usual self. She left here on the Thursday evening, said she'd see us in the morning, and that was that. We never saw her again."

The girl on the reception desk was moving brochures around while trying to hear every word of their conversation.

"Did you see her socially?" Dylan asked.

"Socially? What makes you ask? Why would I?"

James Carlton wore a wedding ring. Was he the man Alice had seen with Sam?

"Sorry, I'm just clutching at straws." He didn't want to raise Carlton's suspicions. "I have to find her but I don't know where to start looking. I wondered if you saw her outside work, and if you knew where she'd be likely to hang out."

"No."

Maybe a little flattery was in order. "Did she tell you about our plans for the show?"

"Not a word." Carlton looked miffed about that.

"Ah. I asked her not to mention it until the ink had dried on the contracts, but she was so excited, I thought the temptation might be too great." He nodded at the gleaming Ferraris. "She was keen to get your business involved and use your expertise."

"Really?"

"Oh, yes. I was all for it too. A lot of blokes want a high-performance car, and it's not only the price tag that puts them off. Sam believed—and I agreed—that your input on maintenance costs would be invaluable."

"Well…" Carlton straightened his perfectly straight tie as if the TV cameras were already rolling. "Yes, that would have been worth considering. So when you start making the programmes—"

"That's just it," Dylan said. "My boss is adamant that it's Sam or no one. That's why I need to find her. And fast."

"You won't find her."

"Maybe not, but I'm going to have a damn good try. So you don't know where she hangs out?"

"No, I never saw her outside work. She spent most of her time with her boyfriend. Sorry, but I don't remember his name."

"What about her other friends? Would you know of anyone she was close to?"

"No, I'm afraid not. I knew nothing of her private life."

"I see." Every time Dylan smiled, he expected his

lip to split. "Would you mind if I spoke to her col-leagues? I won't take up too much of their time."

"Not at all." James Carlton stood, his smile wide and friendly. "I'll show you the workshops."

"Thank you."

"They won't be able to tell you anything though. It's baffled friends and family, the police—no one knows what happened to her."

Dylan made a point of speaking to the reception-ist. "Thanks for your help, um—sorry, I don't think I caught your name."

"Kerry Adams. And you're welcome."

Dylan followed James Carlton onto the forecourt and stopped to admire the building. "This is impres-sive. Trade must be good."

"Very."

"How long have you been here?"

"Coming up to seven years. My father had the busi-ness first and, when he wanted to retire, I took it over. I've expanded a lot since then." He looked proud of his efforts. Justifiably so.

They rounded the corner of the showroom and came upon a Lamborghini. "Wow. Second to the Morgan, that's my dream car."

Carlton laughed. "That's mine."

"Lucky you."

Dylan was about to walk on when he spotted it. When Alice had mentioned those two squiggles that had looked like a letter *S*, he'd thought of sports cars' emblems that might include the letter. An Alfa Romeo Spider, perhaps. Attached to the back of Carlton's red Lamborghini Diablo was a badge that, to Alice Turnbull, would have been two red squiggles that looked like a letter *S*. It was in fact the Senna S, a logo recognisable to any fan of the late, great racing driver Ayrton Senna.

"You were a Senna fan then?"

"Yes." Carlton nodded at the badge. "That's my tribute to the man who had to be the greatest driver ever. Wouldn't you agree?"

"Possibly. The problem is, you can't compare like for like, can you? Who can say that Senna was better than Fangio?"

Carlton smiled at that. "My money would be on Senna every time. Pure genius."

"Either way, it's a beauty of a car," Dylan said. "Had it long, have you?"

"Coming up to twelve months. Before that, I drove a Ferrari. The Maranello 550. It was a few years old, but it never let me down."

"Really?"

Dylan wasn't interested in the Maranello and they walked on.

"This is where the work's done." James Carlton stepped into a large workshop where three cars were in varying states of disrepair. "Bill." He addressed the older of the four men in the building. "This is Dylan Scott, a TV producer. He's looking for Sam Hunt. I've told him he won't find her here. Perhaps you'll have better luck convincing him. Oh, and don't stand around talking too long." This last was said with a smile and a wink at Dylan.

"Thanks very much," Dylan said as Carlton took his leave.

Bill led the way outside. Dylan supposed that his days were spent in the workshop so he'd welcome every opportunity to escape.

"I'm not being rude, but I won't shake hands." Bill was smearing an oily rag across his palms. "Sam, well, that's a blast from the past. It seems to me as the poor lass has been forgotten."

"But not by you?"

"No. You're a TV man, did he say?"

"That's right, yes. I offered Sam a job working on a new programme but then it was stalled. I've just got the go-ahead and need to find my presenter."

"Was she going to be on the telly then?"

"Yes."

"My, she would have loved that."

"What can you tell me about her, Bill?"

"Not a lot. Other than that she was one of the nicest, most genuine people I've ever known."

Bill was probably late fifties or early sixties. He looked comfortable with himself. Confident. As if he'd stand no nonsense from anyone.

"You got on well then?" Dylan asked.

"Oh, yes. Everyone got on well with her." His hands clean, or cleaner, he pushed the oily rag into the pocket of his overalls. "She had time for everyone. Always thought of other folk. That's quite rare in someone so young."

"Very rare." Perhaps, after all, Sam was as perfect as her father claimed.

"Sometimes, she used to sneak her dog in to work with her. It wasn't allowed, but no one had the heart to tell her. Even the dog idolised her. Followed her everywhere."

"She was good at her job, I hear," Dylan said.

"She was brilliant. I couldn't believe it when James told me he'd employed a girl. I mean, I know all about this equality nonsense, but a girl working on cars? I'd never heard the like. Anyway, blow me, she was good. She could tell a lot about an engine just by listening to it. The other lads—" he nodded in the direction of the workshop "—all complain if they have to work late. Not Sam. It never bothered her at all. She was at her happiest lying under a car."

Bill took a tin from his pocket, picked out a hand-rolled cigarette and lit it with a battered Zippo lighter. "Is that your car? The Morgan?"

"It is, yes."

"Sam would have been looking at the engine by now." Bill smiled fondly. "She was a grand lass. Absolutely grand."

"Do you know her family?" Dylan asked.

"No. She had two sisters, I know that." Bill scratched his head. "I met her father a couple of times—he dropped her off here once or twice—but I wouldn't say I know him. Or was it her stepfather? I can't remember now. One of 'em anyway."

"What about her boyfriend?"

"Jack?"

Why was the doubt always there? "Yes, I believe that's his name."

"Oh, yes, I know him. A wrong 'un if you ask me but, there, she thought the sun shone out of his arse."

"Really." Dylan coaxed his throbbing lip into a smile. "What was—wrong about him?"

"What wasn't?" Bill's cigarette had gone out so he relit it. "Drink. Drugs. Fights. You name it, he was involved. He's just about the last person on earth you'd want your daughter mixed up with."

"Really? How old is he?"

"About thirty. No, thirty-two. I seem to think he's ten years older than Sam."

Dylan brought to mind the snapshots he'd seen of Jack. He'd looked the same age as Sam, certainly not ten years older.

"Was there anyone else in her life, do you know? Another man perhaps?"

Bill's glance went to the glass showroom. "There were rumours."

"Oh?"

"You can't take much notice of rumours, can you?"

Dylan could. He loved rumours. It helped no end in his line of work. "When I was talking to her about the programme, I got the impression she was involved with a married man. A married man who owns a car very much like that one." He pointed to James Carlton's Lamborghini.

"Did you indeed?" Bill puffed on his cigarette. "Funny that, but I got the same impression." Deciding the cigarette was dead, he dropped it and ground it into the gravel. "You'll want to talk to the others, will you?"

"That would be good. Thanks, Bill. I appreciate it."

"I haven't told you nothing."

He had. He'd as good as confirmed Dylan's suspicions. Samantha Hunt had been romantically involved with her smooth-talking boss. Her smooth-talking *married* boss.

EIGHT

Rob Hunt poured himself a whisky, carried it into the sitting room and sat near the window. It was his favourite room. He still thought of it as Marion's.

He'd wanted to design a house specially for her but she'd longed for a home that was old, "where people have lived and died," and had a view of the moors. When Wickham House, a Grade II listed building, came on the market, she fell in love with it and insisted they live in the adjoining coach house while the renovations took place.

She used to fill the house, and this room especially, with fresh flowers from the garden. Sid Bentley had been in charge of the gardens for decades and came with the house. He and Marion had chatted and planned for hours. Rob, however, found him dour and gave up trying to get conversation from him long ago.

On top of the piano Marion had sometimes played was a photograph of the three of them—him, Marion and Sam. It was taken in Venice. Sam, just four years old, was almost hidden by an ice-cream cone as Marion held her tight. Happy days.

The room echoed with Marion's memory. A matching pair of tall vases she'd bought at an auction guarded the French windows. She'd chosen the long white drapes. Another of her auction purchases was the small, difficult-to-spot porcelain mouse that sat on a stone ledge at the back of the inglenook. The fireplace was Rusty's favourite spot, winter or summer. Right now, he was staring at Rob, his brown eyes questioning.

Rob picked up the phone and tapped in Marion's number, knowing from experience that this was the best time to catch her. She would have arrived home about fifteen minutes ago and Alan would be driving somewhere. At least, he hoped that was the case because whenever Alan answered the phone, he was loathe to do anything but pass on a message.

Rob despised the man. Thinking of him with Marion, talking with her, eating with her and, worst of all, sleeping with her—

"Hello, Rob. What can I do for you?" She sounded exhausted and Rob wished he was near enough to fuss over her. He'd sit her down and lift her feet onto the sofa, mix her a gin and tonic, and tell her how much he loved her. Then he'd massage the tension knots from her neck and shoulders.

"Hello, sweetheart. How are you?"

"Fine, but busy. What can I do for you?"

He wondered if Alan was home. She tended to be snappy and distant if he was around. "I was wondering if you'd heard from Dylan Scott."

She was lighting a cigarette. He heard the rustle of the pack, the click of the lighter and the inhalation. "Yes, he phoned. He's coming round tomorrow night."

"Tomorrow night? Why not before?"

"Because I'm out tonight. I also have a job, remember?"

"You're out? You have a job?" His heart took up an angry thumping beat. "You could take a day off. Surely Sam's more important than work. You should have been here with me the day he arrived. This was your idea, remember?"

"I know that, but—"

"You insisted I phone Frank. You said I must do whatever it took to get Scott here. You wanted him, Marion."

"And you didn't!" She hurled the bitter words at him. "How could you not want him? We need all the help we can get."

"It's not that I didn't want him, you know that. I just thought we should leave it to the police and look for—"

"Who are getting nowhere."

"If you'd let me finish, I was going to say we should be looking for her ourselves. But oh no, you're not interested. How many places have I suggested we go look for her? Christ, I even bought the plane tickets for Barcelona—you know how much she loves that city. Don't you dare accuse me of doing nothing."

"For God's sake, Rob, we can't traipse round the world." She exhaled. "Look, I'm not going to argue with you. Dylan Scott's coming here tomorrow night and I'll do all I can to help him. As you've already met him and told him everything, there's probably nothing I can add, but I'll do my best."

"You should be doing this with me. Sam's *our*

daughter, Marion. We're supposed to be in this together."

"We are in it together." He heard her inhale on her cigarette. "I'm very busy, so is there anything else you want?"

He forced himself to calm down. Being angry with Marion wouldn't help. "I just wanted to know if you'd seen him yet. I've given him photos, Sam's address book, and all sorts of stuff. He's good, Marion. Everyone says so."

"I know they do. Tell you what, I'll call you when he's been, okay?"

"Yes, do that. It's always good to talk to you, you know that."

"If there's nothing else—"

"I take it Alan's home then?"

"No."

"Really? It sounds to me as if he is. I can always tell. You're a different person around him. I wish you could see yourself, hear yourself—"

"He's not here. Not that it's any of your business."

"A lorry driver, for Christ's sake. How the hell could you take up with a lorry driver?"

"Better than taking up with a snob. What's wrong with lorry drivers? Or van drivers? Or taxi drivers?" She sighed. "Look, Rob, I'm too tired for this."

"Sorry, you're right. If he's your idea of the perfect man, that's fine." He strove to lighten the mood. "So how are you? How are the children?"

"I'm fine, thanks. So are Lydia and Emma." She emphasised the girls' names. It was her way of reprimanding him for not using them. "Sorry, but I really must go."

"Hey, why the rush? Sam's *our* daughter, Marion." He could feel himself growing angry at the brush-off and took a calming breath. "You sound tired, sweetheart."

"I am, and I don't want to fight with you—"

"I don't either. I thought we should see Dylan Scott together, that's all. You haven't forgotten Sam, have you? She still means everything to you, doesn't she?"

"Of course I haven't forgotten her, for God's sake. I just want you to leave me alone. You're on the bloody phone every five minutes—"

"I've called twice this week." He hated it when she swore. The beautiful young woman he'd married had never resorted to that sort of language. It was all Alan's doing. The man loved to punctuate his conversations with obscenities. "That's not every five minutes, is it?"

"It's too much. *You're* too much. I'm sorry you don't like Alan, but that's not my problem. You don't have to live with him, do you? I'm putting the phone down now. I'll call you if this Dylan Scott has anything interesting to say, okay?"

The connection was cut and Rob flung the phone across the room. It hit Rusty, who yelped in a mix of shock and anger before racing from the room.

NINE

DYLAN reached Jack Fleming's block of flats just after seven that evening. He'd called twice earlier in the day and had tried Jack's number several times, but he hadn't been home and wasn't answering his phone.

This time, when he rang the bell for number 51, the main door was opened by a young blonde with what had to be silicone-enhanced breasts. False eyelashes too. The long legs and short skirt were real enough, though.

"Hi. I'm looking for Jack Fleming."

She turned to holler down the hallway. "Jack? Someone to see you."

She waited a moment then shrugged. "It's the first door on the right."

"Thanks."

"You're welcome."

Dylan watched her walk down the road, hips swaying, ankles balanced on precarious heels. Only when she turned the corner and vanished from view did he wander inside and knock on the first door on the right. He waited. Nothing. He knocked again. And again. Finally, a man fresh out of the shower—judging by the wet hair, the damp T-shirt and the jeans he was still fastening—opened the door.

"Jack Fleming?" Of course it was. Dylan recognised him from the photos. In the flesh, he looked older but not that much older. "Dylan Scott. I was wondering if I could have a chat with you about Samantha Hunt."

"Sam?" He couldn't have looked more surprised if he'd tried.

"Yes."

"You'd better come in then. Sorry—it's a bit of a tip."

Given the state of his own flat, Dylan was in no position to criticise. Music magazines were scattered everywhere. Two guitars hung from wall brackets. CDs covered an entire wall.

"Do you play?" Dylan nodded at the guitars.

"Yeah. A bit. I was in a band but it sort of disintegrated. Shame really." He pushed a pile of magazines from the chair to the floor. "Have a seat. D'you want a coffee or summat?"

"No. You're okay, thanks." Dylan took the offered seat.

The flat wasn't bad at all. Dylan would have done a swap with him. The block had been built about twenty years ago, and it still maintained a modern look. Walls—the sections that were visible—were a pale lemon colour and the carpets a grubby beige. Not bad, though.

Jack Fleming was more difficult to assess. Tall, thin and dark-haired. Badly bitten fingernails. Were guitarists supposed to bite their nails? His hands shook too. Drugs or nerves?

He was wearing a black T-shirt with a band's name on the front—Devil's Outriders—and tour dates on the back. Dylan had never heard of them and, judging by the size of the concert venues mentioned, they weren't pulling in big crowds.

"Was that your girlfriend who let me in?" he asked.

"Sal? No, she's my sister."

Silicone Girl had looked like no one's sister.

"She chilled here last night," Jack added.

Chilled here? Spent the night at the flat? It didn't matter and there was no point getting sidetracked. Whether she was girlfriend or sister was irrelevant. Sam had been missing for ten months so Jack couldn't be blamed if he'd met someone else.

"What do you want then? You said you wanted to talk to me about Sam? How do you mean?" Belatedly, or so it seemed to Dylan, he asked, "Who are you anyway?"

Dylan took a moment to think about that. He'd been planning to tell him the TV producer story, but Jack knew the family, and probably knew Hunt was employing him.

"I'd rather you didn't broadcast this, Jack, but I'm a private investigator. Sam's father has employed me to look into her disappearance."

"Yeah?" Jack's face lit up with hope and Dylan was pleased he'd been honest with him.

"What can you tell me about Sam?"

"What do you want to know?" He was either eager to talk or a competent actor.

"Anything and everything. How long have you known her?"

Jack threw himself down on the sofa without bothering to move the magazines first. "Two years. Just over."

"Where did you meet?"

"At a wine bar in the Clough. Cassidy's. It closed down within six months. Sam was there celebrating her birthday. She's never been much of a drinker and when I met her, she was throwing up in the street." A half smile touched his lips. "I bought her three or four strong coffees and we got chatting. We arranged to meet up for coffee the following day. I didn't think she'd remember, but she did. Her dad had bought her a car for her birthday and, that night, she took me out in it."

"A Porsche, wasn't it?"

"Yeah. She loves it. Car mad, she is." He stood and, hands deep in the pockets of baggy jeans, paced a bit. "She isn't really into clothes and stuff. It's all cars. And her dog, of course. Rusty. She's fussy about who goes in her car but the dog's allowed anywhere."

As yet, Dylan had heard little bad about Samantha. The only questionable point was whether she'd been having an affair with a married man. An affair with her boss.

"How did she get along with her colleagues?" he asked.

"Great. They're a good laugh. Bill used to treat her like a daughter."

"What about her boss, James Carlton?"

"What about him?"

Unless Dylan was very much mistaken, he'd touched a nerve.

"Did she get on well with him?"

"As well as anyone gets on with their boss."

"She liked him then?"

He opened his mouth then clamped it shut. After a couple of paces across the room, he said, "Yeah. He's all right."

Dylan was convinced Jack had been on the point of saying something more. Had he known she was having an affair with him?

"Some people believed she thought he was better than all right," he said.

"Yeah. I know."

"A wealthy bloke. Nice car. His own business. Good looking." Dylan paused for effect. "He'd be quite appealing to some women, wouldn't he?"

Jack smiled a secret smile at that. "Yeah. He would."

"But not Sam?"

"No. Not Sam. She's got more sense."

"Rumour says she hasn't."

"You don't want to listen to rumours, mate."

Dylan wanted to do exactly that. The only way forward was to listen to rumours.

He was convinced Jack knew something, but Dylan needed to win his trust so he didn't push it. "What about her mother and stepfather?" he asked. "Does she get along well with them?"

"Yeah. Well, no, not really."

"Oh? Her father thinks she does." Hunt had told Dylan that she'd never really taken to Alan, and Alice had said she'd called him Slob, but there was no hint of any conflict with her mother. Alice had more or less confirmed that.

"Maybe he does. She thinks the world of her little sisters. If it wasn't for them, she'd have nothing to do with them. She can't stand that bloke her mum married."

"Why?"

"Dunno really. She said he freaked her out. She reckoned the kids—her sisters—were always too quiet when he was around, like they were scared of him." He sat again. "We sometimes took the kids out. To the park or summat like that. He seemed okay to me, but I only saw him to say hello and goodbye."

Jack was edgy, unsettled.

"When was the last time you saw Sam?" Dylan asked.

"The day before she vanished."

Thursday. The evening Alice Turnbull saw Sam in the arms of another man, probably in the arms of her boss. Jack had to be lying.

"Where did you go? The pub? Cinema?"

"Nowhere. We only met up at lunchtime."

Perhaps he wasn't lying. It was difficult to tell. Something was bothering him but Dylan couldn't fathom him out.

"You didn't see her in the evening?" he asked.

"No. She had something else to do that night."

"What was that?"

"Summat to do with work, I think."

"You mean she was working overtime?"

"Summat like that."

Again, Dylan had the feeling that Jack knew more than he was saying. But what? Could he have known Sam was having an affair with her boss? If he *had* known, how would he have taken it?

Sometimes you just had to ask outright.

"So the rumours that Sam was having an affair with her boss are completely unfounded?"

Jack's head flew up and something shocked and angry flared in his eyes. "Yeah."

Yet something had been going on. Somehow, and God alone knew how, Dylan needed to win Jack's confidence.

"Is the offer of coffee still open?"

"Yeah, sure." Jack headed for the small kitchen that led off the room. There was no door to it, just an archway. For all that, it looked clean and tidy. "How do you take it?" he called over his shoulder.

"Milk and two sugars if you've got it, please."

Dylan wandered to the window and looked out. It had been another hot, overcast and humid day. The sound of distant thunder had been constant. Lights were on in the house opposite, but they'd probably been on all day. It really was that dark. The road was tidy, the street quiet. This ground floor flat looked out onto a well-cared-for if boring square of garden.

Jack put two big mugs of steaming coffee on the low table.

"Thanks." It was difficult to know where to start. "Do you miss her, Jack?"

The question appeared to take him completely by surprise. Eyebrows shot up beneath his hair. "Yeah. Course I do."

"If she walked in here now—?"

"I sure as hell wouldn't be sitting here drinking coffee with you."

Dylan smiled at that. "So are you going to help me find her?"

"Yeah. Of course."

"Then talk to me, Jack. We both want the same thing. We both want to discover the truth behind her disappearance."

"Anything could have happened to her, though," Jack said, and the hands shook more violently.

"It could." Perhaps he was frightened of finding out that she was dead. This way, the not knowing, was okay. He could tell himself she was alive and well somewhere. But after ten months, he must know that outcome was doubtful.

Or had Dylan got it wrong? Something made him want to trust Jack, just as something had made Sam trust him. Were they both gullible?

"I heard her dad went to see a medium," Jack said. "She said Sam's still alive. But what else is she going to say? It's all fucking bollocks, isn't it?"

"I think so."

Jack was chewing on his fingernails. Or probably chewing on his fingers, given that there was very little actual nail left.

"Come on then, Jack. Talk to me. Start by telling me why you're so nervous."

"Who says I'm nervous?" He was thirty-two, ten years older than Sam, but he looked younger, especially when he wore his belligerent expression.

"I do."

"I just don't want no shit. I swear to God I didn't do nothing to her."

"Who says you did?" The statement came as a shock but Dylan kept his voice casual.

"The police. They thought she'd been done in or summat and I was number one suspect." Amazingly, tears welled in his eyes. "As if I'd bloody hurt her. Bastards!"

"Why would they think you'd hurt her?"

"Christ knows. Well, yeah, I do know. When Sam first met me, I was on probation." The admission came slowly, each word forced out. "I'd locked my ex-girlfriend in her flat after we'd had a row. She'd pissed me off."

"Ah."

"I told them to fuck off. Bastards." He picked up his coffee and blew across the surface. "They burst in here and bloody searched the place. They didn't waste no time asking questions."

"Coppers can be a bit—abrupt. I know, I used to be one. I got kicked out." He waited a moment for that to sink in. "Forget coppers. Tell me what you know, Jack."

"What makes you think I know anything?"

"Just a hunch." Dylan picked up his coffee and took

a few sips. On the edge of his vision, he could see Jack drumming his fingers on the edge of the sofa.

"Okay," Jack said at last. "That boss of hers, James Carlton. The business isn't—or wasn't—doing well. His wife ploughed all the money into it, you know that, do you? None of it was his. His dad used to have a business on the same site, but that was nothing, just small-time repairs. Anyway, Sam reckoned Carlton was gambling. She also reckoned he'd made a couple of dodgy insurance claims. Big claims."

Dylan wasn't in the least surprised to learn this gem. He'd thought James Carlton was a little too smooth to be true. "How big?"

"Big enough. You know the sort of cars he deals with, they don't come cheap. Well, twice, in under a year, he claimed a load of cars had been stolen. That's a lot of money."

One hell of a lot of money. "What makes you think—or what made Sam think—they hadn't been stolen?"

"The second time it happened was a night she'd been going to work late. There was nothing new in that. She was working on some flash car, can't remember what it was, and took it for granted that she'd stay on a couple of hours to finish it. She reckoned Carlton was getting edgy that night. In the end, he practically had her chucked off the premises."

"She didn't confront him, did she?"

Jack shook his head. "What could she say? Without the proof, she couldn't do anything, could she?"

"So she was trying to get close to Carlton to see what she could find out?"

"Yeah." He took a swig of coffee.

The story was feasible. Just. Jack had known about the so-called affair she was having with Carlton. He'd known and hadn't seemed to mind. If he'd been in on it all along—

"Why would she do that?" Dylan asked. "Why would she care?"

"She just did. It didn't seem right to her, that's all."

It didn't seem right to Dylan. And yes, in the same circumstances, he might have tried to find out more. There was a difference between a copper—ex-copper, he reminded himself—delving into people's crimes and a twenty-two-year-old girl. He remembered the paperbacks he'd seen in Sam's bedroom. All whodunits. Sam had probably believed she was the modern-day answer to Miss Marple.

What would Carlton have done if he'd found out she suspected him? If there was a lot of money at stake, not to mention a reputation and a business, there was no knowing what a man would do to avoid a prison sentence.

"Have you told the police any of this?" Dylan asked.

"I tried to, but they weren't interested."

"Why?"

"First off, I told them Sam had been with him the night before she vanished. Carlton said she hadn't and they chose to believe him." He pulled a face. "When someone else said that Carlton and Sam had seemed close, he said she'd been talking over her problems with him. He said she'd dumped me and I'd taken it badly. His story was that she'd gone to him asking for advice." Jack finished his coffee and banged the mug down on a magazine. "He's a lying shit."

Quite probably. "Anything else?"

"Yeah." Jack walked into the kitchen, opened and closed a drawer and returned with a small tape. "She tried my mobile on the Friday morning—the morning she vanished—and couldn't get me. I was out driving. She left messages on my mobile and the landline. The mobile one's gone—Vodafone deletes 'em after so long."

He took a deep breath before removing the tape from his answer machine, inserting the new one and hitting the play message button. Even Dylan shivered as Sam's voice filled the room.

"Christ, babe, you won't believe what I've found out. It's nothing to do with Slimeball Carlton, perhaps he's telling the truth, but this is horrible. Look, I'm running late and can't talk now. I'll see you at lunchtime, okay? Bring me a sandwich, will you, and we'll talk then." Her voice dropped to almost a whisper. "We'll talk about the other as well. Love you, babe. Bye."

Looking into the disappearance of an unknown young woman was one thing. Hearing her voice, breathless and so alive, was something else entirely. Dylan swallowed a couple of times to lubricate his painfully dry throat.

Jack, in a world of his own, hit the play button again.

This time, Dylan listened more carefully. She'd found out something horrible that had nothing to do with James Carlton.

"Did you give this to the police?" Dylan asked.

"What was the point? It didn't make Carlton innocent. And it didn't explain anything else, either."

That was valid. The police would have said "so what?" The answer to that, of course, was that she could have learned something that put her in danger.

"When she said you'd talk about 'the other,' what did she mean?" Dylan asked.

"Dunno." Fingers were being chewed again. Jack paced the length of the room four times before sitting again.

He knew all right.

"Okay," Jack said at last. "There's summat else you should know. She'd just found out she was pregnant."

"What?" Dylan couldn't keep the shock from his voice.

"Yeah. She'd bought one of those testing kits the day before. It was positive. She told me and we—we had a row on the Wednesday night. The neighbours heard us, which is another reason the coppers thought I'd done summat to her."

Dylan despaired. People always had to drip-feed the pertinent facts.

"Was the child yours?"

"Of course it was." The suggestion that it could have been someone else's clearly caused offence.

Why could no one lead ordinary lives? Generations ago, men had worked seven days a week and women had raised children. They'd been content with their lot. They'd had no need for complications.

Why had Sam felt the need to complicate things? Why had she seen herself as Dawson Clough's answer to Miss Marple? And why the hell had she needed to get pregnant, fall out with her boyfriend—

"What was the row about, Jack? She wanted the child and you didn't? Did you think it could be someone else's?"

"No. Nothing like that. She was planning to book herself in for an abortion and I wanted her to have it. I thought we could get married, you know?" He shook his head. "The shit hit the fan when I said that. She accused me of deliberately trying to get her pregnant."

"How come?"

"She used to be on the pill," Jack said, "but it didn't agree with her. You can ask her doctor if you don't believe me. Anyway, she reckoned I'd deliberately used a dodgy condom."

"And had you?"

"Christ, don't you start. Of course I hadn't. What? You think I stuck a bloody pin in it?" He pulled his fingers through his hair. "She was shocked, that's all. It was a stupid fight that meant nothing. Yeah, we yelled at each other. She even chucked a mug at me. It meant nothing though."

They must have kissed and made up. Hadn't she said in her message that she loved him?

"What's your theory, Jack?"

He shook his head. "I dunno. What's yours?"

Dylan wished to God he had one. "It's a funny thing, but on the way here yesterday—" he touched his battered lip "—I was threatened. Someone tried to warn me away from the town."

"Eh?" Jack's eyebrows rose at that.

"Yes. At least, I think they did. There's a slim possibility it was a case of mistaken identity, I suppose."

"Who could that have been?"

"I don't know. I just don't know." Dylan was determined to find out though. "Remember to keep this to yourself, Jack. Okay? If anyone asks, I'm a TV producer."

"A what? Christ." He grinned at that. "Don't worry. Your secret's safe with me."

Dylan hoped so.

TEN

DYLAN had forgotten how quiet Dawson's Clough was when evening descended. Music blared out from some of the pubs, and a few drinkers stood outside to smoke, but Dylan had the streets more or less to himself. That suited him as he was thinking and the process was always easier when walking. Problems could be unravelled with each step.

One of his problems was Bev. Perhaps he hadn't been paying attention during their marriage ceremony but he was damned if he could remember her vowing to love, honour and annoy the hell out of him.

If she was going away somewhere at the weekend, why hadn't she mentioned it? She was playing mind games, that's why.

Two could play at that. Maybe it was time he pretended to take this ridiculous separation seriously. Not that it was a separation, not really. She'd thrown a strop, for no reason whatsoever, declared him impossible to live with and found him alternative accommodation. Dylan was expected to wait until she got over it. She'd come round, she always did. In fact, she *was* coming round. Meanwhile, life was hell and it was probably time he invented a young, beautiful, sexy as hell "someone else" to speed up the process a little. Not that Bev had mentioned a "someone else." No, she was far too devious. She was merely hinting at it so that, when he mentioned it, she could deny all knowledge with complete innocence.

Or perhaps she wasn't playing mind games. Perhaps when he next spoke to her, she'd tell him she'd arranged a game of tennis with her friend Lucy.

There was only one way to find out. It was just after ten o'clock, the ideal time to call her as she'd be relaxing before she went to bed.

He punched in her number and was pleased when she answered almost immediately. He could picture her, sitting with her feet tucked beneath her on the sofa, watching some rubbish on TV.

'Hi, it's me." A bus trundled along and pulled up at the stop right next to him. He stepped back into a shop doorway and put a finger against his ear. "How's things?"

"Fine. Luke's just gone to bed if you wanted to talk to him."

"That's okay, I'll catch him tomorrow. I gather he's staying at my place over the weekend."

"That's all right, isn't it? Your mum said it was okay with her."

"Of course." The bus pulled away in a cloud of black fumes. "Yes, it'll be great. When will you be back?"

"Sunday evening. About sevenish."

"Ah." Still no hint of what she was up to. "Where are you going? Anywhere good?"

There was a pause before she said, "Edinburgh."

Edinburgh? She had no friends in the city. No reason whatsoever to go there. "Really? Is there something on?"

"I'll have my mobile with me if you need me."

He'd assumed as much. She might be a lot of things, including secretive and downright bloody annoying, but he knew she'd be available in case of emergency.

"I've never been," he said, "but I believe it's a beautiful city. Are you sightseeing?"

"Dylan!" She gave a hoot of laughter. "Stop fishing. No, I won't be sightseeing. Was there anything else you wanted? Because I'm in the middle of a film."

"No, I was just ringing for a chat, but it's not important. I'll call some other time. I'm pretty busy myself."

He was about to invent a female he had to meet but dismissed the thought. He hadn't lied to Bev yet and he wasn't about to start now.

As he ended the call, he vowed that, at the weekend, he'd sit Bev down and indulge in a spot of straight talking. It was time this silliness stopped. They were a family—him, Bev and Luke. Families belonged together and that was the end of it. He was damned if he was spending any more time in that confounded flat with his mother. Come hell or high water, he was moving back to the marital home.

With that particular problem mentally resolved, he put his mind to the matter of Samantha Hunt. Saint Sam, as he'd come to think of her.

For all that, he liked the picture he had of her. In

fairness to her, it was only her father and the loyal cleaner, Alice, who believed the sun shone out of her backside. Dylan knew for a fact that she was wilful. She'd resisted her parents' plans for university and she must have faced huge opposition when introducing the boyfriend to her father.

She seemed to get on well with everyone and had a lot of friends, if her address book was anything to go by. Also, she felt strongly about right and wrong. If she walked round the corner right now and introduced herself, he was sure they'd get on well. They could even talk about cars.

Tomorrow he was visiting her mother and stepfather. As both worked, that had to wait until evening. During the day he'd go through Sam's address book and phone the people listed. He would also call Frank and see if he'd managed to get any updates from the file currently held by Lancashire CID. It might be worth visiting the library, too, and looking at the local newspapers around the time she vanished.

He walked past Asda. Even at this hour, people were stocking up on groceries. Farther along the road, people queued at the cash machine. In the distance, a sign told him that the Four Bells offered guest ales. The ideal place to make for.

Tomorrow was a brand new day. He'd celebrate today's lack of leads with a couple of pints.

To get to the Four Bells, he had to walk past a nightclub called Indie Street. A group of young people, laughing and shouting, went inside, treating Dylan to a burst of loud music. He happened to glance at the suit-clad bouncer standing, arms folded, by the door. There was something familiar about the muscles that threatened to split the seams of the black jacket.

"Well, well."

Dylan approached him. Recognition dawned and the bloke took off down the steps and round the back of the building.

Seeing a couple of missing teeth in his future, Dylan followed at a run. Perhaps he wasn't as out of condition as he'd thought because he was gaining on him.

The other bloke had the advantage though. For a start, he knew where he was going.

They ran along a narrow road at the back of the club. Terraced houses, most with metal fire escapes, lined the other side of the road.

Dylan narrowly avoided being mown down by a speeding car as they crossed into another similar road. He had no idea where they were heading or even where they were.

He was gaining on him though. Perhaps acknowledging this, the man ran up one of those fire escapes. Dylan, foolishly, followed.

At the top, Muscle Man hammered on a door and then, when no one answered, turned around and hurled his weight at Dylan, who was still climbing the metal stairs.

Dylan felt every bone in his back crunch as he landed on the ground below. He'd had the good sense to pull the thug with him, though, and the even better sense to roll slightly so he didn't have two hundred pounds of muscle landing on top of him.

Dylan was quicker and more agile. He managed to get astride him and pin him down. It took every ounce of his strength so it needed to be a very quick chat.

"Right, let's hear it." He could barely speak and was struggling to force air into his lungs. "Why do you want me to stay away from this place?"

"Dunno what you're on about."

Dylan managed to knee him in the privates, which had him moaning in pain.

"You fucking bastard!"

"*Angry* fucking bastard," Dylan corrected him. "Right, the cops should be here any minute. Talk to me or talk to them. Your choice."

Muscle Man had an inner debate with himself.

"Okay." Thanks to the orange glow from the street-lights, Dylan saw saliva dribbling down his chin. "A bloke asked me to do a job for him. I don't know any more than that. He told me about your car, said you'd be coming into the Clough on Monday morning, and offered me a grand to send you back to London."

So it wasn't a case of mistaken identity. "Which bloke?"

"Not a fucking clue."

There was a surprise. Not. "Has this man paid you for services rendered?"

"No."

"So—if you don't know the bloke, how is he going to pay you?"

"He's coming to the club. Next week."

"Day and time?"

"Wednesday. A week tomorrow. I don't know the time."

Despite being convinced he'd broken a couple of bones in his spine, Dylan managed to knee Muscle Man in the balls again. Bad move. The bloke had benefited from his rest and struggled out of Dylan's grip. Dylan staggered to his feet, ready to charge into the muscle when, joy of joys, he heard the welcome if totally unexpected sound of a police siren.

Muscle Man heard it too. He kicked Dylan on the shin and raced off into the shadows.

By the time the siren had faded into the distance, he was long gone.

It was feasible that his story was true. Bouncers made far more money using their fists than they did standing outside nightclubs and politely asking people to leave. His employer would be returning to the club a week tomorrow, he'd said. Dylan would be waiting. At least, he'd be waiting on Monday and Tuesday night. Probably Thursday and Friday nights too.

Dusting himself off and deciding that his bones were possibly where they should be, after all, Dylan headed back to the town centre and the Four Bells.

He needed that drink more than ever.

ELEVEN

MARION RODERICK in no way resembled the mental picture Dylan had of the woman who'd once been married to Rob Hunt, the same woman who had given birth to the tomboy Sam. She was tall and extremely elegant. Sleek, copper-coloured hair, worn long, glistened in the reflected light of a gold chain she wore around her neck.

"Dylan Scott," he said when he'd recovered from the surprise. "The private investigator. We spoke on the phone."

She nodded and smiled in a way that made something tingle inside him. "Pleased to meet you, Dylan. Come in."

Bearing in mind that Marion ran a centre for pre-school children and Alan was a lorry driver, Dylan had thought it fairly easy to mentally calculate the joint income. The brand new Mercedes outside the large modern house seemed out of place. Even allowing for the relatively low property prices in Lancashire, he would have thought the house well above their means. Perhaps they had a hefty mortgage.

She led him through a hall, a well-furnished sitting room that boasted superior-quality furniture and top-

of-the-range audio/visual equipment into a large conservatory at the back of the house.

"Take a seat," she said with that disarming smile.
"I'm sorry but Alan's not home yet. He shouldn't be
long."

"That's fine."

He chose a comfy chair rather than the sofa. Ridiculous, but he felt the need to keep some distance
between them. He could still smell her delicate perfume though.

"Thank you so much for agreeing to take on Sam's
case," she said. "I know the police are doing all they
can, but nothing's happening and I feel so helpless.
And I'm sorry I couldn't meet you at Rob's. It's a bit
difficult."

"Ah." He wasn't sure what to say to that. He
couldn't understand his own marital problems let
alone anyone else's. "I gather it's all amicable between
you and Rob though?"

"Fairly." That smile again. "But only because I
have the patience of a saint. I mean, I know we're
Sam's parents, so we can't completely sever the ties,
but even so Rob can make a nuisance of himself."

Of course they couldn't sever ties. Just as he and
Bev couldn't.

"So what can I do to help?" she asked.

"Tell me all you can about Samantha. I gather she
was due here on the morning she vanished?"

"She was, yes. She was working on her car—" She
smiled at that, a laboured sort of smile. "When wasn't
she working on her car? Anyway, because she planned

to walk to work, she said she'd come this way and take the children to school."

"What happened?"

"When she didn't turn up, I called the house. Rob said she'd left some time ago. I kept ringing her mobile but it went straight to voice mail. I left several messages. Anyway, I took the children to school and kept trying her phone. It was so unlike her, you see. She's always been so reliable."

"You get along well, I take it?"

"As well as any mother and daughter get along," she answered with a wry smile. "We fight like cat and dog and then end up hugging."

Dylan smiled, but he couldn't say he understood. Women were a foreign species as far as he was concerned.

Doors were heard closing in the house. Seconds later, a big man came into the conservatory. "My husband, Alan," Marion said. "Alan, this is Dylan Scott, the private investigator."

"Hi." He bent to shake hands with Dylan before giving his wife a quick peck on the cheek and sitting on the sofa beside her.

Dylan held his breath as the sofa protested. Alan Roderick looked as if he spent half his life sitting in a lorry's cab and the other half sitting in cafés eating fried breakfasts.

"So you're the latest waste of time," he said with a smirk. "At least you're not a clairvoyant, I suppose. How's it going?"

"It's early days," Dylan said, surprised by the animosity toward either him or Hunt. "How do you mean, the latest waste of time? Have other investigators been employed?"

"No," Marion said, frowning. "It's just that Alan believes—"

"—it's a waste of time." Alan finished the sentence for her. Pinning on a smile, he patted his wife's hand. "If the police can't find her, I don't see how anyone else can. Still, ours is not to reason why. How can we help, Dylan?"

Alan Roderick wore several hundred pounds' worth of gold—a watch, a thick chain around his neck and three rings. Tattoos banded his neck and both wrists.

"I was asking your wife about her relationship with Sam," Dylan said. "I'm hoping that someone close to her might have heard her mention something— perhaps she said she might be meeting someone or going somewhere?"

They looked at each other and shook their heads.

"She isn't a secretive person," Marion said. "If she'd been going somewhere or seeing someone, she would have said."

"She isn't particularly chatty though," Alan said, and his wife frowned at him.

"Not with you maybe."

A phone rang out inside the house and the Rodericks looked at each other.

"Leave it," Marion said as Alan lifted his weight. "It'll only be Rob."

It could be Sam. Dylan quashed the thought. Sam

hadn't phoned for ten months. Of course it wouldn't be her.

After such a long absence, the most likely outcome was that Sam was dead. Did the people sitting opposite him know that? They must.

Everyone spoke about Sam in the present tense. Dylan struggled to do that.

"What about her boyfriend?" he asked. "Do you know him well?"

"Not really," Marion said. "I know Rob doesn't like him."

"We all know Rob doesn't like him." Alan spoke through thin lips. "The bloke was on the phone morning, noon and night when she started seeing him. As if we could do anything about it. Sam was twenty. More than old enough to make up her own mind."

"Jack's called here a few times with her," Marion said. "He seems all right to me. Polite. Sensible."

"A criminal record," Alan put in.

"Yes, I heard about that." Dylan liked Jack, but he knew how deceptive appearances and first impressions could be. "He had trouble with a previous girlfriend, didn't he?"

"Well, yes, but I expect the story was exaggerated," Marion said. "They had a row and he locked her in her flat. I think he smashed one of the windows too. He didn't physically harm her though."

He did enough to get himself arrested. Yet Marion seemed totally unperturbed by that.

Something else struck him. "Are your daughters out this evening?"

"No, they're upstairs in their rooms." Marion frowned at the question. "There's nothing they can tell you."

"They're—how old? Six and eight?"

"Lydia's nine and Emma's seven."

He was reminded of something Jack said about Sam believing the children were too quiet and too well behaved. Dylan could understand that. Few children would remain in their rooms when visitors were in the house. They were too inquisitive. Even if they'd been sent there, they would make some excuse to see what was going on. They'd want a drink or something to eat.

"They're quiet." Dylan gave them a rueful smile. "My son's eleven and doesn't stop talking."

"We believe in discipline," Alan said.

They were in their rooms, plural. So they weren't even playing together. Unusual.

"Me too," Dylan said. "But children will be children."

Marion smiled but neither commented.

"I've been at the library today," Dylan said, "going through newspaper reports from around the time Sam disappeared. About three months beforehand, a young girl of nineteen vanished, did you know that?"

"Isobel Connor." Marion almost whispered the name.

"That's right." Dylan too lowered his voice as a mark of respect. The girl's body had been found in a disused quarry. "Did Sam know the girl?"

"No. God, it was a terrible time, though. I remember thinking how awful it was for her parents." She shook her head as if to rid herself of the image of the dead girl. "Of course, the next thing, I knew exactly how it felt. Terrifying."

To imagine the two cases were related had been a long shot. A month after the discovery of Isobel's body, police had arrested a man who was currently serving a life sentence.

"She was a prostitute." Alan spoke as if that had made the girl fair game for any killers on the loose.

"But the world's oldest profession shouldn't bring a death sentence with it," Dylan said.

Alan shrugged as if he wasn't convinced. "I'm sure they know the risks they're taking."

He was right in that the girls had been totally different. Isobel had been a drug addict working as a prostitute to feed her habit whereas Sam, by all accounts, would have worked from dawn till dusk and had never even tried a cigarette.

"I gather Sam was fourteen when she went to live with her father," Dylan said. "Is that right?"

"Yes." Marion twisted a ring round her finger. "It happens. She was seeing Rob, and getting spoiled rotten of course, at weekends. She kept on about how great it would be to live with him fulltime."

"I never told her she wasn't welcome here," Alan said.

Dylan wondered if he'd told her she *was* welcome. "The two of you were married by then, were you?"

"Yes." That was Marion's only word on the subject.

Dylan put on his all-pals-together smile. "I imagine she wasn't happy at no longer being the centre of her mum's universe."

"Something like that." Marion stood in one fluid movement. "The police found her scarf, did you know that?"

"I know they found *a* scarf."

She acknowledged that with a nod. "It might not have been hers, I suppose. Rob refuses to accept it was hers. And it doesn't necessarily mean anything, does it? I mean, even if it was hers—well, she could have dropped it and not noticed, couldn't she?"

"Easily."

Dylan couldn't fathom the pair. Alan didn't seem bothered about any of it. It wasn't his daughter who was missing though. It wasn't his flesh and blood. Marion was tense, and definitely unsettled by the thought of the scarf.

The phone rang out again, making Marion start. No one made any attempt to answer it.

"Did Sam talk to you about her boss, James Carlton?" Dylan asked.

"Not that I remember," Alan said. "We didn't see that much of her, though. If I asked her how work was, she'd say fine. She could be a bit stuck up."

"She loved her job." Marion was still twisting that ring round and round her finger. "Alan's away a lot, driving, so he didn't see as much of her as I did." She nudged her husband. "Did you, Alan?"

"No."

"Where do you drive?" Dylan asked. "Long distance?"

"Very." Marion answered for him. "Romania, Hungary—"

"Scotland mostly." Alan's mouth was a hard line.

Dylan smiled. "What an odd mix."

Alan shrugged. "You go where you have to."

A noise had Dylan spinning round in his seat to see that two girls had appeared in the doorway.

"It's seven o'clock," the older one said.

Both were tall and slim. Both had red hair. Both were pale and both wore uncertain expressions.

"It's your lucky night," Alan told them. "We're busy so you can both have another half hour." For Dylan's benefit, he added, "Homework time."

"Off you go." At Marion's command, both girls left the conservatory as soundlessly as they'd entered.

Now Dylan knew exactly what Sam had meant when she'd said they were too quiet. Neither child had seen her father since he'd come in from work, yet there hadn't been so much as a hello, never mind a hug.

In his own home—not that Dylan had been in his own home for months—but when life had been normal, Dylan had always sought out Luke. Or sometimes, if Luke had been in front of the TV or in his room, Bev would have shouted to him, "Your dad's home." Wasn't that normal?

The Rodericks' children had looked too nervous to make a sound.

"They usually do their homework with us at seven o'clock," Marion said. "Children like a routine, don't they?"

Not when it involved homework. At least, Dylan's son didn't. From memory, Dylan hadn't either.

"Perhaps they do," Dylan replied. What did he know? His own childhood, with a dope-smoking hippy, couldn't be classed as normal. "To get back to Sam, her boyfriend thought she had suspicions about her boss. Did she say anything to you?"

Marion smiled at that. "No, but Sam likes a mystery. Sometimes, I think real life's too boring for her."

"Hmm. There was something else that Jack said. He thought she'd discovered something horrible. Did she mention anything to you?"

"Like what?" Alan asked.

"I haven't the remotest idea. I was hoping you might be able to tell me."

"What did she say exactly?"

"Just that," Dylan said. "She found out something horrible."

Alan shook his head. "She has a very vivid imagination. But there, we didn't see that much of her. Most of the time, she called in to see the girls. Sometimes she'd take them out."

"I see."

"The last time we saw her was the day before she vanished," Marion said, "but she was only here five minutes max. She had a quick chat with the girls, promised to take them to school the next morning and was gone."

Rushing off to her date with James Carlton.

Dylan stayed another half hour, but there was nothing they could tell him.

Marion was tense enough to snap in two. Alan was remote. The children were too—spooky. There was something unnatural about their quiet behaviour. Or perhaps they were naturally shy children. Dylan's only experience of children was Luke, and he'd talk to anyone. All day if they could be persuaded to listen.

As he drove away though, Dylan couldn't shake off the feeling that something was wrong at the Rodericks' home.

TWELVE

THE first thing Dylan noticed on entering his flat on Friday evening was the noise. The TV was blaring out and above that came a burst of laughter from his son. For some reason he'd never fathomed, Luke got on well with his grandmother. Dylan just hoped she wasn't rolling joints or convincing Luke he'd enjoy backpacking through darkest Peru.

"Hey, Dad!" Luke raced into the tiny hallway and threw his arms round Dylan's waist. "D'you want a beer? We bought some specially."

"You did? Then, yes. I can think of nothing better." They walked into the minuscule kitchen. Dylan opened the fridge where, sure enough, half a dozen bottles were chilling nicely.

"Hey—your face looks cool. What happened?"

"Cool? So it hasn't marred my good looks?"

"Nah. So what happened?"

"A door took a dislike to me." He wasn't going into details with Luke. "You all ready for the match tomorrow?"

"Can't wait," Luke said. "We'll get an easy three points."

Of course they would. Manchester City would stand no chance.

Dylan's mother came into the kitchen, making it impossible to take a deep breath. He mentally cursed Bev again. She was swanning around the spacious marital home while he existed in this glorified shoebox.

"Hello, love." Vicky Scott dropped a kiss on Dylan's cheek. "Good grief, what happened to you?"

"I walked into a door."

"Really? What a coincidence. I walked into a flying pig."

"Ha, ha. Very droll."

"I'm making myself a camomile tea and taking it to bed," she said. "You'll have to amuse yourselves for the rest of the night."

"Bed?" Dylan checked his watch. "It's only nine o'clock."

Vicky grinned at Luke. "See? I told you your dad was clever. Thirty-eight and he can tell the time already."

Luke hooted with laughter and gave his grandmother a high five.

Dylan was about to take the top from his bottle with his teeth until he remembered that his still-swollen lip might object. He took the opener from the drawer and was soon swigging from the bottle.

"You all right, Mum?" Wearing a long dress that would have camouflaged a peacock and bangles that jangled at her wrists, she looked exactly as she always did. "It's early for bed."

"Good grief, Dylan, it's no wonder Bev's taken off for the Highlands of Scotland. What a fusser you are."

She edged past him to fill the kettle. "Have you had a good week?"

"Fine. And Bev's in Edinburgh not the Highlands."

"Same thing."

"What's she doing there anyway?" He took another swig of beer.

"I've no idea."

"Me neither," Luke said. "All she told me was that she was meeting a friend. I didn't know she had any friends in Scotland."

So she hadn't even told Luke why she was going. Or perhaps she knew that Luke would blab to Dylan. All the same, it was odd.

"It'll be an old school friend, I expect," he said. "Perhaps someone she was at university with."

"Yeah." Luke nodded agreement. "It won't be a bloke, will it?"

"No."

Smiling, Vicky shook her head in a despairing way.

They danced around the tiny space until Vicky had her tea made and Dylan's beer was in a glass.

"Right, see you both in the morning." Vicky kissed Dylan and gave Luke a big squeeze before heading off for the spare room.

This weekend, with Luke in residence, Dylan would be sleeping on the sofa. That was all thanks to this nonsense Bev insisted on.

"How's your Gran been today?" he asked as they walked into the sitting room.

"All right, why?"

"Oh, just wondered." He made a mental note to

keep an eye on his mother. She drove him totally nuts, but he didn't like the thought of her being ill. "So how's your week been, Luke?"

"Great. Well, school's been boring, but Tom had a party and that was brill."

Luke had to be the easiest person to be with Dylan had ever known. He didn't talk for the sake of it, he was interesting. Also, he never failed to see the funny side of life.

A little before nine-thirty, Bev phoned.

"I suppose Luke's still up?" she said.

"Of course he is. It's the weekend." Dylan was more interested in *her* evening. "How's Edinburgh?"

"Brilliant. We've found this amazing restaurant near the castle."

"That sounds nice." He had to ask. "Who's *we?*"

"Just a friend. Pass Luke over, will you?"

"Of course."

While Luke chatted to his mother, Dylan went to the fridge for another beer. Months back, when Bev had thrown him out, she'd called him a drunkard and a bloody loser. It was a Friday night and he was on his second beer of the day. Hardly a drunkard. He wasn't a loser, either. Come hell or high water, he'd learn the truth behind Samantha Hunt's disappearance.

He sat opposite Luke, waiting for the call to end.

"Okay, Mum. Do you want to talk to Dad again?" Dylan reached forward.

"Oh, right. Yeah, okay, Mum, speak to you tomorrow."

With a shrug for Dylan, Luke put the phone back

in its cradle and let out a long sigh. "I wish we were all at home. I mean, this flat's cool, Dad, but I wish we were all together."

"Me too."

"Tom reckons Mum's having a midlife crisis. Do you think he's right?"

"A midlife crisis?" At thirty-six? What could an eleven-year-old know of such things? "I don't know, Luke. Could be, I suppose."

The thought of suggesting it to Bev as a possibility made Dylan smile. He'd see what sort of mood she was in on Sunday.

They talked of simpler things, like the probable team lineup for tomorrow's game, why beavers built dams, and the best ever barbecue food.

"It's eleven o'clock," Dylan said. "Time you were in bed, Luke."

"Okay. Do you want me to have the sofa? I don't mind. Honest."

"No, you're fine. I've got a bit of work to do tonight so I'll be better in here."

When Luke had gone to bed and all was quiet, Dylan got himself another beer, sat back with his feet resting on the coffee table and tried to think of things less confusing than his wife.

Since his visit to the Rodericks' home on Wednesday night, progress had been minimal. Correction, progress had been zero.

He'd met with Frank again but his ex-boss hadn't garnered much information from Lancashire CID and the officers who'd first worked on the case. He was a persistent sod though, so Dylan would be patient.

Dylan had spoken to a couple of parents of children who attended Marion Roderick's preschool group but, while they thought highly of the care their children received, they didn't know Marion well. One of them told him of an Elma Ritchie who'd taken her child out of the group and Dylan was meeting her on Monday morning.

Next on the agenda, Dylan needed to dig into James Carlton's life a little more. Sam had suspected him of fraud. She'd tried to get close enough to learn the truth. The day after she spent the evening with him, she vanished. Coincidence?

Jack Fleming was another enigma. Dylan had liked him and taken his word. On the other hand, few people ended up with a criminal record without cause. Dylan had, of course, but that was different. Also, he only had Jack's word for it that the child Sam was supposedly carrying was his. What if it was James Carlton's? What if Sam had been trying to get close to Carlton and fallen for him? How would Jack have taken that?

But no. Dylan had heard Sam's voice. She'd told Jack she loved him.

Dylan closed his eyes and mentally replayed that recording. On the surface, it all rang true. Sam had sounded breathless, her words coming in short bursts.

Jack was a musician and Dylan would bet that he and his fellow band members played around, recording themselves and editing stuff on their computers.

Assuming Sam had called Jack several times, it would have been easy enough for an expert editor to make her say anything. And who was to say that message had been left when Jack said it had?

The fact had to be faced that Jack didn't mess around where his girlfriends were concerned.

Motive. Dylan needed to think of a motive.

If Carlton had been on the brink of being exposed as a fraud, he could have wanted to silence Sam for good. If the child Sam may or may not have been carrying was his, he might have wanted that silenced too. Carlton's wife was the one with the money. She might not hang around if she knew her husband was getting young women pregnant.

If Sam had wanted to end her relationship with Jack, he might not have taken kindly to the news. Whether or not he'd do something quite so drastic about it, Dylan had no idea.

As for the Rodericks, Dylan still didn't know what to make of them. He felt sure they knew more than they were saying.

His thoughts went round and round and somehow ended up back with Bev. Who the devil was she with?

Coming up with no answers, he went to the fridge for another beer. She'd called him a drunkard so he might as well live up to his reputation.

ON SUNDAY EVENING, DYLAN stopped the car outside the marital home. He was determined to indulge in a spot of straight talking with Bev. Apart from anything else, keeping two homes going—if he could call that flat of his a home—was downright expensive. Also, it gave his mother an excuse to hang around. She'd be far better off back in Birmingham. At least, Dylan would be better off if she was back there.

Luke, his bag swinging off his shoulder, raced on ahead. Bev was home because her car—their car—was on the drive, but the door was locked so Dylan rang the bell. How many husbands had to ring the confounded bell to gain entrance to their own homes?

She opened it and her face was bathed in smiles. "Hello. How are my two favourite boys?"

Oh, for—she'd been drinking. He was the drunkard and the bloody loser. Allegedly. Yet she was the one having to lean against the door frame for support.

Luke looked at Dylan and rolled his eyes. "Hi, Mum. You all right?"

"Never better." She bumped into the wall as she walked down the hall and into the kitchen where Dylan saw an inch of white wine in the bottom of a bottle.

She spun around to look at him and he saw her struggle to bring his mouth into focus.

"Have you been fighting?" She wagged a finger at him as if he were one of her pupils.

"Sadly, no. That was the other bloke." He didn't want to talk about it. "Have you had a good time?"

Straight talking was out of the question. She didn't drink often but, when she did, all she did was giggle. Until she had more than she could handle, at which point she burst into tears about something trivial.

"Great." She picked up the bottle and waved it in front of Dylan. "You want a drink?"

He didn't, not really, but it would give him an excuse to stay. "Why not? Thanks."

She took an unopened bottle of white wine from the fridge and handed it to Dylan to open. At least he still had his uses.

"You're drunk, Mum!"

"Nonsense. A bit tipsy, that's all. So how's your gran? Have you behaved? Did you have a good time?"

"Yeah, it was cool. What about you?" Luke asked. "What have you been doing?"

"Oh, a bit of shopping."

"It's a long way to go to shop."

Laughing, she hugged him tight. "You're as nosey as your dad."

The phone rang out. Bev reached for it, dropped it, picked it up and almost dropped it again before trilling out the number. "It's Tom for you, Luke. Don't chat too long and you can't see him after school tomorrow because it's Lucy's party, okay?"

"Yeah, yeah." Luke carried the phone to the sitting room to chat to his friend in private.

Bev fell into a chair at the table. She looked—well, Dylan couldn't decide. There was an excitable look about her, but that could be alcohol induced. She was wearing black jeans and a loose white shirt. Her hair was blonder than when they'd lived together.

"Are you celebrating?" Dylan sat opposite her.

"Celebrating what?"

"You tell me."

She took an enormous swallow of wine. "No, I'm not really celebrating. I just fancied a drink. Although it's always good to get home, isn't it?"

Her comment warmed him. This was her home and she was happy to be here. So she couldn't have any desire to up sticks and live in Edinburgh.

"I wouldn't know."

"Oh, Dylan." She wagged an accusing finger at him. "Your flat must feel like home now."

"Of course it doesn't. It never will. It'll always be temporary." But he knew there was no reasoning with her when she was drunk. "So what did you find to do in Edinburgh? And who's this friend you've been with?"

She looked at him for long moments. Either she was considering how to answer or she was trying to get him in focus. "His name's Leonard."

Dylan felt the air leave his lungs as if someone had punched him. Hard. Twice he opened his mouth to speak and twice nothing happened.

"I met him on the internet," she said.

"What? You did what? For Christ's sake, Bev." Now he couldn't seem to stop the words tripping over themselves. "How old are you, for Christ's sake? You can't go off meeting strangers. Anything could happen!"

"I'm not stupid."

"You're exactly that if you've gone all the way to Edinburgh to meet some aspiring fucking axe murderer."

She rolled her eyes and sighed loudly. "Dylan, I

am not stupid. I met him over the internet, yes, but through work. I was in contact with him through the school. He's a librarian."

For some reason this didn't make Dylan feel any better. Leonard was still a he. Bev had still spent the weekend with him.

"Christ!" Dylan helped himself to another glass of wine. He'd have to leave his car here and get a taxi home. Which would mean getting another taxi early in the morning. He was past caring though. Well past caring. He drank some wine and took a deep calming breath. "Where did you stay?"

"What do you mean?"

Before Dylan could give vent to his frustration, Luke came back. He grabbed an apple and sat beside Dylan. "Tom's got a new mobile phone. I think I should have one, don't you?" He looked from one to the other of them. Even he sensed the charged atmosphere in the room. "Perhaps now isn't a good time to ask."

"Nonsense." Bev put down her glass and gazed at their son. "What sort do you want?"

"It's not a good time to ask." Luke was confident of that. "I'll have a think and we'll talk about it tomorrow, yeah?"

"Good idea," Dylan agreed. Talking to Bev right now was a waste of breath.

They chatted about mundane things, like the new "weirdo" teacher at Luke's school, but Dylan's mind was still going to dark places that centred around Bev and the unknown Leonard.

By the time Luke went to bed, Dylan was feeling slightly sick.

When they were alone again, Bev descended into silence. Dylan guessed it was the calm before the proverbial storm. Any minute now, she'd be crying about some long-dead pet hamster.

"Let's go and sit down, shall we?" She picked up the wine, steadied herself with the help of the back of her chair as she stood and then swayed into the lounge.

Dylan was surprised he hadn't been thrown out. Then again, nothing should surprise him when she was drunk.

She sat on the sofa and Dylan sat beside her in what had always been his place. She didn't object.

"I didn't sleep with him," she said.

Her statement should have brought relief and reassurance, not another punch in the stomach. "Did you want to?"

She kicked off her shoes and curled her feet beneath her. "I wanted to want to." She turned to look at him. "Does that make sense?"

"Of course it does." He longed to shake her until she saw sense. People fell in love, they got married, they had kids and that was that. Some people fell out of love and got divorced. He and Bev, however, had never fallen out of love. And she knew it. "I feel like that all the time."

Her expression changed from shocked to sad in the blink of an eye.

"When I'm stuck in that flat," he said, "I long to

go out for the evening with an interesting, attractive woman, take her back to my place—no, take her back to *her* place—"

"All right, I get the picture." She banged down her glass on the table. "That's charming, that is."

"I wasn't the one who spent the weekend in Edinburgh with someone else."

She was quiet for so long that Dylan thought she'd fallen asleep. Her eyes were closed, her breathing regular—

"I didn't spend the weekend with him," she said at last. "Our school and his local school are doing a swap in the summer. A load of our pupils are going up there and the Scots are coming down here for a fortnight. The logistics are a nightmare. I'm one of six trying to sort things out this end and he's liaising with the school up there."

"I see." He didn't, not really.

"So, along with two teachers from their school, I met up with Leonard." She sniffed, and then a solitary tear rolled down her cheek. "That was Friday night and the four of us spent an hour together on Saturday morning. The rest of the day I shopped. Today, I had a walk up by the castle and then caught the plane home."

"Right."

She promptly burst into tears and Dylan had no idea why. Was she thinking of the day she buried Goldie Goldfish, was she upset because she'd told him the real reason for her trip to Edinburgh, or was she sad because she hadn't found her way into Leonard's bed?

"You've had too much wine, Bev."

"I know." She rubbed the tears from her eyes, smearing makeup across her face. "Will you stay here tonight, Dylan? Please?"

Mentally, he rubbed his hands in glee. This was the first step. Once he spent the night, it would become permanent. Life would return to—

"You've spent enough nights on the sofa in the past," she said, "so one more won't hurt, will it?"

"The sofa?"

"The spare bed's a mess. I've been sorting out junk in the attic and it's all piled up in there."

It was Sunday. The last time he'd had the luxury of a bed was Thursday night. Hell's teeth.

"Listen, why don't I sleep where I should? In my bed? In our bed?"

She made a noise that could have been yes or no. Seconds later she was snoring like—well, like a woman who'd polished off the best part of two bottles of wine.

THIRTEEN

"STOP snivelling, Crina!" Anca was trying to be patient with her sister, but it was difficult. "It's going to be fine. Better than fine, it's going to be wonderful. You do want to go to England, don't you?"

Crina sniffed and nodded.

"Well then, stop snivelling and give me a smile."

"Sorry."

Crina's sobbed apology softened Anca's mood. Her sister had just had her thirteenth birthday so it was natural that she should be frightened. Anca was fifteen and even she was scared. She knew, though, that their only chance of a decent life was in England.

She couldn't think about the horror stories she'd heard or worry about the statistics surrounding girls forced into the sex trade. All she could do was trust George. He'd said he could only get cleaning jobs because they couldn't speak English. That was fine. Better than fine. For herself, she could cope with anything if it meant a better life for them. The thought brought an involuntary shudder and she amended it to *almost* anything.

George could be trusted, she was sure of it. She must be positive and upbeat.

"We'll sleep in a real bed, Crina. Imagine that. No

more sleeping in the rain. No more begging for food. We'll eat and sleep, earn lots of money—I can work hard, you know I can, and I bet it's not long before we can buy our own apartment. It'll have a bed, a kitchen and everything."

Crina nodded again, but she didn't look excited by the prospect.

As frightened as she was, Anca couldn't wait to get moving. She felt sure they could trust George. He wore clothes unlike anything she'd ever seen. They'd been so fine, she'd longed to reach out and touch his sleeve. She hadn't, of course.

"Come on." Anca reached for Crina's hand. "If we walk slowly, it will be almost eight o'clock when we get to the station."

Crina put her smaller, trusting hand in hers and they set off at a slow pace.

Please be there, George. Please be there.

When they arrived at the station, the big clock told them it was only twenty past seven. They still had forty long minutes to wait.

They sat on a bench outside, close enough to see who came and left, but not close enough for the police to move them on. Even at this early hour, there were a few rich tourists about, but Anca ignored them. If the police caught her, if she missed George—

She couldn't bear it.

Crina was sobbing again. She'd be fine for a few minutes, her attention on something else, then she'd start crying.

"Crina, stop it. Soon we'll be in England. Maybe even tonight."

Crina looked at her, her big dark eyes filled with doubt, and Anca had to look away. Maybe it was foolish to trust George. "Trust no one," had been Dănuţ's advice.

The minutes dragged by.

Anca was hungry, but she couldn't risk begging or stealing food. This was too important. It was worth starving for.

At ten minutes to eight, Anca's spirits dipped. He wasn't coming. It cost a lot of money to get them to England and, although they would pay him back, that would take time. He'd probably found someone more grateful to take their places.

"He might not come," she warned Crina.

"What will happen if he doesn't?"

"Why, you silly thing, we'll get by. We always get by, don't we?"

"Yes." Crina smiled at her.

Anca went inside to check the clock and watched it touch the hour. Just as she stepped outside again, a large car slowed to a stop. It had dark windows so she couldn't see inside. The door opened.

"It's George!" Anca could have wept with relief. "Crina, it's George!"

He walked toward them, looking up and down the street all the while, until he was standing in front of them.

"Get in the car," he said. "Quickly."

Anca tugged on Crina's arm and half-dragged her slow-moving sister to the vehicle.

George opened the back door and bundled them inside. "Good girls."

Anca had never been in a car before or, if she had, she couldn't remember. She certainly hadn't been inside one like this. The seats were a beautiful dark blue leather. She inhaled, drinking in the smell of the hide.

George sat in the front seat. Another man was driving.

The car pulled away and Anca was surprised to discover that, although no one could see inside the car, she had a perfect view of the streets. She felt an urge to wave at the people, to shout out the good news. *We're going to England!*

Crina shivered beside her, which was silly as it was warm inside the car.

"Are we going to England now, George?" Anca asked.

"Soon. First you must have a medical."

"A medical? Why?"

"It's the rule. Don't worry, it won't take long, and then you'll be on your way to England."

He turned and spoke to the driver in a language Anca didn't understand.

Anca was terrified. She hadn't expected them to undergo a medical. She and Crina were both healthy, at least, she hoped they were, but Dănut knew all there was to know about England and he'd never mentioned such a thing.

It felt like hours but was probably only minutes later when the car slowed in front of tall metal gates. The gates opened as if by magic and the car glided round a curve in the road to stop in front of a tall house with shutters at the windows. It reminded Anca of the first orphanage she and Crina had stayed in. The memory made her shudder. They'd had to run from there.

"Is this where we have our medicals?" she asked.

"Yes." George didn't seem as friendly as he had last week. Perhaps he was worried. Anca knew he was breaking the law, and she tried to feel grateful to him.

The house had a grand-looking exterior, but, when they were led inside, Anca thought it shabby. Dirty too.

She and Crina were taken to a small, windowless room and told to wait.

"I'm frightened," Crina whispered.

"Don't be silly. What is there to be frightened of?" The only thing that worried Anca was failing their medical. Once they reached England, they would cope with anything. If the jobs George found them weren't what he'd promised, they would run away and find something else.

A large woman came into the room. "You first." She addressed Crina.

"Can't we both—"

"Of course not." She dismissed Anca's protest. "The room is very small and the doctor is a busy man."

Anca nodded. It made sense and she didn't want to be a nuisance. "Go on, Crina. I'll be right behind you."

With Crina gone, Anca grew nervous. She was supposed to look out for her sister and it didn't feel right to be parted. No harm could come to her though. She was only having a medical and would be back soon.

A couple of minutes later, the nurse returned. "Your turn now."

Anca jumped to her feet, pleased that it hadn't taken long. "Where's Crina?"

"Waiting for you. Come along now."

Anca followed her to another small room where a young man with a stethoscope round his neck told her lie on the couch. Shaking, Anca did so.

"Right," he said, "this won't take a moment." He filled a syringe.

"What's that?" She hated the way her voice shook.

"Inoculation for England," he replied. "Hold out your arm."

Anca thrust out her arm. She hadn't realised inoculations were needed, but was more than happy to have one. This was it. She was going to England.

He plunged the needle into her arm, then took the stethoscope that was hanging round his neck to listen to her heart.

"That's it," he said. "All done."

How stupid they'd been to worry. Their medicals had taken two minutes at most and soon, they would begin their new lives in England.

Anca tried to sit up. The room began to spin, forcing her to grip the sides of the couch. "I don't feel—"

Her voice wasn't working properly. Again, she tried to sit up. She couldn't. Her muscles refused to cooperate.

Where was Crina?

It was her last conscious thought.

FOURTEEN

DYLAN had arranged to meet Elma Ritchie at Starbucks at eleven-thirty and he was there with twenty minutes to spare. As he'd been late setting out for Lancashire, thanks mainly to having to leave the marital home—make that marital *bed*, oh yes—and go to his flat for his clothes, he called that a result.

He ordered coffee and a muffin and read through the local paper while he waited for her. It was preferable to trying to figure out what the teenager at the next table was listening to on his iPod.

A couple of middle-aged women two tables away were discussing their respective diets.

"I always have my main meal at lunchtime," one was saying. "That way, you burn off the calories."

She was at least twenty-five stones. Who the hell would take dietary advice from a woman that size?

Yawning, Dylan folded his newspaper. Tired didn't even begin to describe how he felt. He'd spent a few uncomfortable hours on that sofa with a comatose Bev. She'd woken up around four, decided the sofa was too uncomfortable and suggested they went to bed. He hadn't had a wink of sleep since.

At a couple of minutes after eleven-thirty, the door opened and a woman of about thirty stood in the doorway, looking at the customers. Dylan rose to his feet and she came over to him.

"Dylan Scott?"

"That's me. You'll be Mrs. Ritchie?" They shook hands. "Can I get you something?"

"A cappuccino would be great, thanks. Oh, and I'm Elma."

"Dylan."

He went to the counter and bought two coffees, a cappuccino for Elma and a strong black filter for himself in the hope that it might wake him up.

When he returned to the table, she was removing a white cotton jacket. She was plain with long dark hair tied back from a naturally pale face. Slim and tall, she was wearing white calf-length trousers and a loose red T-shirt.

"Thanks," she said, as he put the coffee in front of her. "I'm sorry I had to meet you here but I'm busy on Mondays. After I've taken Josh and Theo to school, I do two hours at the Red Cross shop, have half an hour here and then cover for an hour in my sister's shop while she has a lunch break."

"You are busy." Dylan smiled at her. "Thanks for meeting me."

"You said you wanted to talk about the preschool group that Josh attended?"

"That's right. I spoke to a friend of yours, a Valerie Goodfellow—"

"Yes, she told me."

"She said you took your child out of the group. Is that right?"

"I did, yes." She spooned the chocolate from the top of her cappuccino. "I'm sure it was a perfectly good nursery, but I didn't think it suited Josh."

"Oh? How do you mean?"

"It's difficult to say." She thought for a moment and was frowning as she continued. "He was only three and a half, but he'd always been so outgoing. He was just a normal, noisy boy who was into everything. After a couple of months there, he became quiet and withdrawn."

Dylan wanted information on Marion and Alan Roderick and the fact that one three-year-old possibly hadn't enjoyed the preschool playgroup managed by Marion meant nothing. Yet Dylan knew it was from these seemingly meaningless conversations that little gems sometimes came.

"And when you removed Josh from the group," he asked, "how was he then?"

"I put him in another one across town. After a couple of months, he was back to normal again."

"Could it have been a phase he was going through? Missing his mother perhaps?"

She sipped her coffee and shrugged. "It could have been that, yes, although he's never been clingy. I've often worried that he'd happily go off with anyone."

Dylan didn't think this was relevant to anything. To find out what happened to Sam Hunt though, he needed to know her family, friends and acquaintances better than he knew himself.

"What about Marion, the woman who ran the group?" he asked. "Do you know her well?"

"Not really. She seems nice enough, and she's certainly well qualified." She looked straight at Dylan. "I can't say there was anything wrong with the group or with Marion Roderick. All I can tell you is that I wasn't happy taking my son there. The change in him may have been down to something else entirely, but I was happier when he was going to a new group."

"I can understand that." It could be that Elma was simply an overprotective mother.

"Sometimes her husband was there. I can't remember his name—a big man. They were having a couple of the small side rooms painted and he was helping out with that. I didn't like him."

"Oh? Why was that?"

"They'd obviously had a row, him and Marion, and although she was trying to be bright and sunny, he was moody and sullen. It was embarrassing. It's difficult to explain, but I just didn't like him."

Dylan hadn't, either. It was a gut reaction.

"How about Sam Hunt, Marion's daughter. Do you know her?"

"No, but I remember reading about her in the paper. She just vanished, didn't she?"

"That's right."

"Sorry, I never knew her."

"Did you speak to any of the other parents at the group? Was anyone else dissatisfied with it?"

"We used to chat when we arrived with our kids or fetched them," she said, "but no, I never heard anyone complain. Having said that, I didn't mention my concerns to anyone. We'd talk about the weather, and how quickly the children were growing—stuff like that. I was friendly with Val, of course, but she didn't have much to do with it. Her daughter's older than Josh and was only there for a couple of months." Elma glanced at her watch and finished her coffee. "It's time I was going. Sorry."

"That's okay. If you think of anything else, or hear anything to do with Josh's old preschool group or Marion Roderick, will you call me?" He reached into his pocket and pulled out one of the business cards he'd had printed. They almost made him feel like a real private investigator.

She gazed at the card then put it in her purse. "Of course."

He watched her leave and wondered if she really was nothing more than an overprotective mother. He couldn't buy that. Marion's own children were equally quiet and withdrawn. Sam had noticed the same thing.

THE TOWN'S LIBRARY WAS AN old stone building trying to drag itself into the twenty-first century. After his last spell in Dawson's Clough, looking into the disappearance of Anita Champion, Dylan was all too familiar with the layout of the building. He was becoming a regular visitor again and was soon looking through old newspapers that had finally made it to microfilm.

He sat at the first of a row of six machines and read through the news from around the time of Sam's disappearance. He didn't know what he was looking for, and wouldn't know until he found it. He spotted the report of Isobel Connor's disappearance and subsequent murder that he'd already seen. He read through it again in case there was something he'd missed. There wasn't. He couldn't imagine the two cases being related.

The only things he found for Marion Roderick's preschool playgroup were adverts saying places were available and one short news piece covering a Christmas party. Photos of children stuffing cake in their mouths dominated the article.

One story caught his eye, that of a young girl who disappeared a month before Sam Hunt vanished. Again, he couldn't see any link. The girl in question, Fiona Partridge, was a few days short of her sixteenth birthday, and interviews with her distraught parents were published almost daily. They told how they'd been separated but how this trauma in their lives had brought them back together. Fiona was reunited with the happy couple nine days later. In a case that highlighted the dangers of teenagers using the internet, she'd met up with a man she believed to be eighteen years old. The thirty-four-year-old sex offender she'd actually met up with was currently serving a jail sentence.

Other than the fact that it had happened shortly before Sam Hunt vanished, there was nothing to link the cases. Sam had shown no interest in the social networking sites.

Dylan trawled more pages but nothing grabbed his interest. Dawson's Clough was a typical working-class northern town where people still knew their neighbours. Very little happened here.

Shortly after one o'clock, he left the library and spotted a young woman dashing inside the café opposite. It was Kerry Adams, the receptionist from Carlton's Classics.

Dylan took his time crossing the road. He wanted Kerry to be seated with her order given before he joined her. She'd been uneasy talking to him and it was possible she'd leave rather than repeat the experience.

To pass a few minutes, he went in the florist's next to the café. One minute he was trying not to look shocked at the price of flowers, the next he was handing over his credit card.

"What message do you want?" the girl asked him.

"Oh—" He thought for a moment. "Hope the hangover isn't too bad."

The assistant smiled. "Will she know who they're from? Or are you a secret admirer?"

Bev wouldn't know who'd sent them because she'd think he had more sense than to spend almost a week's rent on flowers, and he didn't want her thinking she had secret admirers.

"Sign it Dylan, please."

"As in the singer."

He nodded. "No relation."

"They'll be delivered late this afternoon. She'll love them."

Bev might. His credit card wouldn't. Still amazed at such recklessness, he left the florist's and marched into the café.

It was small, only having room for six tables with

four chairs at each. Luckily, it was busy with lunch-time trade.

Kerry Adams was sitting alone, a fork in one hand and a magazine in the other. She looked up at him and returned her attention to her reading. It was impossible to tell if she'd recognised him or not.

She was eating fish and chips. Dylan went to the counter and, despite planning on a sandwich, ordered the curry and rice. He carried his coffee over to her table.

"Hi, Kerry. Mind if I join you?"

Her head flew up and a tide of scarlet flooded her face as recognition dawned. She looked at other tables but, if she longed to demand that he sit elsewhere, she was too polite.

"Help yourself." She put down her magazine and concentrated on her food.

"I've just come from the library." Dylan was determined to get her talking. "What about you? Have you got a day off?"

"I'm on my lunch break." She was eating quickly, risking indigestion.

"I'm no further forward in finding Sam." He took a sip of coffee. "No one will tell me anything. That's odd, don't you think?"

"Not really. No one knows anything."

Perhaps they didn't. Maybe Sam had fallen into the river and been swept away. Doubtful. The river was only a foot deep in places.

"She was having a fling with your boss, wasn't she?"

"Oh, I don't—" She pushed her hair from her face and speared a chunk of fish. "Maybe."

"She must have told you. I've seen photos of the two of you together. I'll bet she told you." He'd only seen one photo, but she wasn't to know that.

She looked up at him and, just as Dylan expected her to deny all knowledge, her eyes filled with tears.

"Whatever's the matter?"

"Nothing." She reached into a cavernous black bag for a tissue. "It's nothing. She—Sam wasn't having a fling with him."

"Oh?"

She put down her knife and fork. Dylan hoped he hadn't stolen her appetite.

"No." She sniffed into her tissue. "She was—if you want the truth, although for God's sake don't tell Carlton I said this—"

"I won't. You have my word."

"Okay." She leaned across the table and spoke in a low voice. "Sam reckoned he was fiddling the books. No sooner had a rumour started that he had gambling debts—" she paused to check that no one was listening in "—than a whole bunch of cars go missing. A break-in. Except Sam didn't think it was a break-in."

"Really?" She'd confirmed Jack's story. "What did she do about it?"

"She asked me to get her some files from his office." Kerry swallowed. "I did—she was very persuasive—but then he noticed they were missing. Of course, I made out that he'd mislaid them—or I had—and promised to sort it out."

"Did Sam return those files?"

"That's just it. She vanished, didn't she?"

"I see." So where were the files now? "Did you tell the police?"

"I couldn't, could I?" She took a breath. "I assume she took them home and they're still there. I'm sure Carlton suspected something, though."

"What makes you think that?"

"Just the way he looked when he kept asking about the files, I suppose." She poked at the remains of her fish, but didn't eat any. "I don't know what happened to her."

"Do you think James Carlton could have been involved?"

She thought for a moment. "No."

"What about her boyfriend?"

"Jack? No way. He doted on her." She took a sip of what had to be cold coffee. "I've thought of nothing else since she disappeared, and I've no idea what happened to her."

"Curry and rice," the waitress said, banging the plate down in front of Dylan. "Enjoy!"

"Thank you."

"I have to go." Kerry shoved her magazine in her bag and strode out of the café.

FIFTEEN

Bev still had her hangover when Luke announced his arrival home from school by banging every door in the house.

"Hey, Mum, Darren's mum's outside in the car. She'll give me a lift to the party. I just need to change and collect the present."

Bev followed him up the stairs. She had her first glimpse of him pulling open drawers.

"That's nice of her. And don't forget it's Lucy's party, not Darren's. Be nice to Lucy, right?"

"Yeah. Where's the present?"

"All wrapped and ready on the kitchen table. I'll just go and say hello to Jenny."

Deciding she probably looked better than she felt—she certainly couldn't look worse—Bev went outside to where Jenny's car was parked.

"This is kind of you, Jenny. Thanks."

"It's no bother and hardly out of the way. Rod's at home today so if any of the other kids are early, he can deal with them." She pulled a face. "I'm beginning to wish I'd taken them all to McDonald's instead."

"Always a safe bet," Bev agreed with a laugh. "What time do you want me to collect Luke?"

"Whenever's best for you. The other kids will be

leaving around sevenish I hope, but Luke can stay as long as he likes. He and Darren are able to amuse themselves quietly."

Luke, duly changed into clean jeans and shirt, and looking as if the unthinkable had happened and he'd combed his hair, rushed out to join them.

"Present," Bev said.

"Oh, yeah." Luke did an about-turn and, seconds later, emerged clutching Lucy's birthday present and card. "See you later then, Mum."

He was soon strapping himself into the back seat.

"Behave yourself." Bev's warning was probably unnecessary, not because Luke was a saint but because Jenny, a geography teacher at Bev's school, could easily handle a few rowdy kids.

"Thanks again, Jenny. Oh, and the best of luck."

"I'll need it!"

Bev waved until the car was out of sight and then wandered back inside to enjoy a couple of hours' freedom. She had a stack of books so she'd have a long soak in the bath and a good read. And no wine, she reminded herself. A glass of wine, bath and book were the height of luxury as far as she was concerned but, lately, that glass had progressed to a bottle. Lately was since Dylan had moved out. Or since she'd thrown him out.

A huge, beautifully wrapped, hand-tied bouquet of flowers, mainly lilies, dominated the room. When she'd answered the door to the delivery girl, she'd been about to tell her she had the wrong house. She couldn't remember the last time Dylan had bought her flowers. Probably when Luke was born.

Every time she looked at them, her stomach, or her heart, gave a tiny lurch.

She was hunting through the pile of unread paperbacks in the lounge when her doorbell rang. She ignored it. She didn't want to buy anything and, more important, she didn't want her solitude stolen.

A figure appeared at the window and tapped on the glass.

"Vicky!" With a hand to her chest to slow her heartbeat, Bev went to the back door and let in her mother-in-law. "You gave me a fright."

"Sorry, love. I was out this way so I thought I'd call in for a cuppa. Luke not here?"

"No, he's just left for Lucy's party. That's Darren's sister." No one was ever "out this way." Vicky Scott had come to deliver one of her lectures.

Bev pushed the unkind thought away. She adored her mother-in-law and it was great having a willing babysitter in London. It was just that, after last night—the overindulgence, the prat she'd made of herself in front of Dylan, the way she'd practically begged him to take her to bed—Bev wanted to lick her wounds in private.

"I'll put the kettle on. It'll have to be PG Tips," she added. "I don't have camomile or—"

"So long as it's hot and wet." Vicky removed a smart linen jacket and two silk scarves, and put them on the back of the chair before sitting at the table.

Bev was glad she'd tidied the kitchen. She'd

wanted to erase all thoughts of last night so, once she'd thrown out empty wine bottles and washed glasses, she'd scrubbed every surface until the room gleamed. If only it was as easy to erase the evidence from memory.

"How was your weekend?" Vicky asked.

"It was good, thanks." It was time she was honest with her mother-in-law too. "It was work, Vicky, nothing more than that. The school funded the trip and, believe it or not, it was cheaper for me to stay on Saturday night and fly back yesterday."

"Ah. Well, it's none of my business, I'm sure."

Damn it. Dylan and his mother both shared the same knack of making her feel guilty.

"Dylan stayed here last night," she said, and her mother-in-law nodded.

"I assumed he had."

No questions were asked and for that Bev was grateful. She made the tea and put Vicky's cup in front of her. "Do you want a slice of cake? Orange drizzle?"

"That sounds good. Thanks."

It was easy for Bev to ooh and aah over cake, and make small talk, but impossible to forget the mess she was in.

"Those flowers are gorgeous," Vicky said.

It was too much to hope that Vicky hadn't noticed them. Or guessed who they were from.

"Yes."

"It must be nice to know someone's thinking of you when he's a long way from home."

"We had too much wine," Bev said. "That's why Dylan stayed here. We—slept on the sofa."

There was no need to tell Vicky that she'd dragged Dylan to bed. Nor was there any need to tell her how good it had been.

That was the problem, of course. Half of her, the stupid half that refused to listen to the sensible part of her brain, still loved him.

"He's changed, love," Vicky said.

"In what way?"

"Lots of ways. I know he's been—difficult."

"Difficult?" Bev laughed at the understatement. "He's been impossible. Night after night—you can't imagine what it was like to come home after a long day at work and listen to all his woes. Then, when he'd depressed the hell out of me, he'd get drunk and maudlin and—oh, downright unbearable."

Bev knew what was coming. Vicky would tell her—again—how difficult it had been for Dylan. How the shock of finding himself on an assault charge, winding up in prison and then losing his job had affected him. She'd remind Bev that Dylan had longed to join the police force almost from the moment he was born.

"He felt useless and redundant," Vicky said. "He worships you and Luke and he felt as if he'd let you both down."

"But I told him time and time again that we were right behind him. God, Vicky, I knew that piece of scum he arrested deserved everything he got. I knew it was wrong that he wound up in prison. I kept telling him he was the same man I married. Nothing made an iota of difference."

It was a trap Bev had no intention of falling into again. While Dylan was spending time in Lancashire, meaning they only saw each other briefly at weekends, it was easy to think they could get back together and everything would be great. Experience had taught her otherwise. She'd been there, done that and burned the T-shirt.

"He's changed," Vicky insisted. "He's more like his old self again. I think, although he probably wouldn't admit it, that he's enjoying his work every bit as much as he did when he was on the force. You know what he's like, love. He likes to be in control. Now he can do the job his way. He doesn't have to follow a rule-book."

Bev wasn't convinced. She knew what Vicky meant, but she also knew it could be a novelty thing. Once that wore off, he'd probably revert to his depressed and depressing self. Besides, she was still enjoying life. These days, when she saw so little of him, she could enjoy his company. She'd certainly enjoyed it last night.

"We'll see," she said. "Anyway, never mind me and Dylan. How are you? Did you have a good weekend with Luke?"

"Yes, and that reminds me. I was thinking about the summer holidays."

"Oh?" Bev knew she sounded wary, but she couldn't help it. There would be no mention of a fortnight in Tenerife.

"I've found this great place—" Beaming with childlike delight, Vicky delved inside her cavernous leather bag and pulled out a brochure. When she'd found the page she wanted, she slapped it down on the table. "Camel trekking in the Sahara. How does that sound?"

If there were words to describe how it sounded, Bev had never stumbled across them.

"It's not all camel riding," Vicky explained. "You drive some of the way. But just imagine trekking across the desert on a camel. The photos are amazing."

The brochure showed artistic photos of camels. And sand. And more camels.

"How many five-star hotels with twenty-four-hour room service are there in the desert, Vicky?"

Her mother-in-law laughed at that. "Who needs room service?"

"Me."

"Nonsense. A holiday is supposed to be something special, an adventure, something to look back on in your old age. Just imagine sleeping under the stars in the desert." She prodded the brochure. "You get a guide and everything. They don't just let you loose with a camel and a map."

"There's a relief."

"Doesn't it sound fun? I haven't mentioned it to Dylan, you know what a stick-in-the-mud he is when it comes to holidays, but I think it would be great. All four of us could go. We'd have a marvellous time, wouldn't we?"

Bev looked from the camels to Vicky. "Do you know what Dylan said to me on our first date?"

"What was that, love?"

"He said 'I'm perfectly normal but my mother's as mad as a box of frogs.' I thought he was joking." She spluttered with laughter. "My God, Vicky, he's right. You are."

"Ah, but I'm not sleeping hundreds of miles away from the man I love." Vicky returned the brochure to her bag. "I've sent off for more information so we'll talk about it then, shall we? Now then, let's have another piece of that cake."

SIXTEEN

It took a moment for James Carlton to remember where he'd seen the yellow Morgan before and, when he did, irritation tensed his muscles. He disliked Dylan Scott as much as he disliked all the probing questions. However, if there was the slightest chance of seeing Carlton's Classics on TV, he had to impress.

It was almost seven and Kerry had gone home over an hour ago. James was alone.

He stood his ground, king of his glass showroom, and smiled a greeting. "Hello. Dylan Scott, isn't it?"

"You've got a good memory." Scott's gaze rested on the highly polished Ferraris.

"What can I do for you?" James asked.

"I'd like another word, if I may."

"I'm about to lock up for the evening, but I can spare a couple of minutes. Naturally, I want to help. Have a seat." James sat behind the smoke-grey glass desk and spoke briskly. "So what can I do for you?"

"As you might imagine, I've got my boss breathing down my neck. He's a right bastard, believe me. If you promise him something, you make sure you deliver. It's more than my life's worth not to find Sam Hunt." Scott had a jovial way of speaking that irritated. "What I'd like is for you to tell me about your relationship with her."

"I've already told you. She was an employee. A good one. Hardworking. She worked for me, I paid her. End of."

"Look, James, we're both men of the world. She was an attractive girl—"

"Whenever I saw her, she was wearing overalls and a baseball cap." Not strictly true but it was none of Scott's business. "I don't know about you, but I'm more a stockings, suspenders and high-heels sort of bloke."

"Name me a man who isn't? But I've been asking around, speaking to her friends, and there are rumours that you got together out of work." Scott smiled again. "That doesn't interest me. Live and let live, I say. But it might help if you'd give me a bit of background. How you got together—socially, I mean. Where you used to go. If anyone found out and objected to the relationship. It could just lead us to Sam."

Only the thought of seeing Carlton's Classics on TV, with the accounts reflecting that glory, stopped James showing Scott the door.

He wasn't in the best of moods and Scott was doing nothing to improve it. James had had a row with Sarah over breakfast, and he was still fuming about her presumption that all she had to do was say "jump" and he'd dash out for a bloody pogo stick. Day in, day out, she reminded him that without her financial backing, he wouldn't be able to "idle days away" at Carlton's

Classics. If he could afford to, which he couldn't, he'd head straight for the blasted divorce courts.

"Okay," he said, "we went out for a drink a couple of times. Three times in total, I think."

"Where?"

"There's a club on Yorkshire Street, Indie Street. We went there a couple of times—just for a drink."

"I know the place. And the last time you saw her was?"

"I can't remember."

"Come on, James. Think." Scott tapped his fingers on the desk. "Just think. It's in both our interests to find her. It isn't just me, you know. You'll make a packet with the right TV exposure."

James knew that. It was the only reason he was tolerating Scott.

"Someone told me," Scott said, "that you were together the night before she vanished."

A silver letter opener lay on the desk between them and James knew a sudden urge to plunge it into Scott's body. "Really? I can't remember."

"You must remember."

"Okay. Perhaps I did. So what?"

"So you saw her on Thursday night and she doesn't turn up for work the next day. That must have struck you as odd."

"Not at first. I assumed she was throwing a sickie."

"But you said she was a good worker. She doesn't sound like the kind of girl who'd pretend to be ill to get a day off work."

"She knew I wouldn't be here that day. I was at an

auction in Manchester." James was sounding snappy, but he couldn't help himself. "If she'd turned up for work on the Monday, I'd have been none the wiser. By then, of course, she'd been reported missing and the police were here asking questions."

"I see."

Scott gazed straight at him but didn't speak. James had trouble holding that gaze and he was reminded of children who tried to outstare each other.

"I'm a married man." James had to break the silence. "She had a boyfriend. Nothing happened. We had a couple of drinks together, that's all. I have no idea where she went or what happened to her."

Scott drummed his fingers on the glass desk for a few moments. "I don't suppose there's a possibility that your wife found out?"

"No. You can rest assured I would have heard about it if she had."

Scott smiled knowingly at that and, not for the first time, James wished to God he'd never heard Sam Hunt's name mentioned. What the hell had possessed him to give her a job he would never know. He'd had doubts from the start but, stupidly, the idea of an attractive female mechanic had appealed to his sense of humour.

There was nothing remotely amusing about Sam Hunt though. She was as big a busybody as Scott. James had to charm her, laugh off her crazy notions—

"But what if she had found out?" Scott asked and James had to drag his mind back to the earlier question.

"My wife? Who knows? Maybe she would have believed me when I said nothing happened."

"I gather her money is behind Carlton Classics?"

Bloody hell. Was there anything this man didn't know?

"She invested some of her money, yes. So did I. But the business is thriving so she's getting a good return."

Thriving was an exaggeration but, for the last quarter, they hadn't made a loss. Given the current financial climate, that meant they were doing well. All they needed was TV exposure. He was about to turn the conversation toward that when Scott spoke.

"Someone mentioned an insurance claim you were forced to make. What can you tell me about that?"

"I can tell you it's none of your damn business." James wasn't going to lose his temper, but he was close. Instead, he tried to use the same jokey manner than Dylan Scott used, as if they were all pals together. "For your information, I made two claims. After the first break-in, I upped security. After the second, I installed the state-of-the-art system you see now. It was hellish expensive, but worth every penny. This place is impregnable."

Scott looked up at the tiny camera in the corner of the room. Nothing else was visible but all windows and doors had motion sensors—

"What did Sam think about the insurance claims?" Dylan Scott asked.

"What was there to think? And what the hell does it have to do with anything?"

"I don't know." Scott chuckled. "I'm so desperate to find her, I'm clutching at anything. I think of those insurance claims then wonder if she thought you were acting fraudulently."

James managed an incredulous laugh at that. "Why would she think that?"

"I've been told she saw herself as a modern-day Miss Marple." Smiling, Scott shrugged. "She strikes me as the type to see crime in the most unlikely of places."

"If she did, she never mentioned it to me. I'm sure she wouldn't have suggested having me—the business—on your TV programme if that were the case."

Scott nodded. "I expect you're right."

"Look, Dylan, I really can't see why Sam is the only person capable of working on your programme. There must be hundreds of more qualified, attractive young women out there. Surely you can make your boss understand that?"

"I've tried, believe me. At the moment, it's Sam or no one. Of course, if I don't find Sam—"

"You'll have to find someone else. Exactly."

"Did you know Sam was pregnant?"

James was picturing himself on the small screen but the question quickly brought him back to reality. "No." He gathered himself. "Not that it has anything to do with me. Or you, come to that."

"It couldn't be your child?"

"What? Of course not." At least he was confident on that score. If she'd been willing, which she wasn't, he would have enjoyed a few afternoon romps with her. He would have protected himself, though. "I told you, nothing happened between us. But even if it had, it's no business of yours."

"You're right. Sorry. As I said, I'm so desperate to get the show up and running, I'm clutching at anything."

James was relieved to see Scott get to his feet.

"Thanks for your time, James. I appreciate it."

"You're welcome. And if you need me for your show—"

"I've got your number." Scott tore a scrap of paper from a notebook, scribbled his name and cell phone number on it, and handed it over. "Here's mine."

"Thanks."

A couple of minutes later, the Morgan was pulling off the forecourt.

As James headed for the coffee machine, he gazed at the scrap of paper with Scott's name and mobile phone number scrawled across it. What sort of TV producer didn't have professional business cards? Tosser.

SEVENTEEN

DYLAN longed for a bed. Any bed. It was an age since he'd hauled himself off the wonderfully comfortable marital mattress this morning for the drive to Lancashire. It was too early for sleep though. Besides, he was going to keep his eye on the nightclub, Indie Street, and see what that bouncer got up to. He'd said he was expecting payment on Wednesday night. Dylan hadn't believed a word of it so he was going to spend his evenings getting to know all he could about the club and its bouncer.

Even at ten o'clock, it was warm. They'd had a couple of thunderstorms but the air remained heavy with the threat of more. No wonder Brits spent all their time talking about the weather. There was more than enough to complain about.

Sadly, there was no pub that offered a view of the club, only a rundown café offering hot drinks, burgers and very little else. Deciding it would have to suffice, Dylan went inside and ordered a coffee.

A young couple left and he slid into a seat at the table they'd vacated. It gave him an uninterrupted view of the club's entrance. A different bouncer manned the door this evening. He was shorter and lighter than his colleague but he wasn't the type you argued with. Like his chum, he opted for the shaved head look.

A few people came and went but it appeared that Monday nights weren't popular with clubbers in Dawson's Clough.

There was no sign of Dylan's chum. If, as might be assumed, it was his night off, there was no point hanging around in this empty café.

He downed his coffee and, just as he stood to leave, he saw him. Dressed in a tight black suit with black tie and black boots, his favourite bouncer looked as if he could be doing a shift on the door after all. Dylan stood for a moment as the bloke spoke to his colleague. They both looked up and down the street as they talked.

Dylan's friend went inside the club. Reluctantly, as the last had tasted like something scooped from one of the puddles in the street, Dylan ordered another coffee and retook his seat with a view.

While he watched, he phoned Frank.

"Fancy a pint tomorrow night?" he asked him.

"Sounds good to me. I was planning to phone you anyway. I'm going to the nick tomorrow to see what I can find out. I don't suppose it will be any more than you already know, but there's no harm in poking around."

Unlike Dylan, who was definitely persona non grata since his fall from grace and a spell behind bars, ex-D.C.I. Frank Willoughby was hugely popular and well respected among members of the police force. They took him seriously and, if he said he wanted to look at files, they didn't ask questions. Or not too many.

"Great stuff. Thanks for that, mate."

"How are you getting on?" Frank asked him.

"Badly. Beaten up twice—"

"Oh?"

"Yes, a bouncer at the Indie Street club claims he was paid by someone unknown to send me back to London. I'm watching the place as we speak."

"Any ideas?" Frank asked.

"None. I can't say I'm making many friends though. Do you know anything about a James Carlton, Frank? He owns Carlton's Classics in the town."

"I know of the business but I don't know who's behind it. Why do you ask?"

"He was Sam's employer and she had her doubts about a couple of insurance claims he made." Which brought him to the man who'd first made those allegations. "How about Jack Fleming, her boyfriend, do you know him?"

"Only what Rob's told me and that hasn't been very complimentary. But it wouldn't be, would it? I gather Rob's a bit possessive where his daughter is concerned."

"And probably his ex-wife too. He's on the phone enough to annoy the hell out of her."

"Oh? I didn't know that."

"See what you can find out, Frank. About Jack Fleming and James Carlton. Oh, and any staff at Indie Street. Okay?"

"I'll do my best."

"Thanks, mate. We can talk tomorrow."

"See you then. Oh, Dylan, don't forget it's your round."

Dylan was smiling as he returned his phone to his pocket. It never failed to amaze him that he and Frank had become friends. When Dylan had worked under Frank on one of Frank's many visits to London, he'd hated the bloke. He'd been a notoriously difficult boss and his underlings, or Dylan and his mate Pikey at least, had been referred to as "soft fucking southerners" so many times that Dylan had longed to deck him.

Things changed, though. Dylan had been kicked off the force and Frank had retired due to ill health. They had more in common now. They both missed working on the force and they both refused to admit it.

Still watching the main entrance of Indie Street, Dylan reached for his phone again and tapped in his home number. It rang and rang before Bev finally answered.

"Hi," she said.

"Hi. You okay? I didn't like to wake you when I left this morning."

"Oh, right. Thanks. And thanks for the flowers. They're—well, they're beautiful. By the way, your mum called in earlier." She spoke quickly and Dylan guessed she wanted to forget last night. He didn't. Couldn't. "She's had an idea for a holiday. The four of us."

"Oh, no. What is it this time? Bungee jumping in Australia? Bullfighting in Spain?"

"It's better than that." He could hear the amusement in her voice. "Camel trekking in the Sahara."

The only thing that surprised Dylan was that he wasn't surprised. "All inclusive?"

"You get a camel and a tent. Oh, and a French-speaking guide."

"Didn't I tell you she's as mad as a box of frogs?"

A man he recognised came out of the Indie Street, ran down the steps and began walking, very quickly, down the road.

"I've got to go, Bev. I'll call you tomorrow." Dylan snapped his phone shut and dashed out of the café.

He ran as fast as he could but soon ended up in a confusing warren of streets. At the crossroads, he stopped. He had no idea which road to take. He could choose any one but there seemed little point.

Jack Fleming was nowhere in sight.

EIGHTEEN

APART from spells in London on police work, Frank Willoughby had lived in Lancashire most of his life. He'd never been to the Dog and Fox in Dawson's Clough though. There were probably lots of pubs he hadn't visited, but the Dog and Fox was particularly appealing.

"It looks all right, doesn't it?" Dylan said.

"It certainly does."

It was split into three smaller areas, one of which was set out as a dining room. The carpet, a deep, swirling red, looked new. A wooden bar and small round tables were clean and highly polished. Glasses sparkled beneath the lights. Things like that mattered to Frank.

About twenty people clustered round the bar. A few more perched on stools or sat at tables.

"Great stuff," Dylan said with satisfaction. "They serve Black Sheep. You having one, Frank, or do you fancy something else?"

"Suits me. Thanks."

While Dylan got their drinks, Frank sought out the best table, one in the corner where they could talk without fear of being overheard.

"What have you got then, Frank?" Dylan put their drinks on the table.

"Not a lot, I'm afraid." As with most missing-person cases, and there were thousands of people reported missing in Lancashire each year, there were dozens of possible sightings. Each one had been followed up but nothing had come from them. "Jack Fleming's a wild card. He was watched for a good period after Sam disappeared. He has a bit of a history too—drunk and disorderly, minor criminal damage, stuff like that."

"I spoke to a couple of Jack's neighbours today." Dylan took a long pull on his beer. "They said that almost everyone in the building heard the argument he and Sam had on the Wednesday night. No one seems to know what they were arguing about though. There was a lot of shouting and name calling, and one woman swears she heard Jack say "I could fucking kill you." They all seem to think he's guilty of something."

"They could well be right."

"Maybe. But Jack told me all about that fight. I don't think he'd have done that if he had anything to hide."

"Why not? If he hadn't mentioned it, the neighbours would have."

"What about James Carlton? Does he show up on police radar?"

"He's got a gambling problem—that's well known—and he was done once for being in possession of cocaine. Other than that, zilch." Frank watched a couple flirting at the bar for a moment.

"What about Alan Roderick?" Dylan asked.

"He's been arrested a couple of times. Drunk and disorderly. Both times, he was causing trouble coming out of Indie Street."

"Yeah? That's interesting. This sodding bouncer, the one who's determined to put me in a wheelchair, reckoned whoever was paying him would be calling at the club on Wednesday night." The flirting couple took the table next to them and Dylan dropped his voice slightly. "Assuming he was lying, I thought I'd watch the place. There's a dump of a café opposite so, last night, I sat there for an hour or so to see if anyone turned up. I didn't see Jack Fleming go in but, while I was on the phone to Bev, I saw him come out. By the time I got after him, he'd vanished. The streets are a bloody maze round there."

"You reckon Fleming wants you warned off?"

"No. I don't know. I like Jack, and I think he's honest enough, but it's a bit of a coincidence."

"He can be a nasty piece of work," Frank said. "He scared the shit out of his last girlfriend."

"He'd only want me frightened off if he knew what happened to Sam."

"Maybe he does."

"No. He's small fry. He has a temper, yes, but he's not likely to kill a girl just because she claims she's pregnant. Even one who could be having her boss's child." Dylan shook his head. "No. I don't believe Jack has anything to do with it. It's interesting to know that

Roderick goes to that nightclub though. Or perhaps it isn't. I asked James Carlton where he and Sam went, and he said they called there for a drink a couple of times. Indie Street is a popular place and, unfortunately, going to a club isn't a crime."

Dylan bent a beer mat and drummed it against the table. "There's more to this than we know. Sam may or may not have accused James Carlton of fraud. She may or may not have told Jack that she'd discovered something horrible. She may or may not have been pregnant." Dylan took a slug of beer. "Her life wasn't what I'd call uncomplicated."

"Who's said she was pregnant—apart from Fleming?"

"No one. But I wouldn't really expect anyone to. According to Jack, she'd taken one of those do-it-yourself tests on the Wednesday. That's why they had the row. I don't suppose she told anyone else."

If Frank had to list Dylan's strong points, being a good judge of character would have been right up at the top. This time, Frank thought he'd got it wrong.

"So perhaps they were still fighting on the Friday morning," Frank said. "Fleming could have lost his temper with her and lashed out a bit too forcefully. Maybe it was an accident."

"No." Dylan was having none of it.

"He has no real alibi."

"I know. He was at home alone that morning." Dylan emptied his glass. "Jack might be a lot of things, but I think he's bright enough to cobble together some sort of alibi."

"Maybe. But there's more to Jack Fleming than meets the eye."

"I know, but—"

"You like him. Yeah, well, I expect some people liked the Krays."

Dylan shrugged at that.

There were times when cases led you straight to a dead end, and Frank couldn't help thinking this was one. Some people *did* vanish without trace. Families were torn apart, forced to spend the rest of their lives waiting and hoping and trying not to imagine their loved ones in a lonely grave.

"I'll find her," Dylan said. "Whether she's dead or alive, I'll find her."

Frank admired his confidence. He only wished he could share it.

NINETEEN

DYLAN could be doing all sorts of things this morning, like finding out how often Alan Roderick visited Indie Street. Instead, he was having to pay Rob Hunt a visit. Dylan only wished he had something to tell him. He didn't. Not a thing.

When he arrived at Wickham House, Hunt was in the garden, putting the wheelie bin back in its place.

"Thanks for coming, Dylan. Let's go inside. It's cooler."

Hunt pushed open the front door and stooped to pick up mail that had been delivered while he'd been out. On top of the pile was a postcard. Dylan couldn't see the picture, but written on the back next to Rob's address was *Weather lovely. Wish you were here.*

Dylan, curious by nature, wondered if it was from a woman. *Wish you were here.* Obviously, it was written with humour but was that the sort of thing a couple or a male friend would write?

Rob and Marion's marriage had been over for twelve years. Perhaps Dylan had been foolish to assume that, because he still wore a wedding ring, Hunt wasn't over his ex-wife. The ring might have belonged to his father or an uncle. He could easily be involved with someone. Perhaps he'd been having affairs during his marriage. Perhaps that's why Marion left him.

The initial thought brought all sorts of other thoughts. Sam had been living with her mother, as most children did in the event of a marriage ending, but she'd soon moved in with her father. Why? Because she enjoyed being the centre of attention and resented her mother lavishing affection on her new family? If that was the case, would she have been equally opposed to seeing another woman in her dad's life?

Hunt carried the mail into the study and dropped it on the low black ash table.

"Take a seat, Dylan."

"Thanks."

"Can I get you tea or coffee?"

Dylan didn't want anything—other than the chance to inspect that postcard more closely. "Coffee would be welcome. Thanks."

Hunt left the room and Dylan was quick to look at it. It was signed with a curling M that gave no clue whatsoever. The picture was of a moored ferry sitting in paintbox-blue water with cliffs in the background, and the caption read *Scrabster.*

Scrabster. The place rang a bell, but Dylan couldn't think where he'd heard it mentioned or in what context.

Hunt returned with the coffee and found Dylan sitting back in his chair, admiring the view.

Again, Hunt seemed as if he couldn't sit still, as if he didn't have time to wait for Dylan to find his daughter. He was terminally ill, so perhaps that wasn't surprising.

"What can you tell me, Dylan? Have you learned anything at all?"

As Dylan didn't think "zilch" was a satisfactory answer, he lifted his cup as he sought a response.

"I know someone wants me far away from Lancashire,' he said at last.

Hunt frowned at that. "How do you mean?"

"You remember the day I arrived? When I was beaten up? Well, I've run into a bit of trouble since." He took a sip of coffee that was too hot for comfort. "Do you know Indie Street, the nightclub in town?"

"I know of it, of course. I think Sam went there a few times with that boyfriend of hers."

"She went there with her boss too."

Dylan waited for a reaction, but there wasn't one. Hunt simply looked more confused than ever.

"And I gather your ex-wife's husband, Alan, sometimes pays the club a visit."

"I've no idea where he goes. We don't mix in the same circles, thankfully. But what does any of that have to do with Sam?"

"One of the bouncers there has been paid to send me back to London."

"Oh, I'm sure there's been a misunderstanding. I can assure you, Dylan, that it has nothing to do with Sam's disappearance."

Perhaps it was easy to sound confident when you didn't have a bruised lip and spine. "What makes you so sure?"

"Well—I just can't believe—" The sentence died away.

Dylan decided that if Hunt wanted to know what he'd found out, then he could hear it all. "It seems your daughter may have been pregnant," he said.

"What?" A flash of anger sparked in Hunt's eyes. "Who told you? That no-good boyfriend of hers?"

"Yes." There was no one else to confirm or deny it so Hunt's outrage could be justified. "Tell me again about your relationship with Sam. I know you say she was happy but was there someone else in *your* life perhaps? Someone Sam might have been jealous of?"

"What?" Hunt seemed to find that amusing. "That's absurd. You think I might have met another woman? Someone to replace Sam's mother? Never!"

Something about Hunt bothered Dylan. Something he couldn't pinpoint.

"Perhaps you'd tell me again about her relationship with her mother and stepfather," Dylan said.

"I've told you—"

"Yes, but humour me, would you?"

"She got along fine with her mother." The answer came grudgingly. "As for Alan, she didn't like him any more than I did. He's—common. I don't want to sound like a snob, but he's a lorry driver. What is there for Sam to like? If it wasn't for her mother and her half sisters, she'd have nothing to do with him."

"Is there anything she said about him? Times she grew angry about him?"

"No. No, there's nothing at all."

Damn it. Hunt wanted his daughter found yet he

wasn't prepared to help. Telling everyone his daughter was a saint wouldn't help find her.

Dylan stayed another half hour, asking questions that received no real answer, and he was pleased when Hunt was showing him out.

"I'm sorry you've had a spot of bother," he said, "but I can promise you it has nothing to do with Sam. Nothing at all."

Even in absence, the precious Sam couldn't be blamed for anything.

TWENTY

MARION RODERICK was preparing the girls' dinner when Dylan Scott turned up. His shirt and trousers were creased, his lip was still swollen and he gave the impression of being a bungling idiot. Yet he still managed to be the sort of man that most women would look twice at. He looked honest, dependable and trustworthy. Tiny creases around his eyes suggested he had a sense of humour.

"Come in," she said.

"Thanks." He followed her into the kitchen where he looked at Lydia and Emma. "Hello," he said, smiling at them. "You'll be—no, don't tell me. You'll be Emma, right? And you'll be Lydia."

The girls nodded. They were both shy around strangers and Marion hated to see them that way. Alan was—

It didn't matter what Alan was, she thought. He wasn't here. They should be fine around her.

Dismissing the thought, she ruffled their curls. "You can go and play for a bit. Oh, tell you what, you can watch your new DVD, okay? You'd better take an apple to keep you going till I get something cooked."

"Sorry," Dylan said. "Have I called at a bad time?"

"No. It's fine. But do you mind if I carry on with the potatoes?"

"Of course not. I don't want to delay your meal."

"Have a seat."

She'd expected him to sit at the table, but he looked comfortable on the bar stool opposite her.

Alan wasn't due back until Friday evening and, usually, as soon as he left, her stress levels returned to normal. She looked forward to time with the girls, to sitting with her feet up watching whatever was on TV. Not this time, though. Her nerves were in tatters.

He'd been in the foulest of moods lately. Everything she did or said, everything the children did, was wrong. He snapped at them, barked out orders, he had them all living on their nerves. Thank God he wasn't here.

"What can I do for you, Dylan? Have you found out anything?"

"Not really, no. I'm sorry, I appreciate this must be distressing for you, but I'd really like you to tell me about Sam, when you last saw her. The frame of mind she was in, things she said, stuff like that."

She could remember every detail of that day. But what mother wouldn't?

"Well." Still clasping the potato peeler, she sat on the stool beside him. "It was the Thursday. Alan had come back from Scotland the day before and had a day off. Because he'd be home for Lydia and Emma, I took the opportunity to do some shopping." She smiled at that. "When you have two girls, it's luxury to get an hour round the shops on your own."

Returning her smile, he nodded.

"Before that, though, Sam had phoned me and said she'd collect the girls from school and walk them home. I called Alan and told him he wouldn't have to bother."

There was no need to tell him that Sam and the girls had stopped off at the park and then gone for an ice-cream. Or that Alan was angry because they were home later than he'd expected.

"I got home at the same time as Sam and the girls," she said. "Sam said she was in a rush—I assumed she was off out somewhere with her boyfriend—and, after promising to collect the girls for school in the morning, she was gone."

"Did she seem happy enough?" he asked. "Did you think there might be something bothering her?"

"Why do you ask?"

"According to her boyfriend, she'd discovered she was pregnant."

"Oh, my." Marion's hand flew to her mouth and she felt the sting of tears in her eyes. "Pregnant?"

"You had no idea?"

"None." There was a possibility she could have been a grandmother and she hadn't known it. "Now you come to mention it, she did seem a bit—distracted when I saw her. I suppose it was that."

A mother knows when her daughter has things on her mind and Marion had thought—well, she hadn't known what to think.

She brought that afternoon to mind and recalled Sam and the girls walking into the kitchen.

"What kept you?" Alan had muttered.

"We've been talking." Sam had answered him defiantly, almost as if she hated him, before hugging the girls close—

And there had been another thing. She'd clung to those girls as if her life had depended on them.

"I'll be here in the morning to take them to school." She'd spoken to Marion, ignoring Alan completely. Yet, as she'd left, she'd glared at Alan.

Alan had stormed after her. He'd been back in less than ten minutes, his face like thunder, cursing Sam, saying he didn't want her around the children—

"Pregnant?" Marion said again. "Who told you that? Jack?"

"Yes. According to him, she'd taken an over-the-counter test the day before. I gather they had a row about it."

Marion wasn't surprised. "It would have come as a shock to both of them. They would have coped though. I know they would. Sam would at least. She's always had endless patience with young children."

"That's useful." He was smiling at that. "With you having two younger ones, I mean."

"Very. Some days, when they were very young, she'd come round and keep them amused so I could have a nap. She's a good daughter."

"She sounds it." He rubbed at his chin. "Do you know the Indie Street club in the Clough?"

"No, I don't think so. A nightclub, is it?"

"Yes."

Marion could have laughed at that. It had been a

long time since she'd been familiar with nightclubs. A long time since she'd laughed too.

In the early days, she and Alan had sometimes had evenings out, but a quiet pub or the cinema had been the height of their social life. Now, they rarely went anywhere together.

People must wonder about their relationship. They couldn't be expected to know that, at first, she'd been totally besotted with Alan. He'd been fun. He'd made her laugh. His devil-may-care attitude had been refreshing. He'd had a knack of making her feel like the most beautiful woman he'd ever seen, the only woman he wanted to be with.

Now, he was the father of Lydia and Emma. Nothing more. They even struggled to pretend they cared about each other when they were with other people.

Marion had stopped feeling sad about it long ago.

"I don't know any of the clubs in town," she said.

"What about Alan? Do you think he'd know it? Does he go out without you?"

"Very rarely. He sometimes goes to the pub after work. Half a dozen drivers go to a pub—the Fox and something, I think it's called."

"The Dog and Fox? What a coincidence. I was there last night."

"That's the one. He wouldn't go to nightclubs, though. I mean, I can ask him if he knows it, but I can't imagine he will. Why do you ask?"

"I wondered if he knew anyone who works there?"

"Not to my knowledge. It's possible, of course. I'll ask him for you."

Alan had contacts of whom she knew nothing. She knew they lived well thanks to those contacts, but she didn't know what was involved and didn't want to.

She stood again, determined to carry on preparing vegetables.

"I'll leave you to your meal. Thanks for your time, Marion, I appreciate it."

"You'll let me know if you learn anything?"

"Of course."

"What do you think?" She had to ask. "Do you think it's possible that, after all this time, she's still—alive?"

He didn't flinch at the question but she could see his doubts. "I'd like to think so, yes."

There was hope, she reminded herself. There was always hope that, one day, she'd see Sam again.

As soon as Dylan had gone, she gave up on the vegetables and stepped outside to light a cigarette. The smoke stung her eyes, reminding her that it was a mug's game. Not only was it a filthy habit, it was also a silent killer. She didn't smoke many, and she didn't usually smoke at all when the girls were around. Alan coughed his way through sixty a day, but because he bought them cheap from his trips abroad, he had no incentive to quit. One of these days Marion would do just that.

Now that she was alone, she wished Dylan had stayed. She'd felt exactly the same the last time he visited. His questions unnerved her, frightened her into thinking that he'd find out what had happened to Sam and that it wouldn't be good. As soon as he'd gone, though, she missed him. She liked him. She had the feeling she could rest her head on his shoulder, tell him her troubles and wait for him to put her world right. He couldn't, though. No one could.

With the cigarette smoked, she pulled herself together and concentrated on feeding the girls. After that was homework. They were too young to have much and she was grateful for that this evening.

Once they were in bed, she stepped out into the still-warm night for another cigarette.

Life shouldn't be like this, on and off antidepressants, dreading the mornings, dreading the evenings, dreading Alan's return. Sometimes she lived her life in a constant state of dread.

Perhaps she'd fallen for Alan in such a big way because she'd been desperate to escape Rob. Their troubles had started when Sam was born, when a bout of postnatal depression had introduced Marion to antidepressants. Rob hadn't understood. He'd wanted sex and she'd wanted to escape.

She stubbed out her cigarette, went inside and poured herself a glass of red wine.

Three times over the next half hour she tried Alan's phone and three times it switched straight to voice mail. She left a message and waited for him to call her.

It was almost ten o'clock when he did.

"Yes?" he said.

The abrupt greeting infuriated her, but she didn't let it show. "Hi. You okay?"

"Fine. You?"

As if he gave a damn.

"Yes. Dylan Scott called in. He was asking questions about a nightclub." She realised she couldn't remember the name of the place.

"Indie Street?"

"That's the one. You know it then?"

She wondered who he met there. She wasn't stupid. She knew he had affairs. Knew but no longer cared.

"What about it?"

"He wondered if you knew it, and if you knew anyone who worked there."

"Why?"

"I've no idea, Alan."

"Right."

"What shall I tell him?" she asked.

"Tell him to mind his own fucking business." His anger made her glad he was hundreds of miles away.

"He's doing his best to find Sam. If there's anything I can tell him that helps, I shall do so." Up yours, she thought viciously.

"You'll say nothing. I've told you, Marion, I won't have him poking his nose into my business."

"He's not. He's trying—"

"He's doing exactly that. There's nothing you can tell him, is there?" She heard him mutter something to someone before coming back on the line. "I'll see you on Friday night." He cut the connection.

Not for the first time, Marion wished she could do a disappearing act like Sam. She would love to gather the girls to her, all three of them, and take off for a life in the sun. A horse-drawn caravan and a pocket full of dreams would be all she'd need.

TWENTY-ONE

I<small>F</small> Dylan lived in Dawson's Clough, he'd make sure his local was the Dog and Fox. It had everything he wanted from a pub—good beer, friendly and efficient barmaids, cleanliness, no TVs blasting out the latest so-called reality programs, or jukeboxes deafening customers with the current tuneless crap.

This evening he'd spotted one of Alan Roderick's colleagues in there. Dylan recognised him from this morning's brief visit to Taylor and Anderson's, the haulage company that employed Roderick. The tattoo of a snake winding down his forearm was difficult to forget. Also, it looked out of a place on a man approaching retirement age.

Dylan walked round the bar to be closer to him. "Sorry, but don't I know you?"

The chap looked at him and shook his head. "Don't think so."

"Ah, I've got. You work at Taylor's, don't you?" At the bloke's surprise, Dylan explained, "I called at the yard looking for Alan and saw you there."

"Is that a fact?"

Typical. Of all the blokes who must work at Taylor's, Dylan had to pick the grumpy bastard. As the

man's glass was almost empty, Dylan downed his pint
and banged the glass on the bar.

"The same again, please, love." As if it was an
afterthought, he added for his companion's benefit,
"Can I get you one?"

The chap hesitated as if torn between pride and
manners. "That'd be good of you. Thank you."

Buying a bloke a pint was the best way Dylan knew
to break the ice. Over a beer, all sorts of friendships
could be made and confidences betrayed.

When the drinks were poured, Dylan handed over
a note. The barmaid looked at it and raised her eyes.
"It's a nice thought, but you can't get two pints for a
fiver these days."

Smiling at his own stupidity, Dylan handed over
another note. "Sorry, love, I was miles away."

"I remember," Dylan's companion said, "when
petrol went up to a pound a gallon. A gallon that is,
not a litre."

"I never knew the Ark ran on petrol, Malc?"

"Cheeky madam!"

The little joke raised a smile and Malc lifted his
glass in a toast to Dylan. "Cheers. Oh, my name's
Malcolm, by the way. Everyone calls me Malc."

"Pleased to meet you, Malc. I'm Dylan."

The ice was broken and they could chat as friends.
All for the price of a pint.

Malc must have passed his sixtieth birthday, but
he looked wiry and fit. He was wearing black denims
and a spotless white short-sleeved shirt, and Dylan
guessed he'd turn up for work in equally clean clothes.

A man with standards. One who wouldn't suffer fools gladly.

"Known Alan long, have you?" he asked Dylan.

"No. I've only met him once. I'm up here from London looking into the disappearance of his step-daughter. His wife's daughter."

"Young Sam. That was a funny do, wasn't it?"

"Dreadful for the parents." Dylan supped slowly on his beer. "What about you? Have you known him long?"

"Five years. Yes, about that."

"Get on well, do you?"

"He's all right. A bit moody at times, but he's okay. I can't complain because he volunteers for all the long-distance trips and I can't abide those. I like to stay local to the north-west. I'll do Scotland at a push, but Alan volunteers for those as well as the Hungary and Romanian runs."

So Roderick volunteered for the runs to Scotland? Dylan had searched for Scrabster on Google and discovered it was a small place on the north coast of Scotland. It was where a friend of his, Jim, had sailed from on his frequent visits to the Orkney Islands.

"I wouldn't be too enthusiastic either. He's got friends in Scotland though, hasn't he?"

"Has he? Not that I've heard of."

"Perhaps I'm wrong. Perhaps it's Sam's real father who has friends there, not her stepfather."

"I wouldn't know." Malc took a slurp of beer that left a white froth moustache above his top lip. He licked it off. "I suppose Alan's got friends there now.

He's been doing that trip for as long as I've known him."

"How far north does he go?"

"Very occasionally he'll go as far as Inverness but usually it's Glasgow or Edinburgh."

Inverness would be about a hundred miles south of Scrabster.

"I suppose it's good money," Dylan said.

"Better than doing the local stuff, but not great."

"What sort of stuff does he carry on his wagon?"

"Oh, it varies. It's just general haulage, you see. If anything wants shifting, we shift it. Hungary and Romania are regular runs. We take stuff that a charity sends out there."

"I wouldn't fancy being away from home that much," Dylan said. "I doubt if my wife would be too keen either."

"Mine doesn't like it. She didn't used to bother but she likes me at home now. Alan and his missus are younger though. I expect she's used to it by now."

"I expect she is."

"She probably welcomes it," Malc said, breaking into a grin.

Dylan laughed at that. "Probably. Even when he's home, they don't seem to go out together much, do they? Alan comes here on his own, he goes to that nightclub, Indie Street—perhaps they get on better if they're away from each other."

"Ay, well, Alan might not be much to look at but he has a way with the ladies. I expect having a wife along with him would cramp his style, if you get my drift."

Dylan shrugged as if Roderick's alleged affairs were of no importance. "Perhaps his wife has a bloke in tow for when he's away. What's sauce for the goose and all that."

"Perhaps she does. I dunno."

"It must be difficult for them," Dylan said. "It's hard to imagine what Marion must be going through with her daughter missing. As Sam isn't Alan's flesh and blood, it won't mean as much to him. Perhaps a situation like that would cause tension between a couple."

"No doubt, and Alan's a selfish bugger. I can't imagine him putting anyone else first. He looks out for number one."

"Yes, that's the impression I got."

"He thinks he's a cut above the rest of us too. Always chucking money about—boasting about what he's bought. A boat, cars—I don't know where he gets his money from but it sure as hell ain't from driving for Anderson's."

"I assume Marion earns a fair bit."

"Perhaps she does. And he'll make a bit on the side, I suppose."

"Oh?" Dylan took a sip of beer as if he wasn't interested, but he'd love to know where Roderick's money came from.

"Yeah. He'll get cheap booze and cigarettes from Hungary and Romania. Most drivers make a few quid at that. Like I said, I'm not complaining. So long as he does the long-distance runs, I can stay local."

Dylan very much doubted that Roderick was making a huge amount selling on alcohol and cigarettes. No, there was more to it than that.

"I'd feel the same," Dylan said.

"He's a good worker, I will say that. He always deals with his own lorry. He reckons that if no one else goes near it, he's only himself to blame if there's owt wrong with it. He's right." Malc emptied his glass. "I'm off now, but I'll buy you a pint before I go."

"No, you're all right, Malc. It's time I was off too. Save it for next time. I'm sure I'll see you again."

"Okay then. See you. And thanks for the drink."

As Dylan left the Dog and Fox, he still had plenty of unanswered questions. Like why did Alan Roderick volunteer for the runs to Scotland? And where did his money *really* come from? Interesting that he didn't like people snooping round his lorry.

TWENTY-TWO

Dylan had been putting this off as long as possible. It was time to ask a few questions at Indie Street and he hated nightclubs with a passion. Given the choice between a couple of hours in a noisy nightclub or camel trekking with his mother—

No, he was kidding himself. A nightclub wasn't *that* bad.

It was a little before eleven and, to his relief, the club wasn't as noisy or as crowded as he'd expected. A long-haired man in his mid-twenties, caged behind a bank of enormous speakers, was playing music. The Black Eyed Peas seemed to be his favourite band. A long, curving bar, lit with neon blue, was staffed by half a dozen teenagers wearing black shirts that bore an electric blue Indie Street logo. A few young people danced beneath streaks of light in every colour of the rainbow.

Perhaps that was why he hated nightclubs. They made him feel closer to sixty-eight than thirty-eight.

He perched on one of the blue upholstered metal-framed stools at the bar and waited to be served. One thing was certain, he wouldn't be drinking Black Sheep. The plus point though was that his car was safe in the hotel's car park. He could drink the place dry if he chose.

"A double whisky, please. On the rocks," he added.

"Coming up, sir," the young girl chirped.

He hated being called *sir* too. Perhaps Bev was right and he was turning into a grumpy old man.

"Thanks," he said as she handed over his drink. "Looks like I'll be keeping myself company. Is it always this quiet?"

"It can be on Wednesdays." She looked the length of the bar, saw that no one was waiting to be served and said, "Is this your first visit?"

"It is, yes. I have friends up here and was hoping to see some of them in here. You know James Carlton, do you?"

"Yeah, but he's never in on Wednesdays. You'd do better to call in over the weekend."

"Oh, right. What about Alan Roderick?"

"He's a driver and he might not even be in the country. You can never tell which night he'll be in."

"Sam Hunt? Jack Fleming?"

"Blimey." She saw that a couple of young women were waiting to be served. "Hang on a minute," she said to Dylan.

She served the two women, then three more customers. It was five minutes before she returned to stand across the bar from Dylan.

"What's your name?" she asked.

"Dylan." He peered at the name tag she wore. "And you're Cindy. Pleased to meet you, Cindy."

"I can tell you haven't been around here for a

while." She didn't have time for the social niceties. "If you had, you'd have heard."

"Heard what?"

"About Sam Hunt. She vanished six months ago. No, it's more like nine or ten months now."

"How do you mean, vanished?" Dylan wanted to give away as little as possible about his own interest in Sam. He had the feeling, though, that Cindy was a born talker.

"Just that. It was in the papers and on the telly for weeks. Just disappeared, she did. I'll tell you summat else too. The police took Jack Fleming away."

"No!"

"Yes. They let him go, but it makes you think, doesn't it?"

"It certainly does, Cindy."

She thought of something else. "Here, she used to work for your friend, James Carlton."

"That's right. I was hoping to see him, but I'll try at the weekend. Does he come in often?"

"No, not often. If he does, though, it's usually a Friday or Saturday night. Mind, I can't blame him. This place is dead in the week."

"Ah. It's a long time since I've been in the Clough." It felt odd calling the town "the Clough," but that's how locals referred to the place. "I'll tell you someone else I thought I recognised, the bouncer who works here. He's not on tonight, but he's tall, big-muscled—"

"That's Stripes. He's only here Thursday through Saturday nights."

"Stripes?"

"Yeah. I haven't seen 'em, but he's got long scars on his back. It's said his dad used to beat him."

"Right." That figured. Violence bred violence, and Dylan had thought Stripes gained far too much pleasure from beating him up. "It's funny, though, but I thought I saw him here on Monday night." He didn't add that he'd seen Jack Fleming too.

"Was he? Dunno about that. Not my night. He comes in to drink, though. He might be in tonight. It's not his night to work, but he might call in anyway."

A gang of about a dozen young men, shirts untucked, trousers low on their hips, laughing loudly, came in. It fell to Cindy to serve them.

Dylan noticed her say something to one of the group. She was nodding in his direction as she spoke. Belatedly, he realised that the one walking over to him was Jack Fleming.

"Hi, Dylan. You looking for me?"

"Not really. I was asking after anyone I might recognise. It's good to see you, though. I didn't know this was one of your haunts."

"I haven't been in the place for ages until this week. These—" he gestured over his shoulder to his companions "—are my band mates. We're gonna try and get the band up and running again."

"Yes? Good for you."

A bottle of Coke was put in front of Jack. "Cheers, mate!" He gave a thumbs up to one of his friends.

Dylan watched as Jack took a swig from the bottle. He would never understand why it was cool not to use a glass. He really was getting old.

Considering Jack was supposed to be a fan of drink, drugs and fights, it was surprising to see him with a soft drink.

He perched on the stool next to Dylan's. "How's it going?"

"I don't know." Dylan had to shout to make himself heard. "A lot of people come in here, don't they? James Carlton for one." He watched Jack's reaction but his companion merely nodded in an "I could have told you that" sort of way. "Sam's stepfather, Alan Roderick."

"Yeah, I've seen him in here a couple of times."

"You must know the bouncer too. I think they call him Stripes."

Jack shook his head. "I don't know any of the staff. Except Cindy. Oh, and Kate. That's about it."

Given that James Carlton, Alan Roderick and Jack Fleming frequented Indie Street, it was impossible to guess who was willing to pay Stripes to break his kneecaps. It could be any of them. Or none.

"Does Sam or her father have friends in Scotland?" Dylan asked.

Jack looked at him as if he were speaking a foreign language. "Not that I ever knew about. Why do you ask?"

"Just curious. What about Sam's stepfather? Does he know people there?"

"I've no idea."

Another gang of youngsters came in and crowded round the bar. Indie Street didn't open till ten so, perhaps by one o'clock, the place would be heaving.

Dylan stayed another hour, talking, or rather shouting at Jack above the noise, and then decided he'd had enough loud music and swirling lights to last a lifetime.

"It's time I was off, Jack. If I hear anything, I'll let you know."

"You do that."

Dylan was relieved to open the front doors and feel the still warm but fresher night air on his face. Stripes wasn't on duty, but tonight's bouncer was only a couple of pounds lighter. He had a shaved head and wore a big gold ring on his short, chunky finger.

"Stripes not about tonight then?" Dylan asked.

"Nope."

"Pity. I was hoping he'd do a job for me."

"Oh?"

"Yeah. I could do with a bit of muscle, if you know what I mean."

"I know exactly what you mean. You'd better come back at the weekend then."

"I thought he worked Thursdays," Dylan said. "Isn't he on tomorrow night?"

"Nope. He's got the night off."

"I'll call in on Saturday then. There's no harm in asking if he's interested in a bit of work on the side, is there? I've been told he'll use his muscles for a price. Is that right?"

"Muscles, knives—"

"Guns?"

He peered closely at Dylan. "You'd have to ask him about that."

That wasn't particularly reassuring. Still, at least Dylan hadn't warranted a knife or a gun. Yet.

TWENTY-THREE

ANCA awoke with a start. Crina was crying. They were in total darkness.

It took only a split second to discover they were locked in a cabinet with smooth sides, something like a fridge or a freezer. She pushed against the sides and top but nothing budged.

"George!" She pummelled the sides with her fists. "George!"

Crina cried all the louder.

"Shush!"

Anca could feel bumps in the road. No, she was wrong. They were at sea. They must be on a boat.

"Help!" she screamed. "Please, help us!"

There was no room to stand, no room to stretch out. Panic rose within her. There was no air. They were going to suffocate.

She dragged in a few breaths, instructed herself to keep calm, and wriggled so that she could put an arm around her sister and pull her close. "Shush, Crina. It'll be all right. You'll see."

Anca's head felt as if it had been hollowed out and stuffed with cotton wool. She tried to think back but could remember nothing after the doctor had given her the inoculation.

She thought she'd been awake earlier, and believed someone had given them something to eat and a drink of water. Or perhaps she'd been dreaming.

"We must be on a boat going to England, Crina. That'll be it." Her voice sounded far more confident than she felt. "George is breaking the law for us, so he'd have to hide us until we were in England."

Crina's cries quietened to sobs and she buried her head beneath Anca's arm.

Anca hadn't known what to expect. She'd imagined them walking onto a plane and flying to England, but they would have been stopped by the police. This way, on a boat, would be better, and it couldn't take too long to get there. Soon, someone would be along to explain everything to them, to bring them food and water. When this boat reached its destination, they would be released to enjoy their first glimpse of English soil.

"We can trust George, I know we can. He said he'd find us hotel work." The idea soothed her nerves. "Dănut said they have lots of big hotels. At first, we'll be cleaners, but one day we might wait on tables. Imagine that, Crina."

She thought Crina had fallen asleep, but she kept talking.

"As soon as we've paid George what we owe him, we'll have our own apartment. Maybe it will be in London with a view of that river. The Thames, it's called. And a garden. Well, maybe not a garden, but we can fill our apartment with plants. We'll be able to buy food and clothes. Hey, we'll see the palace, the one where the queen lives. Perhaps we'll even see her."

Crina was fast asleep and Anca tried not to disturb her sister as she ran her hands carefully over their prison walls. They were smooth yet there must be a gap somewhere. Air must be getting in.

Once again, panic rose inside her, threatening to choke her. Instead of thinking about suffocation, she tried to concentrate on all she knew about England. Her knowledge had come from Dǎnut, who knew about lots of countries. England, he'd said, was very beautiful and no one was allowed to go without food. People didn't have to beg, he'd said, because the government looked after everyone. She knew they had a queen, and a prime minister as well, although she couldn't remember his name. A princess had died in a car crash when Anca was a baby.

With her mind crammed with palaces, princesses and tiaras, she succumbed to sleep.

TWENTY-FOUR

EACH year, Marion bought a calendar, and her first task, even before noting birthdays and anniversaries, was to highlight the third Thursday of every month. For years, before Sam was born even, she'd been organising the Dawson's Clough Library's reading group. An avid reader all her life, she enjoyed meeting with like-minded people. When the children were small, and with Alan away from home so often, the promise of adult conversation had been a fix more potent than chocolate or heroin.

The group tried to keep book choices as varied as possible so she was introduced to authors she wouldn't have thought of trying. Although their numbers had dwindled to less than twenty, the get-togethers remained a bright spot in Marion's social life.

She walked into the library and checked that her garish notice advertising the group's meetings was prominently displayed. It was. So far she'd had no new enquiries but she lived in hope.

Even the sight of books, some face out, some showing creased spines, cheered her. She loved the smell of books, loved to feel them in her hands.

She walked into the back room where Julie was filling the kettle.

"Hiya." Marion took off her jacket and hung it on the peg along with her heavy bag.

"You're early," Julie said.

"My babysitter was early so I thought I'd come and enjoy a cuppa before we started."

"Alan away then?"

"Yes. He's back tomorrow night." The reminder brought its usual feeling of dread.

"I wish I was away from here. Still, we're off to Egypt soon."

While Julie made them tea, Marion arranged the orange plastic chairs in a circle broken only by the table at which she'd sit and hold order. Some books caused controversy and her most difficult tasks were to prevent arguments and to make sure everyone had a chance to air their views.

"Biscuit?" Julie asked.

"Why not? Actually I can think of a dozen reasons why not. What do they say? A moment on the lips and a lifetime on the hips? Never mind, the diet will still be waiting tomorrow."

"You never put on weight, do you?" Julie's gaze was wistful. "I only have to look at a calorie and my jeans cut me in two. Still, better to be overweight and happy than thin and miserable. That's what I always say."

Joy was next to arrive, her flowery perfume filling the room. Other members drifted into the building and to the room at the back that was reserved for their meetings. The library itself was still open for business, but the group was tucked well away and could chat and laugh as much as they liked.

People spoke of the weather, grumbled about problems finding parking spaces and looked forward to holidays in exotic places where they could enjoy a "different sort of heat."

It was a few minutes after eight when Marion began the meeting. She gave them a brief resume of the month's chosen book—*Darkly Dreaming Dexter* by Jeff Lindsay—and asked for a show of hands, first from those who enjoyed the book. As happened most months, half loved the story and half hated it. Some people, Marion was sure of it, hated a book on principle, simply because it had been chosen for them and was out of their usual genre.

"I thought it was brilliant." Polly enthused about most things. If you needed to be taught to look on the bright side, Polly was your woman. "I completely fell in love with Dexter. I wish now that I'd seen the TV series."

"You fell in love with him?" Doris, as Marion had guessed, disapproved strongly. Doris preferred a gentle read and was possibly Jane Austen's biggest fan. "I couldn't finish it. All that gratuitous violence—"

"Hardly gratuitous," Joy piped up. "He's a serial killer and a blood spatter analyst. What did you expect? Picnics in meadows and lashings of ginger beer?"

And so it went on.

They stopped at nine for tea or coffee and a brief chat, then it was time to discuss the next month's read.

"I know you'll be expecting me to choose one of the old classics," Doris said, "but I thought it was time I tried something new. And I sincerely hope there are no bloodthirsty killers in it. My choice is—" she paused for effect, almost as if she expected a drum roll "—Sophie Kinsella's *Confessions of a Shopaholic.*"

There was no drum roll, but there was a shocked intake of breath from several members. Along with Jane Austen, Doris enjoyed Agatha Christie's gentle Miss Marple stories. She liked her heroines to be refined and mature.

"I've read it," Joy said.

"Me too," Mary piped up.

"But you haven't read it with a view to giving us your thoughts," Marion said. "What a good choice, Doris. I'm sure we'll all look forward to reading it."

The next three quarters of an hour were taken up with people sharing knowledge of author Sophie Kinsella and her novels.

"Okay, ladies, I think it's time we called it a night." Marion stifled a yawn. "Same time next month. Oh, and don't forget the library is having a sale next weekend. Get here early to pick up your bargains."

Everyone grabbed coats and bags and, chattering like busy birds, filed out of the room, leaving Marion to lock up.

She thought she might come along to the library's sale, but knew she wouldn't buy any books. She borrowed from the library because she believed libraries were necessary to the community and went by the "use it or lose it" principle, but she preferred new books. Coming across a coffee spill on page 46, melted chocolate on page 104 or, worse, a stray hair, filled her with disgust. These days, when you could throw a couple of books in your supermarket trolley and not notice the cost, libraries were becoming redundant.

Other than a flickering streetlight determined to annoy rather than illuminate, all was dark when she stepped outside. A steady drizzle was falling.

Her car sat forlornly in the car park. She fumbled in her jacket pocket for her keys, silently cursing the rain.

The exact second she pressed the button to unlock the doors, a heavy woollen-clad arm clamped tight around her neck. A gloved hand was rammed hard against her mouth. She could smell damp leather and sweat.

"Your old man isn't answering his phone." The voice was menacing, the man's breath hot against her cheek. "You'd better remind him that he still owes me money."

She felt something cold against her neck. A knife.

When she tried to speak, he tightened his grip around her neck but took his hand from her mouth. The cold blade rested just below her right eye.

"I—I can give you money." Her knees were about to buckle, and she had to force herself to stay upright.

The knife provided a strong incentive. "How much do you want?"

"A grand. That's what we said. Just a bit of rough stuff he wanted to start with, that's all. That's a grand."

"Er—rough stuff?" She didn't know what he was talking about. It didn't matter. She had to get away. "A thousand pounds? I can give you that."

Not tonight she couldn't. She had about a hundred in her purse and maybe a couple of hundred in the house. The cash machine would only release two hundred and fifty a day.

"My bag. There's some in my bag."

Even if he'd released his grip to look in her bag, she wouldn't have been capable of making a run for it. He didn't. The arm around her neck tightened its grip. He used the other hand, the one holding the knife, to search her bag.

"Not enough." He shoved the notes in his pocket.

"There's a cash machine round the corner but—"

"It's a fucking grand!" Hot spittle landed on her face. "A grand for rough stuff, right? He wants more—well, he's not fucking getting it, is he? Not until I've seen the colour of his money."

Marion had no idea what he was talking about. She was more than willing to give him money, though. "I'll give you—"

"Same time, same place. Tomorrow night. A grand, remember?" His voice dropped to a whisper and that hard, gloved hand pressed against her mouth again. "And if I was you, I'd ask him why he wants the bloke who's supposed to be finding your daughter sent back to London."

Shock had her trying to shout, but his hand was too tight against her face. All that escaped her lips was an indecipherable moan.

He laughed at her struggles. "That's about the height of it. Some bloke's employed to find your daughter, and your old man wants rid of him. Makes you wonder, sweetheart, doesn't it?"

He pushed her hard in the back so that she dropped heavily to her knees and banged her head on the side of her car.

She drew in a reviving breath and, when she turned around, he'd gone. All she heard was a rustle of the bushes and the faint sound of retreating footsteps.

She tried to stand, but the movement made her retch. The smell of wet leather and sweat still stung her nostrils.

She finally hauled herself to her feet, staggered to the bushes and was violently sick.

TWENTY-FIVE

"Now then, Mum, about this camel trekking." According to Bev, his mother was on the verge of booking this confounded holiday. Dylan had to put a stop to it. "You're not really serious, are you?"

"Of course I am. It'll be fun."

He was relieved to see she looked better than she had last weekend. Perhaps having Luke to stay had tired her more than it should have. She struggled to sit still for a minute, was always looking to have fun, so it was no wonder that, at her age, she overdid it at times.

"Fun? Mum, it won't. They've done a good job of selling it in the brochure, but it'll be murder. We'd be hot, dusty, dirty, thirsty, uncomfortable—"

"Nonsense. Luke thought it would be wonderful."

"You've told Luke?" How could she do that? More surprising, why hadn't Luke mentioned it? They'd spent most of the day together and he hadn't said a word.

"Of course I didn't." She scowled at him. Great, now she was annoyed that he could think her so stupid. "I merely mentioned it in passing to see if it was something he fancied. He did, which means he's not a stick-in-the-mud like his dad. How I gave birth to you, Dylan, I have no idea."

He needed to head her off before she recalled every painful minute of childbirth.

"It's just not practical, Mum."

"Of course it is. Think of Luke. When he gets back to school after the summer break and has to do the dreaded 'what I did on holiday' essay—which he will because teachers are the nosiest folk on the planet—Bev excepted, of course—he'll be the envy of the school. How many kids could top that?"

"A tent in Skegness would top it!"

She hooted with laughter. "You do talk a load of nonsense, Dylan!"

He took a deep breath and tried not to envy all the men who were living in their own homes, about to go to bed with their own wives, having spent an enjoyable, relaxing weekend with their families, men whose mothers went to bingo on Friday nights and were tucked up with their cocoa at this time on a Sunday night.

"I'm getting a beer. Do you want one?" he asked.

"No, thanks, love."

Dylan went to the fridge, took out a can and rested it against his forehead in a moment of despair. All the beer in the world wouldn't turn his mother into someone normal. Still, it might numb the pain slightly.

When he carried it into the sitting room, she was rolling a joint.

Why me, Lord? Why pick on me? Why do I have to

live in a flat that reeks of scented candles and bloody marijuana?

"Bev thinks that half your problems are down to not knowing your father." She lit her joint and inhaled deeply. "Perhaps she's right."

It would be good if his mother and his wife had more to do with their time than discuss the freak they'd either married or given birth to.

The only advantage to knowing his father as far as Dylan could see was that he could go to the man, throw the joint-smoking woman sitting opposite at him and say "your responsibility, mate, not mine."

"I wouldn't think so," he said. "And I don't think I've got problems. It's the rest of you."

"I can tell you who it might have been," she murmured. "And I know you were conceived in Turkey. They were heady times, love."

"Apparently. And really, it doesn't matter, Mum."

"Well, I've never thought so."

Dylan stretched out on the sofa in an effort to relax. It was difficult when she was in one of her more reflective moods. She rarely looked back, she was far too busy looking forward to camel trekking and other equally ridiculous ways to waste time.

"So how are things going in Lancashire?" she asked and he was glad of the change of subject.

"They're not."

"What sort of answer's that?"

"An honest one. I can come up with several suspects, several people who might have wanted Sam

Hunt out of way, but there's nothing terribly convincing."

Jack Fleming might not have liked the idea of becoming a father, and he also had a temper when his girlfriends upset him, but it was more likely he'd dump Sam and pay a bit of maintenance when necessary.

If James Carlton really was making fraudulent insurance claims, he might want Sam silenced. He was also the last person to see Sam alive—apart from her father, of course. Carlton was an astute, if cheating, businessman and Sam was a twenty-two-year-old who read mystery novels. He was unlikely to kill her to silence her.

According to the message she left on Jack's answer machine, if indeed that was genuine, Sam had learned something horrible before her disappearance. It had nothing to do with James Carlton, she'd said. Before making that phone call, she'd seen her sisters, her mother and stepfather. Was it something connected to Alan Roderick? But what?

"You'll get there in the end, love." His mother was smoking the last centimetre of her happy tobacco.

"I hope so. I'm going to have a chat with her best friend tomorrow so perhaps she'll help." Dylan had been through Sam's address book but Yvonne, who people said was her best friend, had been on holiday for a fortnight. "If Sam confided in anyone, it would have been her. Perhaps."

"And then what? When you've found out what happened to the poor girl, will you concentrate on getting your marriage problems solved?"

"What?" God, she really was the limit. "What the hell can I do? Until Bev sees sense, I'm stuck with the situation."

"You could put some effort in. You need to show Bev that you're not the miserable git who came out of prison. You need to prove to her that you've got your self-respect back, that you're still the man she married."

Of course he was the man she married. Unlike Bev, he was an easygoing, steady type of bloke. He hadn't changed. Ever.

"How can I do that when getting into the house, *my* house, is like getting into Fort Knox?"

"Use your imagination, for heaven's sake."

There was no point arguing with her. No point taking advice from her, either. As the woman had never come close to tying the knot and didn't even know who her child's father was, she couldn't be classed an expert on marital problems.

Instead of dwelling on the idea of his mother having sex with some slinky-hipped waiter in Turkey, or anyone at all come to that, he needed to sort out his clothes for the coming week. Sort out meant wash. He didn't have a single clean shirt. Not one.

The one on his back had been clean until he and Luke had grabbed a quick lunch in McDonalds and Dylan had ended up with ketchup down his front. He'd done his best to mop it up, but still saw the way Bev rolled her eyes and gave a tight smile of satisfaction at the stain.

He was in her good books—flowers had amazing powers—but he refused to give her the impression he couldn't look after himself.

He went to his room, gathered up enough shirts to fill the washing machine—then dropped them on the floor when his phone rang.

It took a minute, tops, to find it but when he tried to return the missed call, no one answered. No one had left a message and he didn't recognise the number.

Any sane person would have forgotten it and washed shirts happy in the knowledge that it was either a wrong number or, if it had been important, someone would call back. Unfortunately, in this instance, Dylan didn't qualify as sane. He checked everywhere he might have made a note of someone's cell-phone number. Nothing. He searched for the number on Google. Nothing.

Two hours later, just as he'd decided to climb over a pile of dirty shirts to his bed, he found the number. It was in Sam Hunt's address book beneath a neatly written *Mum's Mobile.*

Dylan rang the number again, but no one answered.

What had Marion Roderick wanted with him?

TWENTY-SIX

At last. Finally, Anca had found someone who spoke her language. On first sight, she'd thought the woman was about thirty but, beneath the makeup and the long, curling hair, it was clear that she was about forty, maybe even older. She was slim, with painted finger-nails, and was wearing a long silk garment that was like nothing Anca had ever seen. It was tied at the waist with a silk sash and, if Anca guessed correctly, she was naked beneath it.

"This is where we'll be working, yes?"

"Yes. Come along."

Anca and Crina followed her up a staircase that seemed to go on forever. It was late and had been dark for hours.

"What will we be doing? Is this a hotel?"

Anca's question was ignored. Instead, the woman carried on walking up the stairs. Anca was too tired to repeat her question.

Crina didn't look well. Come to that, Anca didn't feel well. She had no idea how long they'd been locked away. At one point, she'd thought they were on a boat. Later, she'd felt wheels rumbling on a road. That had gone on for what had seemed like hours.

When the rumbling stopped, the lid of that chest

had been opened. It had been dark then too. A big man said something in a language Anca didn't recognise. His words must have been kind though because he'd dropped sandwiches and two bottles of water in the chest.

Anca had tried to speak to him, but he'd slammed down the lid. Crina had been asleep at the time and Anca had felt too weak to protest. She was still weak.

The woman pushed open a door and walked into a small room where six narrow mattresses filled most of the available floor space. Harsh light came courtesy of an unshaded light bulb. A set of six drawers sat in the corner.

"Yours." She pointed at two mattresses on the far side of the room. "Sleep now."

"But what about—?"

The woman flicked off the light and closed the door behind her. Anca gasped as she heard a key turn. She grabbed the handle and tried to open the door but it was locked.

"We're locked in." Crina's voice wobbled. "Why has she locked us in, Anca?"

Anca hammered on the door. "Come back!"

"Anca?" Crina cried.

"I don't know." Anca was furious. And a little frightened. "I'll speak to her tomorrow. I expect it's very late and she's had to stay up waiting for us." There was nothing else for it. "Let's get some sleep."

They'd slept for hours so Anca couldn't understand why she still felt exhausted. Perhaps it was the inoculation the doctor had given them.

"It doesn't matter, Crina." She tried to sound optimistic and cheerful. "We'll talk to her tomorrow and find out about the work we'll be expected to do. When we have time off, we'll see about getting a place of our own. We'll have an apartment, just you and me. It'll be fine."

"I want to go home." That was all Crina had said for hours.

"Well you can't. What? You thought it was easy to get to England? Think again. If it was, everyone would do it, wouldn't they?" Anca threw herself down on the narrow mattress. It was so thin she could feel the floorboards through it. She could feel the damp too. "Get some sleep, Crina."

Anca couldn't sleep. Like Crina, she longed for home. It had been more comfortable on the benches outside Bucharest Station. At least they hadn't smelled of urine. She was sure this mattress did.

The sky was inky black but there must have been a streetlight below them because an orange glow came through the tiny slanted window to cast a little light in the room.

A few cars drove past but she didn't think it was a busy street. There were a lot of noises coming from the building. People were walking on the stairs. Men were laughing.

They must be in a hotel, she reasoned. It was late yet there were a lot of people about. It must be a busy hotel. Tomorrow, they would probably be shown their own room. Tomorrow night, they would sleep in a proper bed.

Anca was drifting off to sleep when the door opened. She clutched the thin sheet to her chin and sat upright.

A girl of about her own age came in and Anca heard the sound of the key being turned from the outside again.

Ignoring Anca and Crina, the newcomer threw herself down on the mattress next to Crina and burst into noisy tears.

"What is it?" Anca asked. "What's the matter?"

The crying subsided slightly. "You're Romanian?"

"Yes. From Bucharest." Anca was thrilled to hear the familiar language. "You too?"

"Yes." The sobs turned to hiccoughs.

"Whatever's the matter?" Anca asked again.

"When did you arrive?"

"An hour or so ago." Anca wished the girl would calm down so they could have a conversation. "What about you?"

"Last week." She took a shuddering breath. "Who's that?"

"Crina, my sister. I'm Anca, by the way. What's your name?"

"My name? God, I hardly know anymore. Here, they call me Maria. What are they calling you?"

"What do you mean? My name's Anca."

Maria, or whatever her name was, turned her head and, in the orange glow and with her eyes accustomed to the gloom, Anca saw the bruises.

"What happened to your face?"

Maria touched her cheek. "I said no. A word of warning, never utter that word."

"How do you mean?"

"Do you know why you're here yet?"

"Oh, yes. We've come to work. A man we met in Bucharest—"

"The lovely George?"

"You know George?" A shiver of unease tracked down Anca's spine. None of this felt right.

"Oh, yes. If I hadn't met him, I'd still be at home."

"He brought us here. He said he'd find us work and we could pay him back. Tell me, is this a hotel?"

"A hotel?" Maria laughed. It was a laugh that quickly turned to crying again. "No, it's not a hotel."

"Then what is it? Where are we?" Anca's voice wavered. She knew, deep in her heart, what this place was, just as she knew she'd been taken for a fool.

"Where the hell do you think you are? Hmm? Okay, words of one syllable. The girls here are like you. And me. And her." She pointed at Crina. "The men want young girls, the younger the better, who won't—or can't—say no to anything they demand."

"Sex?"

"Some would call it that, yes."

Bile rose in Anca's throat. She'd been a naive, trusting simpleton. "This can't be right. I mean, not us. Crina's only thirteen."

"Then she'll be extremely popular, won't she?"

Maria lay face down and sobbed into her mattress.

Anca could have wept with her, but there was no point. Tears achieved nothing, she'd learned that much. Instead, she left her mattress and began hammering on the door. She'd got them into this mess. She would damn well get them out of it.

"There's been a mistake. We're in the wrong place. I demand to talk to someone. Now. Do you hear me?"

If they did, they were keeping quiet.

TWENTY-SEVEN

THE following evening, Dylan met up with a bleary-eyed, tanned woman at Jesters, Dawson's Clough's new wine bar. Yvonne, Sam's best friend, had chosen the venue because it was next door to the travel agent's offices where she worked.

He carried their drinks to the table. Without asking, the girl behind the bar had put a straw in Yvonne's Bacardi Breezer bottle. She didn't seem to mind. Or even notice.

"Thanks," she said.

"First day back at work?" Dylan asked.

"Yeah. It's always depressing, isn't it?"

"It is. All you do is think you could be in a sunny beach bar, don't you?"

"Yeah."

"I suppose you get a discount on holidays, do you?" he asked.

"Not like we used to, unfortunately."

A lot of office workers used Jesters. Men and women dressed in suits dropped briefcases on the floor and sat on tall bright red stools to enjoy the first drink of the day. Dylan was pleased that he and Yvonne had managed to grab one of the half dozen tables in the place.

Apart from looking tired and fed up, Yvonne was an attractive girl. The same age as Sam, she was tall and very slim, with long, almost black hair hanging down to her waist. Her makeup was perfect, from pink lips to extra-long dark eyelashes.

He'd phoned her several times over the last week but it was only yesterday morning, when her plane had landed at Manchester, that he'd got a response.

Someone else he hadn't been able to get hold of was Marion Roderick. He'd tried her cell phone all day, but she hadn't answered.

"Why are you looking for Sam?" Yvonne sucked Bacardi up the straw. "Why you, I mean? And why after all this time?"

"Her father's employed me." Dylan was sticking to the truth. If Yvonne knew Sam, it was almost certain she knew Jack. There was no point lying about his identity. "You're best friends, I gather?"

"Yeah. We met on the first day of school, when we were five. We've been mates ever since."

"So you know her well? Well enough to know if she had things on her mind, if she had plans to go somewhere, meet someone?"

"I did—and she didn't. I told the police that. Over and over, I told them that she wouldn't have gone off without a word to no one. Something happened to her."

"What about her boyfriend?"

"Jack's all right. I told the coppers that, an' all. Everyone says he's a bit of a tosser, but I've always got on well with him." She took a swig of her drink.

"The police hauled him off, you know. Bloody idiots. He doted on her." She traced a wistful finger along a scar in the wooden table. "He was forever calling her just to tell her he loved her. He sent her flowers when it wasn't her birthday or nothing. Oh, yeah, and once, he had an I Love You balloon delivered to her at work. He was as soft as shit where she was concerned. I told the coppers all that."

"He had a bit of trouble with a previous girlfriend, didn't he?" Dylan asked.

"Geraldine, yeah. Have you met her?"

"I haven't, no." Perhaps he should. Geraldine might know more about Jack Fleming than anyone.

"She's a right slapper. God knows why he got involved with her in the first place. He stayed with her because she said she was pregnant. She wasn't. She was just trying to trap him."

"Really?" That was interesting. Had Jack thought Sam was trying to trap him? "I heard Jack and Sam had a row before she disappeared. Do you know what that was about?"

"No." She looked annoyed about that.

"But you heard they had a row?"

"Yeah. Sam told me. She was laughing about it so it couldn't have been serious, could it?"

"I don't know."

"She phoned me on Thursday afternoon and she was laughing, said her and Jack had had a right ding-dong. Then she told me she had something exciting to tell me, and that we'd go out on the Saturday night."

Something exciting? That she was pregnant? Would Sam have been excited about that?

"I heard a rumour that she was pregnant," Dylan said and Yvonne jerked back in her seat.

"Pregnant? No, surely not." She took a moment to digest the news. "Well, I suppose it's possible. She did say she had something exciting to tell me. Blimey."

"Would she have considered it exciting, do you think?"

"I don't know." Yvonne shook her head. "Yes. Maybe. She loved kids and they always gravitated toward her. Whether she'd have wanted one of her own though, I don't know."

When Sam had called Jack later that day, she claimed she'd found out something horrible. So something had happened, if Jack was telling the truth and if that tape was genuine, between Sam phoning her best friend and talking of exciting news and phoning her boyfriend to mention something horrible.

"What time in the afternoon did she call you?" he asked.

"Eh? I dunno. Oh, about a quarter to four, I suppose. She was meeting Lydia and Emma from school so didn't have long to talk."

So, after phoning Yvonne, Sam had collected her half sisters, taken them to Alan and Marion's, gone home, phoned Jack, seen James Carlton and been caught kissing him by Alice, slept, woken up, said "see you later" to her father—and vanished.

"Did she seem happy to you?" Dylan asked.

"Very, but she always did. She used to joke that

she had her dream car, her dream job, her dream dog and her nightmare boyfriend." She smiled sadly at the memory. "Everyone liked her. Those coppers kept asking me if she had any enemies. She didn't have none. Everyone liked her. Everyone."

"Did she get on well with her parents?" Dylan asked.

"So-so. Yeah, her dad was all right. A bit of a fusspot, but all right. Her mum—well, tell me a daughter who gets on with her mum. She got on with hers as well as I get on with mine. It's sort of a love-hate relationship, you know?"

"Yes, I know. Did she have friends in Scotland, Yvonne?"

"No. Why do you ask?"

"It was just something I heard. What about her parents? Did they have friends there?"

"Not that I know of. Oh, Alan, her stepdad, might know someone there. He's a lorry driver and he goes up there quite a lot."

"Ah, yes, perhaps I'm thinking about that."

Yvonne looked at him from behind her dark fringe. "She's dead, isn't she?"

It was more statement than question and it took him by surprise. "I don't know. I hope not."

"If she was still alive, she'd have been in touch with me."

The sad thing was that Yvonne was probably right. When people left of their own accord, they usually felt compelled to let one of their old acquaintances know they were alive and well.

Long after Yvonne had left, Dylan was still sitting in the wine bar nursing a drink and thinking about her remarks. Like him, she assumed her friend was dead. What other possibilities were there? If she'd been kidnapped, her father would have received a ransom demand. If she'd chosen to take off for sun, sand and adventure, Dylan would have been able to follow the paper trail that even the most careful of people left in their wake. If she'd been involved in an accident, suffered amnesia—if anything like that had happened, the police would have been notified and an identification made.

Only when people were dead was their exit from this world so clean.

IT WAS ALMOST ELEVEN WHEN Dylan began the slow walk back to his hotel. The rain had stopped, but the pavements were slick, and oil glistened where lights caught the roadside puddles. Traffic was light and there were few people on the streets at this time. Unlike London, a city that refused to sleep, Dawson's Clough called its curfew long before midnight.

Despite the heavy downpour earlier, it was still warm. Uncomfortably so.

As he walked, hands in his pockets, he thought about Sam's life. According to Yvonne, she'd been happy with her lot. There was no reason to doubt that. She hadn't known her father was dying a slow death. Unless—

Hunt was adamant that only Dylan and Frank knew about his diagnosis. He hadn't even told Marion, he'd said. If Sam had overheard a phone conversation though, or found a letter from the hospital, that could easily explain the "something horrible." If she *had* learned that her father was dying, what would she have done? Dylan would imagine her running straight to her mother or to Jack, but he couldn't be sure.

If people were to be believed, she seemed relatively unscarred by her parents' divorce. Perhaps in a society where an unacceptably large proportion of children came from broken homes, it was easier to accept. It couldn't be said that she missed her mother because she had all the access to her, and to her half sisters, she wanted.

She loved her job, everyone agreed on that. That seemed likely given the pictures of sports cars adorning her bedroom walls. If she'd believed she was working for a fraudster, that would have been more likely to excite than depress her.

Sam struck Dylan as a well-balanced individual. Strong-minded and wilful too. If she'd had problems with her boyfriend, she would have been woman enough to leave him.

There was her alleged pregnancy. Would that have depressed her? Frightened her? Yvonne thought Sam could have been excited by the news and Marion had been confident her daughter would have coped.

Dylan couldn't know how she would have reacted, but he'd bet she would have been bright enough to consider all options and either have the baby or arrange a termination.

On the surface, her life had seemed a happy one.

There was her dog too. That she loved the animal was evident from photos Dylan had seen. She wouldn't have left Rusty…

Just as the first few spots of rain fell, his phone rang. He checked the caller ID, saw it was Frank and hit the button.

"Hi, Frank. You're up late."

"What? Oh right, yes, I've been watching the boxing. Have you heard the news?"

"What news?"

"Alan Roderick?"

Dylan ducked into a doorway to avoid the downpour. "What about him?"

"Dead as the proverbial dodo. It's just been on the news."

"What? Alan Roderick? Dead?" Dylan had a vision flash into his mind of the big strong bloke who drove fourteen-wheelers. "How come?"

He expected Frank to say "heart attack." Dylan had thought on their first meeting that Roderick spent too much time eating full English breakfasts.

"Stabbed eleven times."

"You're kidding me. When?"

"Yesterday morning. At home. His wife and kids were out, it said."

Yesterday morning.

Yesterday evening, Alan Rodericks's wife—widow—had tried to phone Dylan.

TWENTY-EIGHT

When the doorbell rang, Marion had been staring at the TV screen and seeing nothing for a full hour. It was the only light in the room. Reporters still hovered outside like vultures waiting for the best pickings.

The bell rang again, more insistent this time. It was doubtful it would wake the children. They were probably still awake but, if they weren't, a full marching band could practice in their room and they would remain blissfully ignorant.

The third time the bell rang, a streak of anger sparked through her like lightning. She refused to speak to reporters or people pretending to offer condolences, while really they were merely hungry for gossip—

She marched to the front door and peered through the viewer. The sight of Dylan Scott took her completely by surprise. She wondered if he'd heard the news. Of course he had. Everyone had by now. A murder in Dawson's Clough made headlines.

She pulled back the chain, turned the lock and opened the door a crack.

"I'm so sorry," he said. "About everything." He shuffled his feet. "I was wondering if I might have a word."

She opened the door fully and stood back to let him enter. Ridiculous, but she couldn't have been more pleased to see him.

"Thanks," he said.

He followed her into the dimly lit sitting room where, stupidly, she switched off the TV and plunged them into darkness.

"Sorry." She fumbled for the light switch and bathed them in a harsh light. "Sit down."

"Thanks." He perched on the edge of the sofa.

"How did you know I was here?"

"I called Rob."

Of course. As soon as Rob had heard about Alan he'd wanted her to stay at his place. No, not wanted. Expected. She and Alan had bought this flat a couple of years ago, as an investment, and luckily, the tenants had moved out a month ago. As they hadn't found new occupants, it was the perfect bolt-hole. Perfect was stretching it a bit perhaps, but it was a damn sight better than staying with Rob.

"Our house—my house—the police—" How did you explain that your home was now a crime scene? She sat down on the armchair farthest from him. "This is okay for a while."

"It's nice," he said.

Nice if you were a dwarf with no belongings and a penchant for grubby beige surroundings.

"Are you okay?" he asked.

"Yes, thank you. The children are asleep." Why had she said that?

"What happened, Marion?"

The simple question came like a kick in the stomach. "Would you like a drink? I know I could do with one."

"Thanks. I'll have whatever you're having."

"Whisky?"

He didn't bat an eyelid. "That would be good."

Deciding she couldn't tolerate the cold light, she switched on the TV, muted the sound and switched off the main light. It was better.

Shopping bags still sat on the small counter in the kitchen. On the way here, she'd stopped at the supermarket for the children's meal. She hadn't eaten all day, but she'd needed to feed them. All she'd bought for herself was a jar of coffee and a bottle of whisky.

She pulled the bottle from the bag, twisted off the top and found the two best glasses in the flat. They were cheap but serviceable.

"Do you want anything in it?" she called to him.

"As it comes is fine, thanks."

A lettuce was wilting on the worktop. She couldn't be bothered to put it in the fridge. Couldn't be bothered to do anything. A part of her was furious. The other part, by far the larger part, was numb.

The measures were too generous but she carried them through and handed his to him. As the sitting room didn't boast such a thing as a coffee table, he had to balance it on the arm of the sofa.

"Are you sure you're okay?" he asked. "Is there someone who could stay with you?"

Didn't she look okay? She hadn't bothered with makeup, and couldn't remember if she'd brushed her hair. "To be honest, I'd rather be on my own at the moment."

He nodded as if he understood, but how could he?

He took a sip of whisky and seemed to find it to his liking. It was only a blended one, Bell's or Grant's perhaps, she couldn't remember. As long as it did its job, she didn't care.

"Alan wasn't working yesterday," she said. "He'd done a run to Scotland and had a couple of days off." A large swig of whisky offered warmth as it slid down her tight throat. "He was supposed to be going to look at a motorbike with his mate. Geoff was thinking of buying it and wanted Alan's opinion. It was Geoff who found him." She cleared her throat and took another slug of whisky. "He was lying in the conservatory. He'd been—" She swallowed hard. "He'd been stabbed."

"I'm sorry."

"I was at the swimming pool," she said. "I always take the girls there on Sunday mornings. Two police officers, a man and a woman, came to tell me."

What did he care if it was a man and a woman? Why was she talking nonsense?

"And your daughters?" he asked. "Are they all right?"

"They're sleeping." She'd already said that.

She didn't know if they were all right or not. Like her, they seemed numb. From now on, life was going to be very, very different for them. Neither had shed a tear as yet. Perhaps that was natural. They were both too young to understand the finality of death.

"Was it a burglary?" he asked.

Although he was sitting back on the sofa, taking small sips of whisky now and again, looking relaxed and sympathetic and the sort of person you could confide in, Marion felt like a small insect he was examining under a microscope.

"No one knows."

"I see."

He was quiet for long, long moments. The only sound was the distant rumble of traffic and the humming of the fridge coming from the kitchen.

"You tried to phone me last night." He wasn't asking her, he was making a statement.

"Yes." She was tempted to lie, but what was the point? "Silly really, but I wanted to talk to someone. A stranger, you know?"

"I've been trying to return your call ever since."

She knew that but her courage had deserted her. "Reporters," she said. "They keep calling."

He nodded again.

"I have to be honest with you, Marion," he said at last. "Someone didn't want me in Lancashire. I was warned off twice." He touched a finger to the lip that had been bloodied and bruised when she'd first met him. "I can't say for certain, but it's possible that Alan wanted me off the case."

Her grip on the glass was so tight she thought it might splinter in her hands. "Alan? Why would he?"

"I was hoping you could tell me."

"No." She shook her head. "I can't say he was keen on the idea of employing you. He believed we needed to accept that Sam was gone and get on with our lives. He couldn't understand that the not knowing was stopping us doing that. It's difficult to sleep at night when you don't know if your daughter's safe."

He looked for somewhere to put his empty glass and, in the end, handed it to her. "I assume Alan had friends in Scotland?"

"Not that I know of."

"What about Rob? Does he have friends there?"

"None. Why do you ask?"

"Just thinking aloud really."

They talked for another half hour—about Alan and about Sam. They even complained about the oppressive heat and how, even at this late hour, it was no better.

When he stood to leave, she wished she could have begged him to stay.

"You've got my number, Marion. If there's anything I can do, you know where I am."

"Thank you."

She walked to the door with him and, when he'd gone, she locked it behind him. Then she refilled her glass, carried it into the sitting room, switched off the TV and sat in the dark.

There was no phone at the flat and she'd switched off her mobile hours ago. No one could reach her. She would sit here until daylight came.

TWENTY-NINE

Rob Hunt woke up gasping for breath as he tried to extricate himself from the tangle of sweat-drenched bed sheets.

He jabbed a shaking finger at the switch, and the bedside lamp cast its slightly blue light. The blinking figures of the alarm clock told him it was 4:15 a.m.

He punched at the pillows until they made a backrest and sank into them, wiping the sweat from his face with the sleeve of his pyjama jacket. He felt like an eight-year-old convinced that monsters lurked in dark corners.

The dream was always the same. He was standing on a street, one he didn't recognise, where tall buildings glowered down on him. It was too dark to see much, except there, at the bottom of the road, was a figure waving to him. It was impossible to tell if it was Sam or not.

He'd run along the street, trying to catch her. He was running and she was walking slowly with her back to him, yet he couldn't get any closer.

Marion appeared in front of him. She was dressed all in white, in her wedding dress perhaps.

"You can't leave me, Rob," she said.

Of course he couldn't leave her. Sam—if it was

Sam—was disappearing from his view, but he couldn't leave Marion.

He'd been lying on the cold ground next. His arms were being pulled from their sockets. The pain was excruciating. Teeth tore at his skin.

Marion, her white dress soaked in blood, pulled his left arm. Sam pulled on his right.

"Sam!" He spoke her name and she turned her face to his.

Except there was no face. No eyes. Nothing.

He closed his eyes and took several deep breaths. It was just a dream. Nothing more than that.

God, what a bloody mess they were in. It was all Marion's fault. If she hadn't met that man, if they'd had more children—

How old had Sam been when she'd first decided she wanted a sister? Five? Younger? He and Marion had laughed, he remembered, and told her it wasn't quite that simple.

"Everyone else has got one," Sam had said, long curls hiding her eyes and twisting round her pouting lips. "A brother then? If I can't have a sister, can I have a brother?"

In the end, she'd had to settle for a hamster.

Rob could remember turning to Marion that night in this same bed. His hand had rested on the curve of her belly. Three months had trundled past since they'd last made love and he ached for his wife.

"Perhaps we should give her a brother or sister,' he'd murmured. "Perhaps it's time, Marion."

"Don't start that again. Not tonight."

He stroked her soft pale skin and traced a line down to her thighs. She didn't offer encouragement, or indeed give any indication that she noticed, but at least she didn't push him away.

He pulled the sheet back and dropped a kiss at the base of her throat. She lay tense beside him. "Sweetheart," he murmured, licking a trail down to her breast.

He inched closer to her, so close that she would be able to feel him hard against her thigh. The ache increased, sweat broke out, his heart raced. His fingers, trembling now, stroked her thigh and, of their own volition, moved upward until they touched her crisp hair.

"Rob, stop it. Not tonight."

"Aw, come on, Marion."

He lifted his leg to rest it across her thighs. He moved against her, seeking to soothe the ache, and climbed on top of her.

"Sweetheart," he gasped, "I need you. Please, don't push me away."

"Rob—"

If he didn't take her, he would explode. He forced her legs apart with his knee.

"Rob!"

"Rob, what? I'm your husband, remember? I have rights."

"You don't have the right to force yourself on me."

"Don't I? We'll soon see about that."

He rammed himself inside her—God, it felt good. Blood pumped so furiously in his head that he couldn't hear her protests. He was aware of nothing but easing his need. He held her arms immobile as he thrust deeper and deeper, pushing her body upward so that her head banged against the headboard.

Minutes later, he slumped across her. Exhausted. Spent.

"You bastard. You fucking bastard!" She brought her knee up sharply and wriggled from beneath him. "You fucking bastard!"

She stormed into the spare room and, when Rob tried to gain entry to apologise, he realised she'd dragged the dresser in front of the door.

They never made love again.

THIRTY

FLASHING lights competed with ear-splitting music and indecipherable lyrics to give Dylan a migraine.

He'd been sitting on the bar stool at Indie Street for an hour and hadn't recognised a soul.

Three days on and, as far as he knew, there was no suspect for Roderick's murder. There were no outpourings of grief, either. He'd expected tears at the least from Marion Roderick but she wasn't the grieving widow. All Dylan had sensed from his brief chat with her was a sense of relief. If that was true, and life with him had been hell, why hadn't she divorced him? She'd divorced Hunt, so she clearly didn't have strong views on marriage being till death parted those concerned.

Dylan had spoken to Hunt—the bloke was never off the phone—and, although he'd sounded shocked by the news, there was no sympathy for Roderick from that quarter. Dylan hadn't expected any really. It was no secret that Hunt had disliked him. Jealousy, Dylan supposed.

Jealous enough to kill him?

Alan Roderick had been a big, strong brute of a man whereas Hunt was terminally ill. It seemed unlikely that Hunt would be capable of overpowering him.

Dylan tipped back his glass, swallowed the contents and was ready to leave the club. He was two steps from the bar when James Carlton walked in.

Dylan did an about-turn and reclaimed his glass. He could suffer another half hour in this place. Just.

After reminding himself he was a TV producer, and deciding a drunk one would be even better, he turned to see Carlton approach the bar.

"Hi!" Dylan waved his arm to attract the bloke's attention. "What's it to be? I'm just getting another."

"Oh, hello." There was no way Carlton could refuse the offer but it was plain from the frown pulling his brows together that he wanted to.

"I'm having whisky," Dylan slurred. "I've had a few already."

The frown was replaced with a reluctant smile. "So I see."

People felt less vulnerable when talking to drunks. They dropped their guard.

"I'll have the same then," Carlton said. "Thanks."

The heavy thump of music vibrated the bar. Dylan would be glad to get away from it and to his bed.

"Two doubles—on the rocks," he told the young barmaid. "And have one yourself, love."

"Oh, thanks. I'll have it later," she replied.

While she dropped ice into their glasses, Carlton sat on the stool next to Dylan.

"What brings you here?" he asked.

"I thought I'd give it a try." Two glasses were

plonked in front of them. "Thanks, love." Dylan raised his glass in a toast. "Cheers."

"Cheers," Carlton echoed, taking a sip.

"What about you, James? Is this one of your regular haunts?"

"I nip in for a nightcap sometimes." He nodded at the dance floor where a small crowd, mostly young girls in various states of undress, were dancing. "The scenery's good."

"Too true."

They both swivelled round to get a better a view of the dancers, and Dylan tried to gauge the ages of the girls. Apart from two who were probably in their thirties, the others looked to be about eighteen.

"I thought you'd be long gone," Carlton said.

"I wish. Nah, I've got my boss breathing down my neck. I have ten days to find Sam, otherwise—" He ran a finger across his neck.

"You won't find her."

"I'm beginning to believe that." He winked at Carlton. "Still, I'm in no hurry. As you say, the scenery's pretty good and my wife's more than two hundred miles away."

Carlton laughed at that.

"Anyway," Dylan said, "I haven't given up hope on Sam. I might be lucky. Who knows?"

"No chance, mate."

"You reckon she's dead?"

"I've no idea." Carlton shrugged.

"It's funny," Dylan said, wobbling on his stool as the finest drunks did, "but usually, when I tell girls I

work in the TV business, they're mine for the taking."
He tossed back his drink. "Admittedly, I only saw
Sam briefly, but I got the impression she wasn't interested in anything—er, extracurricular, if you get
my gist."

"You didn't try hard enough."

"Obviously." Dylan laughed as if they were the best
of pals. "You had more luck than me?"

"No, I didn't. I was getting there though." Carlton
returned his gaze to the gyrating bodies on the dance
floor. "Plenty more fish in the sea, eh?"

"More than enough. Hey, you know that bloke—
Christ, I've forgotten his name. The bloke who married Sam's mother—"

"Alan Roderick. Yeah, I heard about that."

"Alan Roderick." Dylan pretended to try the name
for size. "That was bloody odd, wasn't it? Christ, if I
was a member of that family, I'd be demanding police
protection."

"He wasn't family. Well, not really. He just happened to marry her mother."

"All the same. Did you know him?"

"No."

"Murdered."

"That's about the height of it."

Talk about blood and stones…

Dylan's phone rang and he hunted in his pocket
until he found it. A quick glance at the display told
him his mother was calling for the eighth time that
day. He hit the button to reject the call.

"That was my boss again," he lied for Carlton's

benefit. "Time's running out for me. I have to find Sam."

"You won't do that, believe me. What I can't understand is why your boss is so hung up on her. There are dozens of suitable girls out there." He jerked a thumb in the direction of the dance floor. "Any of those for a start."

"It's a nice thought, but I doubt they even know what a carburettor is." He didn't like Carlton, but he didn't want to alienate him yet. "I'll keep feeding my boss the plenty-more-fish-in-the-sea line and hope he takes the bait. If he does, I'll be in touch with you and see if we can use your expertise."

"Thanks for that. I'll be only too pleased to help in any way I can."

"The biggest help would be to find Sam and make my boss's day."

"I wish I could." Carlton emptied his glass. "There's nothing happening here tonight so I'm heading home. I'll buy you one before I go—"

"No." Dylan waved the offer aside. "Save it till next time. I'll be off myself in a minute or so."

"Okay. Be seeing you."

"Yeah, sure."

Dylan watched as Carlton, hands in the pockets of his jacket, walked toward the exit. He was still watching when the bouncer Stripes walked in. The two almost collided. Words were exchanged. Carlton left the building and Stripes, after looking round the room, spotted Dylan and walked over to him.

"Yeah, yeah," Dylan slurred, "you don't want me here. I already got the message."

Stripes shrugged and settled his muscular bulk on the stool Carlton had vacated. "I've done my bit. I gave you a warning. If you don't take any notice, that's not my problem, is it?"

So the person wanting Dylan warned off had given up. Or was dead. If Dylan were a betting man, he'd stake his house on the latter.

"It's not Alan Roderick's problem either now, is it?" Dylan said.

"Alan Roderick? Nope, the name means nothing to me."

"A pity you never learned to read then. He's on the front page of all the papers."

"Oh?"

"Yeah. A murder in Dawson's Clough always ranks higher than a stolen Mars bar."

"I wouldn't know. I've been in Birmingham."

"How convenient."

"I was visiting my sister and my new nephew. I haven't heard any local news."

Dylan glanced up to see if any neon blue pigs were flying in formation.

"You must have known him though," he said.

"What was his name again?"

"Alan Roderick."

"Nope. Never heard of him."

"Funny." Dylan shook his head in bewilderment. "I saw the two of you chatting in this very club." There were times, as he often told Luke, when a lie was necessary.

"Yeah? Perhaps he was asking me for a light."

"Perhaps he was."

The barmaid finally came to take his drinks order.

"Same again?" she asked Dylan.

"No, thanks. It's time I was off." He wasn't going to learn anything from Stripes.

"Watch how you go," Stripes said.

"Don't worry, I will. I don't want to end up like Roderick."

It was bliss to step outside. The bouncer stood at the bottom of the steps, arms folded across his broad chest, feet spaced the regulation twelve inches apart. He nodded as Dylan reached the bottom step.

"You on your own tonight?" Dylan asked. "I've just been talking to Stripes." He nodded back at the building and the noise. "He's not on tonight, is he?"

"Nope, just me. They won't waste money paying two of us. Unless they're expecting trouble, that is."

"Do they get much trouble?"

"Not really. It can get a bit lively on Friday nights—well, the early hours of Saturday mornings—but that's about all."

"Sounds a cushy number you've got then."

"It is. So long as you can handle yourself."

"Yeah." It was at times like this that Dylan wished he smoked. Stepping outside for a cigarette was the perfect excuse for striking up conversations with strangers. Instead he had to make do with shoving his hands in his pockets, gazing up at the cloud-laden night sky and pretending he was taking a few deep breaths and enjoying the air. "That was a surprise, wasn't it? Alan Roderick getting done in."

"It was. Have they got the bloke who done it yet?"

"Not that I heard."

"Me neither." The bouncer, probably breaking club rules, did light a cigarette. He put a Zippo lighter back in his pocket as he inhaled. "He was a funny bugger though, wasn't he?"

"Yeah, but he didn't strike me as the sort of bloke to argue with."

"There's all sorts of tales going round." The bloke leaned closer to Dylan to whisper. "Mafia. In Romania. He sometimes drove his lorry there."

"Mafia?"

"Yeah. It makes sense too. He wasn't making the money he spent driving a bloody lorry."

"That's what I always thought," Dylan agreed.

"You don't tangle with them bastards if you've got any sense. There's loads of mafia in Romania, you know."

"I wonder why they didn't kill him there then. Seems odd to come over to England and kill him in his own home." Dylan smiled at his companion. "I thought the mafia walked into restaurants with machine guns hidden in violin cases."

"Dunno." He pulled deep on his cigarette. "Now you mention it, it does seem bloody odd that they'd come over here."

Odd because the mafia had nothing to do with it. Roderick's killer was much closer to home, Dylan was sure of that.

THIRTY-ONE

DYLAN stopped the car outside Alice's bungalow just as his phone trilled into life. He unfastened his seatbelt and fumbled in his pocket for it. Expecting yet another call from his mother, he was pleased to see Frank's name beneath Caller ID.

He hit the button. "Frank? How's things?"

"I've just heard that they're about to make an arrest for Roderick's murder. You'll never guess who it is."

It wasn't Hunt because the bloke had been on the phone demanding a meeting with Dylan. "I won't bother trying then."

"Jack Fleming."

"What?" A mental picture of Sam's boyfriend came to mind—the confidences he'd shared with Dylan, the way he'd kept that last phone message from her—except, of course, there was no guarantee Sam *had* left that message. "Surely not."

"They've got a strong case. He was spotted on CCTV near the area, a neighbour swears she saw him at the back of the house, and a shoe print that matches his was found in the garden."

"Christ, that *is* a good case. What's his story, Frank?"

"I gather he denied all knowledge at first. Well, he

would, wouldn't he? He's now claiming he was there, but that's all."

"What the hell was he doing there?"

"I don't know."

"Hmm." Dylan noticed curtains twitching at Alice's bungalow. "Do you fancy a drink later?"

"Sounds good to me."

"The Dog and Fox? Sevenish?"

"Yup, suits me."

Dylan cut the connection and jumped out of his car. Judging by those moving curtains, Alice was growing curious.

He strode up to the front door and rang the bell. She must have been expecting him, but he had to ring twice before she opened the door a crack and peered out at him.

"Hello, Alice. I'm on my way up to Rob's so, as I was passing your door, I thought I'd drop in and say hello."

"Come on in then. The kettle's on."

"Thanks." Dylan kept his elbows tight by his sides to avoid smashing owls that stood sentry the length of the hall.

He followed her into the small, tidy kitchen where yet more owls stared at him from tea towels, cups, oven gloves and fridge magnets.

"You like your owls, Alice." Unable to think of anything else to say, he decided to state the obvious.

"Oh, yes." She smiled. "They're wise old birds. People could learn a lot from owls."

It seemed to Dylan that people had learned a lot—like the art of silence.

"Did you hear about Alan Roderick?" He had to raise his voice over the sudden whistle of the kettle.

"What a shock. I couldn't believe my own ears. Those poor daughters of his. What will life be like for them now?" She removed the teapot's lid, but made no attempt to fill it. "You can't take it in, can you?"

"Terrible."

"And his poor wife. Rob's ex-wife. How must she be feeling knowing she has to face life alone?" She finally filled the teapot and reached up to the top cupboard for what had to be her best cups. Surely, the ones she used most often would be within reach. "Life can be cruel, can't it?"

"It can, Alice." Life hadn't murdered Alan Roderick, though. Dylan wasn't convinced Jack Fleming had, either. God, how he wished he had the resources of the local CID at his disposal.

"You were passing then?" Alice asked.

"Yes. I'm on my way to Rob's and thought I'd nip in and say hello while I was here."

"That's nice."

Her pleasure had Dylan feeling like a total heel. He felt obliged to make small talk.

"My wife would love this kitchen. She longs for a kitchen that catches the sun. Ours is north facing and it's like a freezer at times."

"Then tell her from me to be careful what she wishes for." Alice pointed at the window. "I have to keep the blinds down in the summer or I'll roast. There's no need to have the oven on."

"Ah. Yes, I can see that being a problem."

The tea was made and Alice was about to pick up the tray. "We can go in the conservatory if you like. It's not too hot yet. I've got the blinds down and the doors open."

Dylan took the tray from her. "Lead on, Alice."

"Ooh, look at that," a familiar voice screeched.

"Is the parrot still swearing?"

"He is, and I'm at my wits' end. It wasn't as if Sean swore often. Just occasionally, you know?"

Dylan wasn't surprised to see small owls dotted on the white uPVC windowsills in the conservatory. A circular piece of stained glass, depicting a barn owl, hung from a plastic sucker.

The furniture was wicker, covered with thick blue cushions. Dylan set the tray on the glass top of a matching wicker table.

"I don't suppose you've heard anything about Sam?" Alice peered at the tea, decided it was strong enough, and began to pour.

"Not really, Alice. It's a mystery, isn't it?"

"That it is."

"I do know who you saw her with that night, though. The married man, remember? That was her boss."

Alice frowned and tutted, disapproval in every wrinkle.

"She might have been kissing him," Dylan said, "but I don't think there was anything between them.

I think she suspected him of dodgy dealings. He'd made a couple of insurance claims and Sam believed he was on the take."

Alice's eyes widened at that. "And was he?"

"I wouldn't put it past him."

"Well, well. So she wasn't cheating on young Jack?"

"On the contrary. It was Jack who told me why Sam was with her boss."

"You see? I knew she wouldn't have done something—bad. She hated cheats. If her boss was on the fiddle, she wouldn't have liked it."

"I can understand that. But if he was—well, there was a fair bit of money involved, Alice. He wouldn't have taken kindly to her meddling in his affairs."

Alice was about to take a sip of tea, and the cup shuddered to a stop two inches from her mouth. "You don't think—"

"I don't know, Alice. I'm not sure he even knew she was trying to find out what he'd been up to."

"He sounds a nasty piece of work, if you ask me." Alice took a sip of tea and, deep in thought, returned the cup to the tray. "Oh, look at me. I've forgotten the biscuits."

Dylan had finished a full English breakfast less than an hour ago, but he didn't have the heart to tell her so. Besides, like a bird darting from tree to nest, she was gone.

A few moments later, she returned with a plate of homemade biscuits and two small muffins. "I was so surprised to see you, I forgot the biscuits. I am sorry."

"You spoil me, Alice."

She chuckled at that and pushed the plate toward him. "Help yourself. Don't be shy."

Dylan had been called a lot of things in his time but shy wasn't one of them. He took a biscuit and murmured his pleasure as the buttery taste melted in his mouth. As far as he could remember, his mother had never baked a biscuit or a cake in her life. She adhered to the "chew on a few seeds" philosophy. As for Bev, she could never be bothered to cook when Tesco was just around the corner. You couldn't buy biscuits like these at a supermarket, though.

Dylan didn't know what he wanted from Alice. Any information he could get on Sam, he supposed. And anything on her family and friends.

"Between you and me, Alice, I feel quite bad about this. For not finding out much about Sam, I mean. I'm quite costly, you see. It's the expenses that mount up. I hope Rob isn't going to be too shocked when I hand in my final account."

Dylan wasn't worried because, given his current dodgy financial situation, he'd asked for, and received, a substantial advance up front.

"Oh, I'm sure he won't. He'll understand, just as I do. I'm sure he knew how expensive it would be."

"I hope so." Dylan tried to make light of it. "I'd hate to think I wouldn't get paid."

"Goodness me, you've no need to worry on that score. Rob always pays promptly." Alice dropped her voice to a whisper. "He's very well off, you know."

"I've come to realise that. I still can't get over the

size of his house. Still, so long as he can afford it, it's his choice, isn't it?"

"It is a big place, especially now he's rattling around in it on his own. Mind you, none of us like change, do we? I wouldn't want to move house. Such an upheaval."

"True."

Dylan remembered something else. "The other day—" Dylan, too, dropped his voice to a whisper despite knowing that only the parrot was within earshot. "The other day, I saw a bundle of cash at Rob's. We're talking a lot of cash too. At least a thousand pounds. Maybe even two. It was lying on the table. I mean, it's good for me to know he has money, but that's not wise, is it?"

Alice tutted. "I've told him about that. One day— oh, it was two or three months ago—I saw him putting a huge amount of cash in an envelope. 'You can't do that,' I tells him. It looked for all the world as if he was going to mail it to someone. Well, I tells him, that's just asking for trouble. You can't trust the mail these days. What doesn't go missing gets pinched."

"Isn't that the truth." Dylan nodded sagely. "Did he take note of your warning?"

"He got a bit stroppy, to tell the truth. I suppose that's only natural. After all, he's got money to burn and I get by on what he pays me. All the same…" Her voice trailed away.

"I expect there's nothing to worry about. He was probably going to pay it into his bank account. He's far too sensible to have that much cash lying around."

"Maybe." Alice looked doubtful. "More likely is that a builder, a tradesman of some sort, had persuaded him to pay a bill in cash. They do, don't they? That way they don't have to tell the taxman about it."

"I'm sure Rob's wise to that one. We'll be worrying about nothing."

He beamed at her and helped himself to another biscuit. Despite having demolished a huge breakfast, he could, quite easily, clear the plate.

His mind was working overtime though. Why would Hunt have large amounts of cash lying around?

A distant rumble of thunder was heard and Alice scowled out at the darkening sky. "I thought we were supposed to have a nice day today. What with the heat, the thunder and lightning and all that rain, I won't be sorry when winter's here. I know you shouldn't wish your life away, but it's too hot for me. I don't like it at all."

"Me neither." His mind was still ticking over. "A friend of mine has just come back from Scotland and he said they'd had lovely weather. No thunder. No rain. He said it was glorious."

"I can believe that."

"Someone else—" He pretended to think. "Oh yes, I saw a postcard that came for Rob. He must know someone who's holidaying up there."

"Oh no, they're not on holiday. Those postcards come all the time. They're from someone who lives there."

"Really?" What did "all the time" mean?

"It's a man." Alice frowned. "Oh, it'll come to me."

"Alan Roderick must have had friends there too." Dylan helped himself to a muffin and took a bite. "At least, I assume he did. He used to volunteer for the Scottish trips so I imagine he had friends there."

"I wouldn't know about that. I expect it was good money driving up there. These drivers can make a fortune, can't they?"

Not as large a fortune as Alan Roderick had managed.

"It's long hours, though, and half the time they sleep in their cabs." He took another bite of muffin. Delicious.

"It's Mattie," Alice said. "That friend of Rob's. I'm sure he said his name was Mattie. He's an old army chum, I think. I asked him once. I mean, I don't like to be nosy but I can't help seeing them when I pick up the mail for him. Anyway, they're signed with an *M.* It's nice that they keep in touch after so long, isn't it?"

"It is. People form strong bonds in the army, don't they? I suppose it's a different world and they gel together. Some find it hard to accept life as a civilian."

"I don't think Rob ever did."

"No. Some do, though. All those postcards, Alice, how long have they been coming for Rob?"

"Oh—" She thought hard. "About six months, I'd say."

"Really?"

"Possibly longer. There have been more of them lately, sometimes four a month. It's lovely that they keep in touch. Nice for Rob to have friends when he has so many problems. Sam, I mean."

"Yes." Dylan emptied his cup and resisted the very strong temptation to have another biscuit. "Talking of Rob, it's time I was off, Alice. Thank you for feeding and watering me. You're very kind."

"You're more than welcome. Any time you're passing, just call in. I'm usually here if I'm not up at Rob's."

"You'll never get rid of me." Dylan gave her his warmest, most teasing smile as he left.

When he started the car, Alice was waving from the window. He returned the wave and pulled away.

Hunt had been seen with large bundles of cash on two separate occasions and there had to be times when he hadn't been seen. There could be all sorts of reasons for that.

Blackmail made it to the top of Dylan's list as he drove the short distance to Hunt's house. Who might enjoy a spot of blackmail? Who had lived beyond his means?

Alan Roderick.

Then there was the matter of the postcards. Was it rare for two men, ex-army colleagues, to keep in touch via frequent postcards? Yes, it was. Damned odd. It was odd for blokes to keep in touch at all in Dylan's experience. Even if they were the best of mates, a phone call now and again would be more usual. They lived too far apart to meet up for a quick beer so what the hell did they have to say to each other?

He wasn't sure it mattered whether they kept in

touch via postcards, phone calls or homing pigeons. Nor did it matter if Hunt was being blackmailed. His job was to learn the truth behind Sam's disappearance. Nothing more.

Something was niggling though.

Hunt was waiting for him. The front door was open before Dylan was out of his car.

"Morning," he greeted Dylan, ushering him inside. "How's it coming along?"

Hunt was hard work. He was also paying Dylan a lot of money and it was difficult to admit that, so far, he was paying for nothing. Dylan was no nearer to discovering the truth behind Sam's disappearance than he had been the first time he heard her name mentioned.

Today, though, he had questions for Hunt. For once, the conversation wouldn't be one-sided.

He refused offers of tea and coffee—he'd be awash with the stuff if he had any more—and they were soon settled in Hunt's study. Apart from Sam's bedroom, it was the only room Dylan had seen.

"What have you heard about Alan Roderick's murder?" Dylan asked.

"Only that someone broke into his house and stabbed him. I assume he disturbed a burglar. Why do you ask?"

"I wondered if it struck you as odd—Sam disappears, Roderick is murdered."

Hunt didn't bother to hide his surprise. "He was nothing to Sam. Just because her mother chose to marry him—no, he was nothing to her."

Dylan was sitting. Hunt was up and down like a fiddler's elbow. He seemed even more fidgety than usual, if that were possible.

Dylan wondered just how frail he was. If Hunt hadn't told him he was terminally ill, Dylan would have put the dull pallor and the occasional breathlessness down to a man out of condition. Dylan had seen heavy smokers who looked worse.

Hunt wasn't a strong man but anger and jealousy could pump adrenaline like nothing else. The element of surprise was a strong ally, too, although it was unlikely he'd be able to overpower a man like Roderick.

"No one seems sorry he's dead," Dylan said.

"Low life." Hunt spoke as if that explained everything from his murder to the lack of outpourings of grief.

"How's Marion coping? I assume you've spoken to her?"

"Of course. She'll be fine. I've told her there's a home here for her. His daughters too."

His daughters? Such bitterness.

"Tell me," Dylan said, "have you been a victim of blackmail?"

"I—sorry?"

"I asked if you'd been blackmailed by anyone."

Hunt shook his head as if Dylan were crazy. "Of course not. Why the hell would anyone want to blackmail me?"

Dylan only wished he knew.

Why, though, would a man like Hunt have a thousand pounds, maybe more, lying around as he had on

Dylan's first visit and on the occasion his cleaner had felt obliged to warn him? Hunt was wealthy. Why would he pay for anything in cash? American Express was accepted everywhere.

"We all have skeletons," Dylan said. "Everyone's done things they'd like to keep secret."

"Not me. What the hell are you suggesting exactly?"

Hunt was growing angry, with every right probably. Even if Roderick had blackmailed him, it wasn't Dylan's problem. If Hunt had decided to put an end to it, to put an end to Roderick, that wasn't his problem either.

His job was to find Sam Hunt. Dead or alive.

"Oh, I was just curious," Dylan said. "Ignore me."

Hunt visibly relaxed. "It's the heat. It makes us all a bit frazzled. Let's sit outside, shall we? It's probably cooler out there.

"Good idea. Do you think I could use your bathroom first?"

"Of course. Along the hall—third on the left."

"Thanks. You go ahead and I'll join you."

Dylan wasn't sure why he wanted to see the rest of the house. He wasn't going to find bloodstained clothes or the knife used to kill Roderick. Nor was he going to find a blackmail note from Roderick. It was doubtful he'd find evidence of another woman in Hunt's life.

As he walked along the hall, he heard Hunt slide open the French windows. Moving quickly, Dylan opened a door into the dining room. Like the rest of the house, apart from Sam's bedroom, this was furnished in an ultra-modern style. It didn't hold his interest.

He opened the third door on the left. The bathroom boasted toilet, washbasin, shower and shimmering blue walls. A quick look in cupboards revealed nothing more than dozens of fluffy white towels and a few toiletries. The room looked as if it was rarely used. That wasn't surprising as Dylan guessed Rob's bedroom had its own. In case Hunt had ventured back inside and was within earshot, Dylan flushed the toilet.

He headed for what he knew was the kitchen. If questioned, he'd claim a poor sense of direction. Again, the room looked more for display than use. There wasn't so much as an unwashed cup to be seen.

A pile of mail sat next to a gleaming stainless steel kettle and Dylan flicked through it—a letter from the local hospital, one from Sky TV, several leaflets from local Indian restaurants and kebab houses and there, right at the bottom, a postcard. Dylan assumed it was the one he'd seen on his previous visit until he turned it over. This one showed the same picture of the ferry in the harbour at Scrabster but read *Thank you. Most welcome.*

Dylan pulled open a few drawers and cupboards but found nothing more than crockery, utensils and food. Hunt was supposedly terminally ill but Dylan hadn't seen so much as an aspirin in kitchen or bathroom.

Knowing he couldn't poke around anymore, he marched to the study and stepped into the garden.

Off to his right was a decked area complete with table and four chairs. Several stone tubs offered a burst of blue and yellow colour. Hunt sat in one of the chairs.

Dylan sat opposite him and wondered again how ill Hunt was. Looking at him now, he seemed okay. Not a picture of health admittedly, but okay.

"What a lovely spot," Dylan said, looking around him. "A real sun trap."

"On the rare occasions we get any sun." As he spoke, another rumble of thunder echoed round the hills.

"A friend of mine has just returned from a holiday in Scotland." Dylan watched Hunt closely but there wasn't so much as a flicker. "He said the weather's been better up there. Hard to believe, isn't it? He's been in the Highlands. I've had a couple of holidays there, but I can't say I know the area. Do you?"

"I don't. All I know is that you get eaten by midges in Scotland. The heather attracts them."

"True." Dylan ran his hand over the wooden table, pretending to think. "Someone else—oh, of course, Alan Roderick knew Scotland well, didn't he?"

"I doubt he soaked up the culture." Rob's tone was sneering. "He drove his lorry there and back, that's all."

"So he did. Someone said—can't think who it was—that you have friends in Scotland?"

"Me? No."

"I must have it wrong then. I could have sworn someone said an old friend of yours was up there."

There was a long pause. Even the birds held their breath as they waited for Rob's response.

"Not me. Now, to get back to Sam," Hunt said. "What do you think of that boyfriend of hers, Jack Fleming? I'm sure you can understand why I didn't want her seeing him."

Dylan wasn't going to push the issue of the postcards, but he knew Hunt was lying. Why?

"Jack seems okay to me. There's nothing to suggest he had anything to do with Sam's disappearance. Nothing at all."

"I'm not saying there is. No one would call him likeable though." Hunt drummed his fingers on the table. "So what have you been doing?"

"Talking to people."

Dylan wasted the next half hour by telling Hunt what he'd been doing. He told him about every meeting he'd had, every phone call he'd made, every place he'd visited. All the while, he tried to figure out why Hunt was lying...

"Right," Dylan said, standing up. "I'll call you if I learn anything interesting. I'll have to dash off now as I have an appointment, but I'll be in touch."

"Of course. And thank you, Dylan. I appreciate all you're doing."

Dylan put up his hand in acknowledgement and walked the length of the garden round to the front of his house and his car.

AT TEN MINUTES TO SEVEN, Dylan sat in the Dog and Fox with a welcome pint of cold beer in his hand. Life wasn't so bad after all. It was so good, in fact, that his glass was empty in under ten minutes.

"Same again, please, love." As soon as he'd spoken, he heard the echo of Bev telling him that calling young women "love" was "too patronising for words." This one didn't seem to mind.

The door opened, letting in unwelcome traffic noise.

"Frank, that's good timing. What are you having?"

Frank peered at the beers on offer. "The same as you, please."

They took their drinks to a fairly secluded table, sat down and took quick swigs.

"What do you know then?" Dylan asked.

Frank licked froth from his top lip. "Not a lot—other than the fact that Jack Fleming is in custody. What do you think of that?"

"I think they've got the wrong man." What did he know? He was basing that on pure instinct, whereas CID would be looking at the facts. "What have they got?"

"I don't know anything more than I've already told you. Apparently, Fleming was caught on CCTV—there are a couple of shops at the bottom of the Rodericks' road and he was caught passing there and turning into the road. They reckoned he looked shifty and they also knew he was known to Roderick so, when they found a shoe print outside the Rodericks' house, they checked out his shoes and found a match." Frank played with the beer mat. "Fleming claimed he'd never been near the house until they presented him with that piece of evidence. He's now saying he was watching Roderick."

"He admits to being at the property?"

"Yeah. That was a damn fool thing to do but he did that before his lawyer arrived."

It was an insane thing to do, but Dylan knew what it was like for suspects. They had no idea of the procedure. Rights were read, of course, but suspects didn't understand what was happening and were often too shocked to ask.

"Why was he watching Roderick though?"

"I don't know, mate."

Dylan and Frank were alike in that they were both outcasts from the force. Unlike Dylan, though, Frank was still respected. Officers would talk to him. They'd have Dylan escorted from the building.

"I still reckon they've got the wrong bloke. Jack Fleming's no killer." He was just a bloke who locked girlfriends in their flats and scared the living daylights out of them. "What motive would he have?"

"No idea, but who needs a motive? He knew Roderick. He was there. That's enough." Frank drank his beer. "Christ, that went down well. I'll get us another. Same again?"

"Please." Dylan's glass was still half full—or half empty—but it would save getting up again.

While Frank chatted to the barmaid, Dylan closed his eyes and tried to come up with a reason for Jack snooping around the Rodericks' place. When Dylan had mentioned Alan and Marion Roderick, Jack hadn't seemed duly concerned by either of them.

He'd claimed he only saw them to say hello to. He'd also claimed that Sam hadn't liked Alan. That wasn't reason enough to kill the bloke though. Besides, Sam had disappeared months ago. It was old news.

"There you go." Frank put two full pints on the table and sat down.

"There's something bloody funny going on." Dylan was getting adept at stating the obvious. "For one thing, I think Rob was being blackmailed. Probably by Roderick."

Frank was reaching for his glass. He stopped. "You're kidding me!"

Dylan probably was. He had no evidence.

"I know of two occasions when Rob had a wad of cash, at least a grand, lying around. When I saw it, it was in an open envelope. His cleaner saw him with a lot of cash, too, and she thought he was putting it in the mail."

Frank gave him his "is that it?" look.

"Think about it, Frank. Roderick was a lorry driver. No way could he afford that lifestyle of his."

Frank's expression didn't alter, but he was prepared to humour Dylan. "Okay," he said, drawing the word out. "What would anyone have on Rob? What skeletons could he have lurking?"

"I don't know. It could be anything. Something Marion knew about. She must have discussed Rob with her husband, and Roderick struck me as the sort of bloke to leap on any opportunity."

"No. I can't see it. Rob's too—clean. Too respectable."

No one was *too* clean.

"Then there's this Scottish thing," Dylan said.

"Scottish thing?"

"Yeah." He was thinking aloud, throwing random thoughts in Frank's direction. "Roderick volunteers to drive his lorry there. Everyone else hates that run, but he volunteers to go to Scotland. He goes to Hungary and Romania, too, but it's still odd. Next, I see a postcard that's been sent to Rob from up there. A week later, I see another postcard—same view, different short message. He claims he knows no one up there. His cleaner, though, says one of his old army chums lives up there. The postcards are signed with an M and his cleaner says his mate's name is Mattie. Your friend's lying about something, Frank."

"Rob?"

Dylan might have tried to convince him the earth was flat.

"Yes. He claims he knows no one in Scotland and yet I've seen two postcards. According to Alice, his cleaner, he sometimes gets four a month."

"Get a grip. Rob wouldn't lie."

"One card said 'Wish you were here' and the other said 'Thank you. Most welcome.'"

"He wouldn't lie." Frank took a slug of beer. "I mean, for God's sake, why would he? What does it matter how many friends he has in Scotland? Who would care if he kept in touch with some bloke he was friends with in the army?" Frank was growing more defensive on Hunt's behalf and, at the same time, less certain. "Why would he lie, Dylan? All he wants is the truth behind Sam's disappearance."

A middle-aged couple strolled into the pub and seemed disappointed not to know any of the customers. Dylan knew that feeling. When he and Bev went to their local, it was always a let-down to see strangers there. It meant they had to talk to each other and they could do that as easily at home. It spoiled the night out.

Forgetting them, he turned his attention back to Frank. "I don't know. I *do* know that Roderick had a much better lifestyle than your average lorry driver. That money came from somewhere and it sure as hell wasn't driving. He was up to something. It was either to do with blackmailing someone or it was connected with the long trips he made. I also know that Rob denies all connections with Scotland and is obviously lying."

"Bloody hell, Dylan." Frank's eyes were as wide as his pint glass. "First you reckon Rob's being blackmailed by Roderick. Now you're implying that they're up to something together."

"No, I'm not."

Dylan didn't know what he was implying. All he had were a few half-baked ideas.

All the same, Sam had said on that phone message left for Jack, the phone message that could be a work of fiction, that she'd learned something horrible. If she'd found out that her father and stepfather were involved in something illegal, she would have confronted her stepfather. She would have believed her father to be pure in body and spirit, and would have assumed that the blame should rest with Alan Roderick.

"There's James Carlton too." He was speaking his thoughts aloud. "Those cars that were allegedly stolen. I wonder if they turned up in Hungary or Romania. Or anywhere else Roderick liked to go. I wonder how full those lorries are when they head for the continent."

"You're forgetting something," Frank said. "Jack Fleming's the one currently banged up on a murder charge."

Frank was right. Where the hell did Jack fit in?

"I'll call in at the nick tomorrow," Frank said, "and see if I can find out anything more. No promises but, if I hang around long enough, I might hear something."

"Great, Frank. Thanks." He drummed his fingers on the table. "Those postcards are of the view at Scrabster. Remember Jim Franks?"

"Oh, God, yeah. Constable Bloody Jim. Is that where he used to go?"

Constable Bloody Jim was an ex-colleague of Dylan's. A keep-fit fanatic, he'd enjoyed climbing and he often visited the Orkney Islands to climb the Old Man of Hoy. He'd insisted on boring them to death with his snaps too.

"It is. He used to drive up to Scrabster and catch the ferry over to Orkney. As far as I know, and I wish I'd paid more attention now, the only thing at Scrabster is that ferry terminal."

"If it's the terminal for Orkney," Frank said, "it'll be as far north as you can get."

"That's right." Roderick, as far as his colleagues were concerned, never took his lorry north of Inverness. All the same— "It's a bloody funny place to send a postcard from, don't you think?"

"Well—"

"Of course it is. There's nothing there. You'd only go to Scrabster if you were catching a ferry to Orkney. You'd send a postcard from your destination, not the ferry terminal."

"In which case, there'd be no point having post-cards printed in the first place." Frank's tone was dry.

Dylan supposed he had a point. Someone must buy the damn things or they wouldn't bother printing them.

It was no use, they needed another drink. Dylan had known this would be at least a four-pint problem.

THIRTY-TWO

DYLAN overslept, missed breakfast at the hotel, and wandered into town and to Tesco's cafeteria.

As he munched through a full English breakfast and downed two cups of strong black coffee, he tried to put his thoughts into some sort of order. Sam Hunt wasn't in Lancashire, he was sure of that. Hungary and Romania insisted on flitting through his mind, but neither settled. Scotland then. Hunt received postcards from over the border and Roderick drove his lorry up there.

Perhaps Frank was right in that there was no link. Maybe Hunt was so wrapped up in his own problems—and he had plenty of those—that the regular postcards from his ex-army chum meant nothing to him. Perhaps those trips north that Roderick happily undertook were nothing more than a way to get paid while enjoying some spectacular scenery.

Dylan would do well to concentrate on facts and ignore gut instinct.

With his breakfast eaten, he wandered through the store. He'd once bought shirts for a fiver here but none caught his eye today. In any case, he'd mastered the washing machine since then. He hadn't actually used it for weeks, and the shirt he was wearing was a little grubby round the cuffs, but he'd put that right tomorrow. He was spending Sunday with Luke, but tomorrow he'd concentrate on the washing machine.

He left the store and wandered down Dawson Clough's pedestrianised shopping centre. Dark clouds scowled down on him, threatening heavy rain before the day was over. Great. There was nothing like a five-hour drive when filthy spray hurled up from lorries on the motorways made visibility nothing more than a dream.

That long drive wasn't appealing. He and Frank had stayed longer at the Dog and Fox than they'd intended, and Dylan had woken with the headache from hell. Not a hangover, just a headache. All the same, he could do without it.

The town centre had been redeveloped and was dotted with bronze statues of weavers and miners. The shops were nothing special, though. Boots sat next to W H Smith's, then came Argos, Next and M&S.

Dylan spotted a familiar face just as the first drop of rain fell. He dashed toward her. "Marion?"

She swung round to face him, reminding Dylan of a cornered fox about to be torn apart by a pack of baying hounds.

"Oh, hello." She didn't seem to know what else to say.

Plump raindrops landed on Dylan. "Looks like we're in for a shower. Time for a coffee, I think. Can I get you one?"

Nerves had her so taut that Dylan half expected her to snap in half.

"Okay. Yes, thanks."

By the time they strode the fifty yards to Costa's and Dylan pushed open the door, the rain was bouncing off the pavement.

"What would you like?" he asked.

"Coffee, please."

"Black? White? Cappuccino?"

She looked as if she'd forgotten how she took her coffee. "Regular. Black, please."

They were lucky and managed to grab a table near the counter. A steady stream of rain dodgers followed them in. Some shook water from their hair like dogs leaping out of lakes.

For a moment, they both watched people dashing to escape the sudden storm.

"Perhaps this lot will clear the air," Dylan murmured.

"Yes. They said it should feel fresher tomorrow."

So she was aware of that. If Bev had been murdered, God forbid, Dylan couldn't imagine giving a toss about weather forecasts.

"How are you doing?" He turned his chair slightly so he was directly opposite her.

"Okay. The girls have gone back to school today."

"That's probably for the best."

She nodded. "I think so."

She stirred her coffee as if she were mining for gold, and expressions flew across her face like shadows—anxiety, panic, fear. Dylan spotted all those but no grief.

"I'll be opening the nursery on Monday," she said.

He tried a gentle smile. "The children will have missed you."

She picked up her cup, sending a wave of coffee into the saucer. "They've, um, arrested Jack." She cleared a throat that sounded as if a sheet of sandpaper had been stuffed down it. "They've arrested Sam's boyfriend. They—they think he murdered Alan."

She was beyond nervous.

"Yes, so I heard."

"He didn't kill Alan, for God's sake. Why—why would they think that? It's insane."

"That's exactly what I thought." Dylan added more sugar to his coffee. "I don't claim to know Jack well, but I can't imagine him as someone who would do that. Why would he? It makes no sense, does it?"

"He wouldn't. God, it just goes to show how the justice system works in this country."

There was no need to tell Dylan about the country's judicial system. One moment he'd been doing his best to protect Joe Public from a known thug and habitual offender. The next, he'd been banged up on an assault charge.

"Have the police spoken to you about it?" he asked.

"Not a word. If they had, I'd soon have told them. For God's sake, why pick on Jack?"

"I thought they had evidence that he was on your property."

"What? No. Surely not."

"It seems unlikely, but that's what I heard."

There was no doubt about it. Jack had confessed to being at the property. God alone knew what he was doing there. If Sam had thought she was Dawson's Clough answer to Miss Marple, Jack must believe he was Sherlock Holmes.

Dylan was in no position to criticise. He had no real experience of how a real private investigator worked. Having been thrown off the police force, he'd taken the next logical step and registered as an investigator. He'd thought it would be a good career move, but he wasn't so sure now. He'd had three boring matrimonial cases and this was his second missing-person case. No one would call him experienced.

"What if I went to the police?" she asked. "What if I told them Jack's innocent?"

"They would want evidence. They would want to know why you were so sure."

Her face was invaded by a tide of red. "I suppose they would."

Something jolted in the region of Dylan's heart. His throat was dry, leaving him unable to swallow.

"What makes you so sure he's innocent?" He made his voice so casual he might have been asking her why she thought it might rain next Tuesday.

"You just know, don't you?"

No. You didn't.

Around them, people chatted over coffee while keeping one eye on the weather through windows blurred by condensation. Dylan almost envied their mundane conversations. They spoke of the weather, of plans they had for the weekend, and how young Johnny was doing at school. He and Marion spoke of murder.

"If you did go to the police," he said, "they would assume that, if you knew Jack was innocent, you would also know who had murdered your husband."

"That's what I thought." Her voice was soft, little more than a whisper.

"What happened that morning?" His heart rate was a powerful thud, thud, thud.

"I've already told you." She peered through the window. "It's stopped raining. Thanks for the coffee, Dylan, but it's time I was going."

"Marion—"

"I was with the girls at the swimming pool, re-member?" Already standing, she gazed down at him for long moments. "The police arrived to tell me Alan was dead." She grabbed her bag. "Thanks for the coffee."

Dylan felt the warm, damp air settle in the room as she left.

Slowly, his heart rate returned to normal.

All around him, people chatted about what was showing at the cinema, how evil their boss was and how wine was currently half price at the supermarket. It was easy for them. They hadn't had coffee with a woman who had murdered her husband.

THIRTY-THREE

"I could do with a favour, Dylan."

Dylan and Luke had only taken one step into the hallway of the marital home when Bev accosted them.

"Come into the kitchen," she said. "I'll get you a coffee. Luke, you can make yourself scarce."

If she was offering coffee, it was a Big Favour.

Still, he wasn't going to argue. Usually it took every ounce of deviousness he possessed to progress as far as the kitchen. *His* kitchen.

Luke grabbed a slice of chocolate cake, Tesco's finest, and, with a wink for Dylan, dashed off to the lounge and the TV. Moments later, Bart Simpson shrieked at something.

"Do you want a piece of cake?" Bev splashed cold water over her arms as she attempted to fill the kettle. "Or a sandwich or something?"

This was an exceptionally Big Favour. Perhaps he'd agree to it on condition she allowed him back to his home.

"Coffee's fine, thanks."

Watching her deal with the coffee, he was reminded of the first days they were together. They'd lived in a cramped flat for six months before they were married, and Bev had been so eager to make their relationship work that she'd tried to convince him she was a domestic goddess. She wasn't, never had been and never would be, but he'd appreciated the effort.

They'd both changed since those heady days. Dylan knew he had. He'd been new to the police force and had seen a glittering career ahead of him. Now, he was more cynical. And bitter.

Bev had changed too. She'd been in the early days of her teaching career and frightened to death by half of her pupils. Now, she stood for no nonsense. She was sensible and responsible most of the time. Motherhood had changed her too.

For all that, Dylan looked at her and saw his wife, the only woman he wanted to spend the rest of his life with.

"So what's this favour?"

She sloshed coffee into the saucer and cursed beneath her breath. "I've got a job interview."

What had he said? That it would serve her right if she was offered a job in the Outer Hebrides? The frame of mind she was in, she'd probably take such a position.

"Oh? Where?"

"Blackburn."

"What?"

"Do you want milk or cream?"

What the—he'd never had cream in his coffee in all the years she'd known him so he didn't even dignify the question with an answer.

"Blackburn? As in Lancashire?"

"Yes." She thrust his coffee at him. "There you go. That's a coincidence, isn't it?"

Coincidence? Sheer bloody madness was the term that sprang to Dylan's mind.

"But why go for the interview?" he asked. "What the hell's the point?"

"The point," she said, all nerves gone as she slipped into teacher mode, "is because it's a good job. A head's job, Dylan. A better salary. More responsibility. More say in everything."

"It's in Lancashire."

"God, you're quick."

"So you're telling me that, if they offer you the job, you'll up sticks, leave your family and friends and move up north?" He couldn't keep the sarcasm from his tone.

"Yes. I'm telling you exactly that. Why not?"

Surely, she couldn't be serious. "And you'd expect Luke to leave his family and friends behind, not to mention his football team, just because you think a head's job will be everything you've ever dreamed of?"

"His football team?" She laughed at that. "Even I know there are teams up north. Blackburn for a start."

"No son of mine will support Blackburn!"

"Man United then. Liverpool. For God's sake, Luke would settle anywhere."

"And if he didn't?"

"Then I'd think again."

"What about me?" he asked. "Would I be expected

to travel up there at weekends to see my own son? To see my own wife?"

"You're spending more time up there than in London."

"What? Of course I'm not. This is the second job I've had north of London in thirty-eight years."

She shrugged at that. "You're still practically living there."

"Yes, but I won't be. A couple of weeks, when I've finished looking into Sam Hunt's disappearance, I'll be home. In London."

All Dylan could do was shake his head in despair. He wondered if the menopause was responsible. Bev was a couple of years off forty, so it was probably a bit early, but something had to be behind such madness. She throws him out. She refuses to have him back. She's heading north for job interviews. Sheer bloody madness.

She took a sip of her coffee. "What's wrong with Lancashire? I thought you quite liked it up there."

"It's grown on me, yes, but I wouldn't want to live there."

"Why not?"

"Because it's—it's up north for a start."

"What sort of answer is that?"

A very poor one.

"So what's the favour?" he asked, ignoring that question.

"My appointment's at two o'clock tomorrow afternoon. As it's only—what?—twenty miles down the road from where you'll be, I was wondering if I could beg a lift?"

The unexpected request momentarily robbed him of speech.

"I can get the train back easily enough," she said, "but I don't like relying on public transport for important appointments. I'd hate to miss a connection or find the train was cancelled."

That was some favour. It meant sharing the confines of his car for at least five hours. Presumably, he'd be allowed to take her out in the evening—

"And it would mean Luke staying at your place tonight," she added. "And tomorrow night. I've mentioned it to your mum and she's more than happy to have him."

"Sure, that's fine."

"Aw, thanks."

"We'd have to leave about seven. This will be news to you, Bev, but there are two seven o'clocks in the day and one's in the middle of the night."

She rolled her eyes at his sarcasm. "Thanks. I shouldn't think for a moment they'll offer me the job, but the experience will do me good. It's been ages since I had a job interview."

Even if they offered it to her, she wouldn't accept it. The reality of it would make her see sense.

Bart Simpson was still yelling out when Luke came into the kitchen. "Well? Have you kissed and made up?"

Dylan looked at Bev. She gave him her he-gets-that-from-you look.

"So how do you fancy spending the night at your dad's?" she asked him.

"Tonight? Wow, cool. Yeah, brill. Does that mean—Vicky will be taking me to school?"

"Vicky?" Dylan and Bev repeated in unison.

"She doesn't like me calling her Gran now. She says it makes her sound old."

Dylan saw his amusement mirrored in Bev's expression. His mother was a lot of things but one thing she would never be was old.

"Do you have everything ready for school?" Bev asked him.

"Yeah. No."

She rolled her eyes. "And that is supposed to mean?"

"Football kit." He raced off, feet pounding up the stairs.

"I'd better sort out his uniform," Bev said.

Left alone, Dylan realised that he no longer felt at home in this kitchen. It was the same as it had always been—except the walls had been painted—but he felt out of place. He'd be hard pushed to find the can opener or the coffee.

Still, he wasn't going to dwell on that. When Bev saw sense, when she got over this particular strop and invited him back, he'd soon feel as if he'd never been away.

Half an hour later, Luke had everything he needed for his stay at Dylan's, and Dylan could think of no plausible excuse for hanging around any longer.

"I'll be here at seven then," he told Bev.

"I'll be ready."

He crossed his fingers for luck. Experience had taught him that when a Morgan with eighty thousand miles on the clock broke down, it did so in a spectacular cloud of exhaust fumes.

THIRTY-FOUR

That evening, Arthur Bryant caught up on the local newspapers that had been pushed through his letterbox while he'd been fishing in the Lake District.

He didn't recognise the name Alan Roderick, but there was no mistaking the big, bull-headed man staring out from the grainy photographs that dominated the pages. Arthur knew the address too.

The story of Roderick's murder occupied almost every page but that wasn't surprising. Very little happened in the Clough. A good murder was a gift for journalists more used to covering cute baby competitions or schools' sports days.

It was difficult to sift the pertinent facts from the hearsay, but there was enough to tell Arthur that Roderick had been murdered last Sunday morning.

The same morning Arthur had had the misfortune to meet him.

Deciding he had more important things to worry about, Arthur began the chore of cleaning his fishing equipment and putting it away until his next trip to the Lakes.

He liked to keep himself to himself. Alan Roderick's murder was nothing to do with him. Nothing at all.

It was almost nine o'clock but he didn't leave things

undone. He wasn't that type. Washing was put in the machine, his teacup and saucer washed and put away. All rubbish was taken outside to the bin.

His sister called him fussy. He called her sloppy. On the rare occasions he called at her house, he could smell cat. She had three and was too frightened to let them out. "Get a cat flap," he'd say, "so they can go outside and get some air." She wouldn't listen. Too many cats got hit by cars, she said.

The only times he visited was when he delivered the parish magazine. It was a chore that had fallen to him last year when his wife died. Barbara had done the job for over twenty years and, on her death, it was assumed Arthur would take over. He didn't go to church, nor was he religious, but he hadn't been able to say no. It had been Barbara's job, one she'd enjoyed, so he'd been fairly happy to take over.

Walking round the parish, dropping the newsletter through letterboxes—whether people wanted it or not—wasn't a particularly arduous task. In fact, Arthur quite enjoyed it. He hadn't enjoyed delivering Alan Roderick's last Sunday though.

The letterbox had been stiff, he recalled, and he'd scraped his knuckles as he'd struggled to pushed the newsletter through. The second it dropped onto the mat, the door was yanked open and a big man, a man he now knew to be Alan Roderick, stood facing him.

"What the fuck are you up to? I saw you sneaking about in the garden."

"I beg your—now, sir, I don't know what your

problem is but I'd appreciate it if you'd keep such foul language to yourself."

Roderick grabbed him by the lapels of his suit jacket and lifted him on to his toes.

"What's your fucking game?"

"Game?" Arthur repeated, a little afraid. "It's no game. I've delivered your parish magazine. I've been doing it every month for years."

"Wait here!"

Arthur was left to straighten his lapels as Roderick dashed off to the back of his garden.

"Oi, you!" Arthur heard him shout. "Get back here, you fucking runt!"

Confound it. Arthur wasn't hanging around here waiting to be insulted. He'd taken two steps from the door when Roderick returned, gasping for breath.

"The bastard's scarpered. Some little shit was in the garden—I thought it was you."

If that was meant to be an apology, it was a poor one.

"Right," Arthur said with as much dignity as he could muster, "I'll wish you good day then."

Arthur strode away from the front door, breath held as he waited for the monster to come after him.

So much for wishing him a good day. Soon after that, he must have been murdered.

Arthur put it all from his mind and went to bed. Sleep refused to have anything to do with him though.

He supposed he should go to the police. Some people would like that, they'd enjoy being the centre of attention, telling the police that he was one of the last people to see the man alive. People like that were on the TV all the time. They revelled in the media interest. Arthur kept himself to himself. Always had and always would.

He gave his pillow a good thump and closed his eyes.

What did it matter? They'd arrested a man for Roderick's murder so it was too late now. Arthur could tell them he'd seen Roderick, and seen him chase someone out of his garden, and the police would say "So what?" They might even arrest him for wasting their time.

No one had seen Arthur delivering the newsletter and getting into an altercation with Roderick. At least, as far as he knew, no one had seen him. Even if they had, so what? He couldn't be charged with withholding evidence, could he? No. He had no evidence. He knew nothing about it—other than the fact that Roderick was a nasty piece of work and the world was a better place without him.

THIRTY-FIVE

THERE were times, and this was one, when nothing made sense to Dylan. Nothing.

He wasn't even attempting to sleep. He was lying on his bed, hands linked behind his head, and he was thinking.

The last time he'd stayed in this hotel, his room had been freezing. Now, it was hot and stuffy. He had the window open, could hear pigeons cooing above the sound of the traffic, but the curtains didn't move.

It was no use. He was going to make a trip to Scotland. And Orkney. He wasn't mentioning it to Hunt either.

Damn it, that was annoying him. If the person employing him insisted on lying, what hope was there?

Dylan wasn't sure what he was looking for. All he knew was that the ferry on the postcard, one in the livery of Northlink Ferries, ran between Scrabster on the northern tip of Scotland and Stromness in the Orkney Islands. He knew that a man named Mattie— Matthew?—sent postcards to Hunt on a regular basis, and he knew that Roderick chose to drive to Scotland.

Talk about a stab in the dark.

He'd used the internet facilities in Dawson's Clough's library to find the ferry company's timetable. The *MV Hamnavoe* made three sailings a day from Scrabster to the Orkney Islands.

According to his sat nav, the journey to Scrabster was four hundred and eighty miles and should take around nine and a half hours.

He was tempted to fly to Wick, a small airport near Scrabster, but that would mean hiring a car to explore the area. As he didn't know where he'd end up, that could get complicated.

It was almost two o'clock when he decided it was time he forgot Sam Hunt and embraced sleep.

His mind flitted to Bev and the interview she'd had. She thought it had gone well, and she was clearly excited about it. They still had several more applicants to see though, so Dylan wasn't going to worry about it.

They'd enjoyed dinner together, even shared a few laughs. They hadn't spoken of the way they'd shared a bed, but he'd bet they'd both thought of it often. It had been a good evening. Dylan would have liked to repeat the experience, but Bev had insisted on staying in a hotel near the station and was catching the train home first thing in the morning.

He tossed and turned for an hour or more then drifted into a restless sleep during which he dreamed of James Carlton unloading gleaming red Ferraris from a blue-and-white ferry.

His phone woke him just after seven.

"Yes?" He was too bleary-eyed to focus on the caller ID.

"Dylan? It's me. Frank."

"God, Frank, can't you sleep?"

"Eh? Oh, sorry, I forgot it's a bit early for you soft fucking southerners."

"Ha, ha. Very funny."

"I thought you'd want to hear the latest on Jack Fleming," Frank said.

"Latest? Has something happened?"

"He's been released."

Dylan struggled into an upright position and wished his brain would follow suit.

"Another witness came forward," Frank said. "Some chap who was delivering something to Roderick's house that morning."

Dylan wished his brain would keep up. "Delivering something on a Sunday?"

"A magazine. Something to do with the church. Anyway, you know Fleming had said he was in the garden snooping? Well, apparently, he'd also claimed that Roderick chased him off the property."

"And?"

"This bloke—the one delivering the magazine—said he was there when Roderick chased someone out of the garden."

Dylan tried to picture the scene—and failed.

"Why's it taken so long for this bloke to come forward?" he asked.

"He'd been away. On a fishing trip in the Lake District."

"So Jack's been released? He's back at home?"

"As free as a bird."

It was good news. Dylan had believed all along that Jack was innocent. Just as Marion had.

Sitting in that café with her, Dylan had been convinced she'd murdered her husband. She couldn't have though. She'd been at the pool with her daughters. Even if she hadn't been, she wasn't capable of taking a knife to a man. She wasn't strong enough either. Dylan would bet his life she knew who *had* killed him though.

"I'll go and have a chat with Jack," Dylan said. "Then I'm thinking of going to Scotland."

"I honestly can't see a Scottish link."

"It's all too coincidental for my liking." All the same, he was only following what was known in the trade as a gut instinct. "I want to know who's sending Rob those postcards. I know you don't like to hear this, Frank, but your mate's lying to me. I also want to see if there's any connection between that person and Alan Roderick."

"It's your decision, of course, but I can't helping thinking—"

"It's a waste of time." Frank was probably right.

"Yeah. But let me know if you find anything."

"Will do."

When he ended the call, Dylan dressed quickly and, feeling more awake now, went downstairs to the hotel's dining room. Breakfast called. For all the hotel's faults, the breakfasts were mouthwatering and he was soon washing down sausages, bacon, egg and mushrooms with a cup of strong tea. Perfect.

Then it was time to pay Jack Fleming a visit.

THIRTY-SIX

Anca had overheard a conversation between a man and woman but, as they'd both spoken in English, she hadn't understood it. The only word she grasped was *dead*. She had no idea who was dead. Nor did she know why it affected her and Crina. That it did was obvious from the way they were bundled into the back of a horsebox in the early hours of the morning.

Crina had refused to get inside and had been knocked to the straw-covered floor by an Englishman.

To prevent further argument, he covered their mouths with thick tape that smelled of oil and tied their hands behind their backs. All they could do was make frantic noises as they were pushed inside a wooden structure at the far end of the horsebox. He ignored them and banged the lid down. Anca heard a padlock snapping closed. The glow from streetlights came through a tiny gap in the lid and she could smell wet straw.

The vehicle set off, bound for God only knew where, but Anca knew their destination wouldn't be pleasant.

Mile after mile passed. Hour after hour.

Daylight was slow to come but it was visible through that small gap in their wooden prison.

Crina mumbled behind her gag. Anca didn't have to understand the words, she knew what they would be. "I want to go home." Those five words had become Crina's mantra.

Anca longed for home too. She'd been too frightened to sleep, she hadn't seen food for hours, she was battered and bruised—

She couldn't think about that. If she did, if she remembered the smell of the man, his hot breath—no, she couldn't think about it or she would be sick again. Instead, she would give thanks to God that no one had touched Crina.

Anca longed for home, but could think of no way of getting there. They had no friends, not one, and she daren't speak to a stranger, even if she was lucky enough to find someone who understood her, because they would call the police. She and Crina would find themselves locked in a filthy cell for years.

The horsebox drove into a tunnel and stopped. Anca's heart, beating fast with terror, threatened to jump out of her ribcage.

Chains clanked around them. People spoke. Men shouted to one another. Anca didn't understand a single word. A horn sounded. A mechanised voice came over a loudspeaker system.

Within minutes, Anca realised they were at sea.

Her heart soared and plummeted with a mix of terror and hope. Perhaps they were going home after all. Something had happened. A man had died. Perhaps that's why they were going home.

Anca could think of no other explanation.

Winters would be lived cold, wet and hungry, but at least they would be home. People would speak their language. The sights, sounds and smells would be blessedly familiar.

Whoever it was, she was glad the person was dead. If it meant she could go home, they could all die.

She didn't know how long they were on the boat, but guessed at a couple of hours. Chains clanked again, men shouted again. Soon, Anca saw a welcome slit of daylight and could feel the road beneath the horsebox's wheels.

Not long after, it all happened again. The daylight didn't vanish, but she heard chains crashing against each other and she heard men shouting to each other again. Unbelievably, she soon realised they were on another boat. It must be a small one. As she could still see daylight, they must be on the deck.

The boat bobbed on the water and she and Crina kept bumping into each other as it rode the swell. Anca began to worry that they might be seasick. Their mouths were sealed. They would choke on their own vomit.

Anca put her nose to the gap and inhaled the fresh, salty air. Whatever they did, they must not be sick.

After a while, the sea grew calmer. Instead of being tossed around, they gently rose and fell with the waves.

The horsebox was driven off the boat and, once again, Anca listened to the rumble of the wheels on the road. This was a bad road, full of ruts and deep holes that jolted them.

She had to concentrate on the sounds and smells. If she thought of the man—

The vehicle stopped. All was quiet. Anca could hear birds. She also thought she could hear the sea, but that might have been nothing more than another dizzy spell.

She could cope with the nausea, the dizziness, the bruises, and even the fear. Anything was preferable to having that man force himself inside her. He'd been delighted to make her bleed, had even laughed when she'd staggered off the bed and collapsed to the floor. Yes, anything was preferable. Even a cell in an English prison.

The lid was yanked open by that brute of an Englishman. He was big and ugly with tattoos on his neck and forearms. He cursed as they stumbled drunkenly on legs that had gone numb hours ago. Shouting, he pushed and shoved them toward the door of a large house. Anca knew an urge to run, just run, but she was too weak and her legs wouldn't cooperate.

There was no time to check out the interior of the building. They were being pulled down some steep steps and into a cellar lit only by one small bulb. It smelled damp. It *was* damp. Anca's shoes squelched on the soft earth.

The lone occupant was a young woman with close-cropped black hair. She was chained to the wall by ankle cuffs but she leaped to her feet and screamed at the man in what Anca assumed was English. He didn't answer her. She pummelled his chest but he knocked her aside as if she were an irritating fly.

The man said nothing. He yanked the tape from Crina's mouth, then Anca's, untied their hands and strode back up the stairs, switching off that light and slamming the door shut.

The woman continued to shout at them in English. The only word Anca understood was *kill*. She pointed at her heaving chest and at Anca and Crina as she said this.

Crina dropped to her knees, banged her fists over her ears and screamed.

THIRTY-SEVEN

DYLAN thought Jack looked wary when he opened the door of his flat. His jeans were in need of a good wash and his dark blue sweater had lost its shape long ago, but his clothes looked a lot better than he did.

"Oh, it's you. D'you wanna come in?"

"Thanks." Dylan stepped inside and followed him to the small kitchen where he was in the process of making tea.

"Do you want one?" he asked.

"No, you're okay, thanks. I just called in to see what's been going on?"

"You tell me." Jack cursed as he spilled milk all over the counter. "Fucking police have got it in for me."

"They say you were on Alan Roderick's property the morning he was murdered."

"So?"

"So?" Dylan echoed in amazement. "So it makes you chief suspect in a murder inquiry."

Jack shrugged.

"What the hell were you doing there, Jack?"

He leaned back against the counter, a mug cradled in shaking hands. "Just having a look."

"But why?"

"Dunno," Jack said. "You'd come up from London asking questions about him. You kept going on about him. Then I listened to that message Sam left me again, the one where she said she'd found out something bad. I dunno. I just wondered if she'd found out summat about him. About Roderick."

"But what—?"

"I was going to break in and have a look round, that's all. But the bastard chased me off. I told the police that at least a hundred bloody times, but they wouldn't listen. If that bloke hadn't come forward and said he'd been there when I was chased off, I'd still be there now."

"Did you see anyone else? Notice anyone you knew hanging around?"

"No." Jack blew across the surface of his tea before taking a sip. "I wish I'd never gone near the bloody place but you don't expect folk to be done in like that, do you?"

"Hardly."

"Fucking police," he muttered. "Christ, if I'd done him in, I'd have been covered in blood, wouldn't I?"

"Unless you'd changed your clothes, yes."

"They knew full well I hadn't. Tossers."

Anger emanated from every pore. Dylan knew Jack had a temper, though. For the moment at least, he was holding it in check.

"It's a good job they have CCTV around there," Dylan said.

According to Frank it was the CCTV that had saved him. CCTV that had captured first Jack, then Arthur

Bryant delivering his newsletters, Jack fleeing from the house, Bryant walking away.

Given that, one would like to think that Roderick's killer had been captured on that same camera. Apparently not. No one known to the police or, as far as they knew, to Roderick, had been seen. Witnesses said an old blue Transit van had been parked on the other road near Roderick's house. There was no CCTV along there though.

Dylan was blocking the arched entrance to the kitchen. When he stepped aside, Jack followed him.

Dylan looked out at the quiet street. He would have expected reporters to be queuing up waiting for a word with Jack. He was glad there were none around. Jack was sure to say something damning.

"The coppers have always had it in for me." Jack scowled at his tea.

"That's what happens when you lock girlfriends in their flats and frighten the life out of them," Dylan said.

"Yeah, well." Jack shrugged at that.

"Tell me about Alan Roderick." Dylan perched on the arm of a chair. "Everything you can think of. What Sam thought of him. Things he's said or done. Anything."

"Sam didn't like him." Jack spoke slowly, thoughtfully. "Dunno why, though. I don't know that he ever did or said anything to her."

"Perhaps she didn't like seeing her mother with another man. A lot of children resent new people in their parents' lives."

Jack put his cup of tea on the windowsill and stared out at the street. "Nah. It was more than that. She wasn't particularly close to her mum so she didn't care who she was living with."

"She never told you why she didn't like him?" Dylan found that hard to believe.

"No. She said he gave her the creeps, that's all." Jack turned to look at him. "D'you reckon she found out something about him?"

"I don't know what to think." That had to be the understatement of the decade.

"It's funny she found out summat and then vanished."

"It is."

"Especially now he's been done in." Jack picked up his tea with shaking hands.

"Yes."

"She didn't like the way he was with the kids," Jack said. "I do know that. She reckoned it'd kill him if he saw 'em having fun."

Dylan could believe that. Those children had been much too quiet when he'd called at the house. He wouldn't exactly say they'd seemed nervous around him, but they were certainly well behaved. They hadn't been playing together—not that it meant anything. For all Dylan knew, they'd fallen out that day and preferred their own company. Perhaps, if they'd wanted, they could have played together and made as much noise as they liked.

"She said once that she wished he'd stay in Scotland," Jack said. "She said, 'If he likes it so much in

Scotland, why doesn't he piss off and live there?' She just didn't like him, but I don't really know why."

Dylan didn't either.

He wasn't getting any answers from Jack. Or from anyone else come to that.

It was time for a change of scenery. If the answer wasn't in Dawson's Clough, maybe it was in Scotland.

THIRTY-EIGHT

"CHRIST!" Dylan cursed as rain pelted the car like bullets. He drove into a lay-by and switched off the engine. It was like a sodding monsoon.

That wasn't why he was lost though. His sat nav, with its usual efficiency, had taken him along close to ten miles of single track roads that, judging by the tall grass verges, were rarely used. It was also obvious that the last half hour had been spent driving round a complete circle.

He'd arrived in Scotland on Wednesday evening and had stayed at a hotel in Thurso, a few miles down the road from Scrabster, for the last two nights. He had photographs with him—one of Hunt, one of Roderick, both of which had been cut from newspapers, and one of Sam. Those photos had been shown to the small local population of Scrabster and hadn't elicited so much as a flicker of recognition. The name Mattie had been met with equally blank expressions.

When the rain eased slightly, Dylan tried to start the Morgan. As fond of wet weather as Dylan was, the car reluctantly coughed into life at the third attempt.

It was Saturday morning and, instead of being at home enjoying time with Luke, Dylan was driving to the terminal to catch that ferry to the Orkney Islands.

The wipers swished across the screen, doing their best to cope with the rain. *Madness, madness, madness,* they squeaked.

Dylan should face facts. If he hadn't seen two postcards sent to Hunt, he wouldn't be anywhere near Scotland. Roderick had driven here, true, but he'd also taken his lorry to Hungary and Romania, and Dylan hadn't, as yet, been tempted to race off to eastern Europe.

Once aboard the ferry, Dylan showed his photographs to every member of the crew. No one recognised the subjects or the names he mentioned, so he sat in the bar and enjoyed a drink to pass the time. The sea, fortunately, was flat calm although he'd heard that the Pentland Firth was notorious for parting travellers from their breakfasts.

The sky had cleared and was a perfect blue when the ferry docked in the small Orkney town of Stromness. Everything looked picturesque, unhurried, low-key—and small.

The population of Orkney didn't warrant a Starbucks or a McDonald's on every street. Only around twenty thousand people lived here and they were scattered across the many islands. It seemed unlikely that Roderick had brought his lorry over here. There would be no point.

Perhaps the only reason Roderick volunteered for the drives over the border into Scotland was because he enjoyed them. Dylan had dreaded a nine-and-a-half-hour drive but, surprisingly, it had been good. Compared to England, the roads were deserted. The scenery was stunning too—lochs and mountains, even a golden eagle had soared above him, the first Dylan had ever seen. Perhaps Roderick had been equally enchanted. Maybe he'd never set foot on Orkney soil. Maybe the person who was sending those postcards to Hunt hadn't either.

After checking in at the Stromness Hotel, Dylan strolled through the town and wandered around the harbour.

Tiredness had him yawning as he walked, but restlessness and a lack of purpose wouldn't let him sleep for hours. Sometimes, problems solved themselves as he walked. The problem of Sam Hunt, however, remained a tangled mess in his head.

For all he knew, she could have just taken off with someone she met. It was unlikely, but possible. There was her father, her mother and half-sisters, her boyfriend, her best friend, her job and her dog. He couldn't imagine her taking off without a word to anyone.

Dylan didn't know her, admittedly, but he believed he understood the sort of girl she was. She was responsible. She knew right from wrong. She also had an overactive imagination but he supposed she couldn't be blamed for that. No, she had intended picking up her sisters and taking them to school on that fateful morning.

The most likely explanation was that she was dead. That was no reason to give up though. If she was dead, she was in no position to bring the culprit—if indeed there was a culprit—to justice.

Dylan intended to do that for her.

Deciding he'd think better with a glass in his hand, he stepped into a pub. It was busy, crammed with people putting the world to rights, and Dylan took the opportunity of asking around and showing his photographs. Nothing.

"He's a lorry driver," he said, pointing at the picture of Roderick that he'd cut from Dawson Clough's local newspaper.

People shook their heads. They apologised. The names, the faces, they said, meant nothing to them.

"He's friendly with a man called Mattie." He pointed to the poor photo of Hunt. "Mattie used to be in the army."

More shaking of heads.

He spent an hour in that bar before walking slowly back to the hotel.

Apart from asking around and showing off his photos, he wasn't sure what he could do. When he'd been on the force, he'd always been able to come up with ideas, avenues to tread, theories to test. Now he was clueless. He'd thought he was up to this job, which just proved that he'd started to believe his own hype.

Orkney was noted for various things—its history, its beauty and its lack of crime. If it hadn't been for Jim, who'd visited Orkney to climb and had bored Dylan with hundreds of photos of deserted shorelines, fishing boats, sheep and cottages dotted here and there, he probably wouldn't have heard of the place. To Dylan, it was simply a cluster of islands that, along with the Shetland Isles, were dumped to the side of Scotland on TV weather maps.

It wasn't the sort of place where crimes were committed. Or solved.

THIRTY-NINE

Bᴇᴠ didn't know what woke her. She only knew that her head hurt like hell if she attempted any sort of movement. No, scrap that. It hurt without the movement.

She closed her eyes, but it was no use. She needed the bathroom, followed by coffee and a couple of aspirin.

She eased herself out of bed, pulled her dressing gown from the hook and decided she was getting too old for girls' nights in with Lucy. How many bottles of wine had they demolished?

She brushed her teeth gently but that didn't help. God, why did they do it?

Envelopes scattered across the mat told her what had woken her. Their postman couldn't do anything quietly. At best, he whistled as he walked round the estate. Sometimes he sang "Oh, what a beautiful morning…" He also took great delight in pushing mail through letterboxes with an enormous clatter and then throwing red elastic bands to the ground. The fact that it was before seven and most people were still asleep didn't bother him at all. Sadistic sod.

She picked up her mail and flicked through it as she headed for the kitchen. The three circulars would go straight in the recycling bin, and the reminder that the car insurance was due would be put aside until she had time to compare more quotes. The other envelope was official and addressed to Ms. B. Scott.

She ripped it open, aware that, despite telling herself it didn't matter one way or the other, her heart was racing.

"Oh my God—" She read the words again. *We are delighted to offer—* "Oh my God!"

She definitely needed coffee now.

While it was percolating, she swallowed two aspirins and put three empty wine bottles in the bin. The letter watched on. "What are you going to do now?" it seemed to ask.

Bev had no idea. At the moment, she barely knew which day it was.

She stared at the letter, disbelieving, shocked and, yes, a little proud.

Her mug was almost empty when she heard the slow pad of feet on the stairs. Lucy put her head round the door. "Couldn't you sleep?"

"Our lovely postman, the one I usually refer to as Evil Bastard, woke me. And I needed aspirins. They're over there if you want some."

"Just water. And coffee." Lucy took a glass from the cupboard, filled it with cold water from the tap and drank it straight down. "How come I'm so thirsty when I drank so much last night?"

"Ha, ha." Bev poured her friend a coffee and then handed the letter to her.

"What's this?" Lucy's eyes widened and she let

out a shriek that had Bev wincing. "Woo-hoo! You've got the job, Bev. You've only gone and got the bloody job!"

Bev laughed at her friend's enthusiasm. "I certainly have."

"Oh. My. God." Lucy read the letter again, more carefully this time. "What are you going to do?"

"That's easy. I'm going to accept it or turn it down. Yeah, one of those." She laughed at herself. "I honestly don't know."

She and Lucy had been debating this issue ever since Bev had been for the interview, but this was different. It was easy to say what she would or wouldn't do when it was all speculation. Now that they'd actually—unbelievably—offered her the job, she didn't know what to do.

It was all so fast. She'd expected to wait weeks before she heard anything.

"What a pity this didn't come yesterday. We'd have had an excuse to get legless." Lucy smiled ruefully.

"We managed without an excuse."

"Yeah."

"Do you want breakfast?" Bev asked.

"I probably want a stomach pump."

Their girls' nights in were rare these days, but Luke had spent the night with his grandmother, and Lucy's boyfriend was on a course in Nottingham. The temptation to enjoy a long gossip over DVDs, wine and Chinese takeaway had proved too great. They'd had enormous fun too. It was the morning-after feeling that was the killer.

"So what am I going to do, Luce?"

"I don't know. It's a terrific opportunity. I mean— fancy being offered a head's position. The salary is fantastic." She pulled a face. "It'll be a long way to go for our girlie sessions though. And what will Dylan say?"

"What can he say?"

Lucy laughed at that. "A lot!"

She was right, of course. Dylan had already made his views known and he didn't like the idea of her whisking Luke off to Lancashire.

"He thinks I'm suffering from an early menopause," she confided with a smile.

Perhaps he was right. All Bev knew was that she wanted change in her life. Work-wise, if she stayed where she was, she was going nowhere. Relationship- wise—well, that was a disaster from start to end.

"I suppose I'll have to turn it down," she said.

"You'll have to do what you think is right. You have to think about Dylan and Luke too."

"I know."

Bev recognised the look on Lucy's face as her friend added, "You and Dylan—you belong together, you know that."

That's what everyone said, and she didn't want to think about Dylan right now. It was more fun to bask in the pleasure of being offered the best job in the world.

"You have a tough decision to make," Lucy said. "You can't accept or turn down this job until you've decided what you're going to do about Dylan."

Bev smiled at that. "You make him sound like vermin. Should I put poison down or use a humane trap?"

"You love the bloke," Lucy said simply. "I can't see why it's so difficult to sort things out."

"Ha." Bev refilled her coffee cup. "I keep remembering what he was like when I threw him out. I couldn't have tolerated another minute in his company. Moody, depressed, finding fault with everything, drinking too much—honest, if I hadn't got rid, I would have had to kill him."

Lucy shrugged at that. "Yeah, but he was going through a rough time of it."

"God, and now you sound like his mum. Everyone forgets that it wasn't exactly easy for me and Luke either."

"Ah. So you want sympathy."

Bev looked at her friend in amazement. "Of course I don't."

"Are you sure?" Lucy shrugged. "It seems to me that you want the world to say good old you for going through all that, for having a husband with a promising career that you could be proud of and ending up with a man who, through no fault of his own, lost all that."

"That's crap."

"You could have it all now, Bev. Dylan's working again—okay, so he's never going to be a detective sergeant again—but he's working. He's got his purpose in life back. And, of course, there's the small fact that he loves you and Luke to death." She took a big swallow of coffee. "And given that you love him, it all seems fairly peachy to me."

"Peachy?" Bev giggled at that, but that was probably due to last night's wine.

"Yeah, peachy."

"We slept together, you know."

Lucy almost choked. "You and Dylan? Slept as in had rampant sex? When?"

"Yes, yes, and the night I got back from Edinburgh. I was drunk. We fell asleep on the sofa, then I woke up and it was uncomfortable. I said we should go to bed and the next minute—well, the next minute we were making love."

"Wow."

Bev laughed at the surprise on her friend's face.

"Was it good?" Lucy asked.

Bev grinned. "It was freaking awesome."

She could say what she liked, but she knew she couldn't let Dylan go. She couldn't bear the thought of him not being in her life. They were going to have to work something out. She'd have to welcome him home and hope he didn't turn into the morose, moody git she'd thrown out.

"Maybe," Lucy said, "this new job is exactly what you need. Dylan's last two jobs—"

"His only two real jobs."

"And they've both been in Lancashire. It proves there's work there and he seems to be making a bit of a name for himself. Perhaps he'd be happy to live there. The three of you—you could all start again."

That thought had gone through Bev's mind. She'd

made a right hash of this so-called separation, she knew that, and she also knew that, if she and Dylan got back together, it would have to be permanent. It wouldn't work if it was one of those "see how it goes" things.

The thought of moving all the way to Lancashire without Dylan—no matter how exciting the new job offer—was terrifying.

"I'll sleep on it tonight," she said.

"Does the job really appeal to you?"

"Yes. It's a dream school, the staff are young, energetic, enthusiastic, the kids all seemed—normal. Yes, it's really exciting."

"What would you do if it was in London?"

"My written acceptance would have been in the mail by now."

"Sounds to me like you have your answer then."

She didn't. She had more questions than answers. A lot more.

FORTY

By Tuesday night, Dylan was thoroughly disheartened.

There were worse places to waste time than Orkney, though. Its beauty had surprised him. People smiled, almost smugly, as they enjoyed a slower pace of life than their mainland counterparts. The sea sparkled like a bed of diamonds in the sunlight. History was everywhere. It was a different world.

The long hours of daylight were an added bonus. No doubt the islanders paid the price in winter but, at this time of year, darkness didn't arrive at all.

It was a special place, but it wasn't where he needed to be. He'd spent almost a week here and it was time wasted. He had to be on the wrong track.

He was catching the ferry back to the mainland first thing in the morning and then—well, hopefully inspiration would strike and suggest his next course of action. He couldn't give up. *Wouldn't* give up.

After a couple of pints in the hotel's bar, he wandered down to the harbour where two men were busy painting a small fishing boat. Nothing ventured, nothing gained. Dylan walked along the path and leaned over the railings to shout to them.

"Hi! I wonder if you can help me."

They straightened and then climbed off their boat and over the railings.

"I'm looking for a man named Mattie," Dylan said. "I believe he sometimes visits Orkney. Does the name mean anything to you?"

It obviously didn't.

"How about these?" He showed them the well-worn photos of Sam and Rob Hunt, and Alan Roderick. "Do you recognise anyone?"

Dylan waited for the usual apologetic shaking of heads.

"I've seen him before." One of the men pointed at the photo of Roderick.

"Oh?" Dylan tried not to get his hopes up. It was possible that news of Roderick's murder had come this far north.

"Aye."

Dylan waited to see if the furrowed brow, the finger tapping against the chin would bring forth anything. It seemed doubtful.

Suddenly the brow cleared.

"Got him!" He was clearly pleased with himself. "I saw him in Glasgow with Sullivan." He turned to his mate. "You know Sullivan? Got the place on Westray. A place on Hoy, too, that he's going to do up."

"I know him,' his companion said with obvious distaste.

"Aye, a miserable sod. English. No offence, mate."

"None taken," Dylan said.

"He came up here about five years ago. Don't know much about him because he keeps himself to himself.

A real loner. He tows a horsebox. Once, my daughter asked me to lift her up. Horse mad she is. It was empty and he had a right go at me. Told me to mind my own business. Terrible language he used. In front of a five-year-old too." He handed the photo of Roderick to Dylan. "That's where I've seen your man. In Glasgow. With Sullivan."

"Thanks." The name Sullivan meant nothing to Dylan, but Roderick could easily have been seen in Glasgow. "You say this man Sullivan lives on the island of Westray?"

"Yes, but he's probably over on Hoy at the moment. I saw him towing his horsebox on to the ferry yesterday. Someone said he'd got an old run-down cottage there that he's going to do up. Mind, there's a lot of rumours fly around about incomers."

"Thanks for your help," Dylan said. "I appreciate it."

Some Orcadians, Dylan had discovered, weren't fans of the English, the incomers as they called them. In a way, Dylan could understand their concerns. They lived a quiet, peaceful life on the islands, had for centuries, and the incomers arrived from England to settle and enjoy that lifestyle. They found the life too quiet though and often tried to change things.

He'd been to Westray and no one he'd spoken to had known a man called Mattie or recognised anyone in his photos. Then, though, he hadn't had the name Sullivan to offer them.

He'd tried to visit Hoy yesterday, but there had been

no room on the ferry and, as the population only num-
bered about four hundred, he'd decided not to bother.

He walked back to his hotel, his mind racing with
possibilities. Perhaps he was on to something after all.
He had no idea exactly what he might be on to, but he
was in a far more positive mood.

THE FOLLOWING MORNING, still feeling optimistic, Dylan
cancelled his booking for the mainland and drove onto
the small inter-island ferry bound for Hoy. He stood
on the deck for the forty-minute crossing with the
brisk wind whipping his face and the sun making him
squint.

He'd had the good sense to call at the tourist information office and pick up a map of Hoy as well as
a couple of brochures dotted with photos of Pictish
ruins and comical puffins.

While he was on the island, he'd make the short
journey to Rackwick. If the brochure was to be believed, a three-mile walk would give him the perfect
view of the Old Man of Hoy. He'd like to see if it was
as challenging a climb as Jim had led him to believe.

For now, though, he had more important matters
on his mind.

First, he drove the other way to the small village of
Longhope. He went in the shop, bought himself crisps
and chocolate, and showed his photographs to the girl
at the till.

She studied them closely, then shook her head.
"Sorry, I've never seen these people."

"Would you know a man named Sullivan? I believe he owns a property on the island?"

"English, is he?"

"Yes, I believe he is."

She shook her head. "Sorry."

Dylan wondered if she would have known him if he'd told her he was Orcadian.

"I gather he tows a horsebox," he said.

"No, it means nothing to me."

"What about a man called Mattie? Does the name ring a bell?"

"Mattie? No. Sorry."

He showed his photos to half a dozen more people, drove round looking for horseboxes, then left Longhope and drove to Lyness. Nothing. No one recognised the people in his photos, no one gave so much as a flicker of interest when he mentioned the names Sullivan and Mattie, and he didn't spot a single horsebox.

He drove on to Rackwick where the scenery grew even more spectacular. The drive took him along fairly good roads with plenty of passing places where sheep crossed with no heed to traffic. Not that there was much traffic. In the last five miles, Dylan had met one lone tractor.

Hills dropped steeply to the sea. About twenty seals basked on rocks. A few crofters' cottages looked as if they hadn't been lived in for decades. The island was largely unpopulated, covered in open moorland, and there were few signs of life. As the brochure had told him, Orkney boasted more sheep than people. He didn't even see a horse, never mind a horsebox.

He parked his car at Rackwick and walked down to a beach that was sided by tall sandstone cliffs. Apart from a lone seal who put its head above the water, and a noisy gathering of oystercatchers, it was deserted.

He set off up the hill, following a well-worn path that should lead him to the best viewpoint for the Old Man of Hoy. Perhaps he should have packed sensible walking boots, but he hadn't planned on being a tourist.

The peaty earth was spongy underfoot and, after a while, the walk levelled off. Birds, mostly gulls and skuas, circled overhead, perhaps warning him to keep away from their nests. There was nothing manmade in sight. No houses, no fences, and certainly no horseboxes.

Dylan was soon looking down at the water from the edge of almost sheer cliffs and there, rising four hundred and fifty feet out of the water, was the famous rock stack—the Old Man of Hoy. It was as impressive as Jim had said. Dylan wouldn't have fancied climbing it, mainly because it looked as if it could crumble into the sea at any second.

A couple of small fishing boats bobbed on the water and, on the horizon, some sort of cargo ship went on its way.

There was no one in sight, but it was noisy. Gulls nesting on the cliffs' crags and crevices made sure of that.

Instead of taking the path back, he wandered on,

heading for St. John's Head, the tallest sheer cliffs in the U.K. Dylan didn't do heights so he wasn't going to stray too close to the edge.

An hour later, he was lost. And furious with himself. It should be impossible to get lost on such a small island.

He walked on, heading in what he hoped was the right direction, although the heather and the lack of a clear pathway suggested otherwise.

Off to his right was an old single-storey crofter's cottage. He made for that, hoping it was still a home to people rather than wandering animals and, more important, that someone could point him back to the path.

Although he hammered on a rickety wooden door, he wasn't surprised when no one answered. In a couple of years, when the door had given up its job, the cottage would provide shelter for the sheep.

He walked along the side of the cottage and stopped. There, in a dilapidated, doorless wooden structure that would struggle to pass as a garage, was a horsebox.

He peered inside. Apart from some straw, it was empty. The towing ball was clean though, so it had been used recently.

It meant nothing. Orkney was a land where fields and hills met the sea. There must be dozens of horse-boxes on the islands.

He inspected the horsebox more closely. The tyres were in good condition, as was the box itself. There were no registration plates, but he wouldn't expect to

see any. They would be fixed when the box was attached to the towing vehicle.

He tramped back to the cottage, through long grass
and spiky tufts of heather. He banged on the door.
Nothing. A grimy window was half-boarded with a
wooden sheet. He pulled back a corner of the wood
and peered inside. All he saw was an empty room that
didn't look as if it had been used in decades.

He returned to the front door, banged on it and
shouted. No one answered.

He was walking along the side of the cottage
when he almost tripped on a sturdy clump of spiky
heather. Frustration made him kick out at it. Something winked back at him. A tiny gold locket reflected
the sun's rays.

It was warm in his hand. He knew exactly where
he'd seen it before. Around Sam Hunt's neck.

He slipped the locket in his pocket and stood for a
moment. He wasn't thinking what to do, he was trying
to figure out how he'd talk his way out of a breaking-
and-entering charge.

"Right."

The half-boarded window was his best bet. He
pulled more of the wood away and, not stopping to
worry about the consequences, put his elbow through
the glass. He closed his eyes as thin splinters flew everywhere.

It was enough. He climbed through, cursing as he
caught his leg on a shard of glass.

The room was empty. Wallpaper had given up

trying to cling to damp walls. A door stood open. All was silent.

Not knowing what he was looking for, but knowing that Sam Hunt's locket—or one similar—nestled in his pocket, he walked into the hall where there were three more doors.

One led to a kitchen with a dirty black range, half a dozen cupboards and a small grubby table. The range was warm so someone had been here recently. A mug and spoon waited to be washed in a cracked porcelain sink.

Every muscle in his body was tensed, ready for anything.

Another door led to a bathroom that offered an old enamel bath, a toilet with no seat and a grimy wash basin.

The third door opened into a bedroom. Apart from a single bed and two drawers, it was empty. There was another door leading off the bedroom, a flimsy door in an equally flimsy wall. He tried to turn the handle but it was stuck. No, it was locked.

He'd already smashed a window, albeit one that was already broken, so he may was well go for it. To hell with it.

He charged at the door. The door remained locked in its frame, but the frame parted company with the thin plastered wall. Flexing his shoulder, he charged again.

"Holy shit—" The door flew open to reveal three figures. They were each gagged and chained to a metal bolt attached to a crumbling stone wall. And they were terrified.

He held up his hands in a gesture of peace. "Don't be scared. I can help."

He carefully pulled a length of thick black tape from a small girl's mouth. She took a deep breath and screamed in terror.

"It's all right," he shouted above her screams. "I'm here to help."

She made even more noise if that were possible. Undaunted, Dylan took the gag from her companion. She tried to soothe the crying girl by speaking in a language that he didn't understand. He'd guess at Hungarian or Romanian.

The other girl was thin with short dark, almost black hair. She was barefooted. He removed a strip of tape from her mouth too.

"Quick!" This one was English. Her voice was hoarse and shaking. "Oh, please, be quick!"

There was something about her voice.

"Quick!" She pointed to the plaster and wood splinters on the floor. "He kept the keys above the door. They'll be on the floor somewhere. For fuck's sake, hurry up. He'll be back any minute."

There were three keys, one for each girl, each padlock.

The youngest girl, still screaming, was first to be set free. Her companion was next.

"Run!" the English girl yelled at them. "For fuck's sake, I don't know which planet you're from, but surely you know how to fucking run."

Dylan turned to look at her. The long red hair had gone, the freckles weren't visible beneath the dirt—

"Sam?"

She backed away, eyes wide with terror.

"It is you, isn't it?"

She didn't answer, but she pushed herself as close to the wall as she could, clearly frightened for her life.

"It's okay," he said. "Come on, let's get you out of here."

He soon had her free. The chains were thick, but the padlocks were small, cheap and easily undone.

Dylan's leg was bleeding from his argument with the window, but it was nothing compared to the state of the girls' ankles where the chains had rubbed their skin raw.

Sam was already at the door, not caring about running in bare feet.

"He'll be back any minute." Panic turned her voice into a squeak. "Run!" She punched the taller of the other girls in the back. "Fucking run!"

There was a panicked scramble to get out of the building.

"My car's at Rackwick," Dylan said. "Do you know the way?"

Sam didn't bother to answer, preferring instead to set off down the hill like a gazelle.

"Come on," Dylan urged the other two.

They raced after Sam and, after a mile or so, Dylan recognised his surroundings. The best part was that it was all downhill from here.

On and on they ran until, finally, Dylan spotted his

car. He caught up with Sam and grabbed her hand. "This way!"

Gasping for breath, he stopped by the Morgan.

The foreign girls stared at him, clearly frightened. Sam stared at his car.

"This is yours?" She traced a grubby finger over the paintwork.

At any other time, Dylan would have laughed at the absurdity of the situation. She looked half-starved, she was terrified and filthy. Tears had made white tracks down her dirty face. He still had no idea how he'd found her. Yet she could admire his car.

"It is. If I'm rescuing damsels in distress, I want to do it in style." However, there wasn't room for three passengers. Correction. There *had* to be room. "Get in."

"Who are you?" Her teeth were chattering despite the warmth of the day.

"It's a long story. It'll keep. Come on."

Somehow, and Dylan never knew how, the girls, amid much cursing from Sam, managed to pack themselves in the car.

He had two towels and an overcoat and he did his best to hide them.

They had to wait for over an hour for the ferry but when it finally moved out onto the open water, Sam burst into tears.

Dylan couldn't blame her.

He stood out on deck for the crossing, his back against the Morgan's passenger window to hide the bulk of his surprising cargo from prying eyes.

He sent a quick and urgent text message to Frank asking his friend to find out all he could about a bloke named Sullivan. As the ferry made its way slowly across Scapa Flow, Dylan sent Frank another message that he wanted translating into Hungarian and Romanian.

When the ferry berthed, Dylan didn't stop to think. He drove straight to Balfour Hospital, the only hospital in Orkney. It was small, not the sort of place you could get lost in, or more important, lose someone in, but it would have to suffice.

As he stopped the car, Frank's messages came through.

Dylan carefully wrote what he hoped was his message in Hungarian and then Romanian. It was supposed to say: *You can trust me. I want to help you. You must sit here until someone comes to take care of you.* He hoped it did.

He uncovered his passengers, all of whom seemed happy enough to remain hidden, and gestured for them to get out. They could hardly move, but they managed.

"Sam," he said, "I want you to stay in the car. I won't be more than a few minutes, but I'm going to lock you in, okay?"

She nodded, not, he suspected, because she trusted him but because she could think of no other option.

"Here." He took her locket from his pocket and handed it over.

"Where did you get that?" Her eyes were dark with suspicion.

"Outside the cottage. I've got to go, but I'll be back in a few minutes."

He urged the two girls toward the hospital's entrance. The older girl was studying the note he'd given her. She nodded, which was promising.

Once inside, he pointed to some chairs. The girl nodded again. Grabbing her young companion by the arm, she led her to the chairs where they both sat.

Dylan didn't want to abandon them, but he had little option. They would be safe here.

Satisfied that was the case, he walked out and back to his car. He drove about half a mile to a public phone box and called the local police. "There are two girls, Eastern Europeans, at Balfour Hospital. They need help."

"Who's calling?"

Dylan cut the connection and returned to his car.

It was time to check out of his hotel and smuggle Sam back into England. First, he needed to buy her some clothes and footwear.

Then he had to talk to Marion Roderick. He had a lot of questions for her, and he needed answers. Fast.

FORTY-ONE

TEARS stung Sam's eyes as Dylan Scott drove off the ferry and onto the Scottish mainland, but she wasn't about to let them fall. Ever since he'd found her, she'd been bawling her eyes out. He said it was shock, and he was probably right, but he must think her a complete moron.

He didn't seem to mind though, and he hadn't forced conversation yesterday. After calling at the ferry terminal and booking them on the next available sailing, he'd driven to his hotel and taken her to his room.

"We can't get out of here until the morning," he said, "so we'll spend the night here. Sorry, but I'm going to lock you in. Answer the door to no one. I mean it, Sam. No one. I'll be back as soon as I can. I'll get you some clothes and something to eat."

"What about those girls?" she'd asked.

"They'll be okay at the hospital. Someone will help them—the police and hospital staff. I couldn't take them to the police station. There would have been too many questions to answer. Now, remember, open the door to no one."

He'd been out for about an hour, but he'd returned with jeans and T-shirt which were about three sizes too big, a pair of trainers which were too tight, and best of all, fish and chips. The gesture had touched her and she'd eaten every hot, tasty morsel.

She'd then locked herself in the bathroom for a couple of hours until she'd felt clean for the first time in months.

All he'd told her was that he was a private investigator and that her father had employed him to look for her. He'd said nothing else. Probably because mention of her dad had had her blubbering like a baby.

She was better this morning though. She was going home. She still couldn't believe that. Too many days and nights had been spent believing she'd *never* go home.

Photo ID was required for all ferry passengers, so he'd kept her hidden until the car was actually on board.

"I think you'll be safe to come out now," he'd said.

She'd sat on a plastic seat on the upper deck as the ferry had taken them ever closer to the Scottish mainland.

It had taken an age to get off the ferry but, finally, they were on dry land. Sam could have wept.

He'd only driven a couple of miles from the ferry terminal before stopping to fill up with fuel. When that was done, he dangled the keys in front of her.

"Do you want to drive for a while?"

"Me?" The unexpected kindness had her blinking back fresh tears. "Well, yes, please. Are you insured for any driver?"

"Yes." He seemed to find the question amusing.

"For someone under twenty-five?"

"Come on, let's be reckless!"

It was ten months since she'd been behind the wheel and she'd never driven a Morgan. Never. Yesterday, she'd been chained like an animal, knowing someone wanted her dead. Today she was holding the keys to a 1956 Morgan.

Her heart was racing, her nerves were ragged, but she scrambled into the driver's seat and fired the engine. The Morgan purred with pleasure and she closed her eyes to thank God that, hopefully, her nightmare was over. Hopefully. She felt safer with Dylan Scott, but she wouldn't be able to relax until she was home.

She moved the car off the forecourt and drove.

The Morgan gobbled up the miles and her hands slowly released their tight grip on the steering wheel. The car was a joy to drive. It handled better than she'd expected and was more responsive too.

"The shocks need looking at," she said.

"Yeah? It's just as well I know the person to do it then."

She smiled at that and wondered if he'd known she'd needed to drive. It was impossible to tell because his expression was unfathomable. She detected anger. He wasn't angry with her, he was kindness itself, but there was a tightly controlled fury there.

Even the Morgan took four hours to reach Inverness. Sam didn't care. She simply followed the signs for the south, knowing that every mile took her closer to home.

They were almost at the border for England when he suggested they stop for a coffee and to stretch their legs.

The sun smiled down on them and they took coffee and blueberry muffins to a wooden table that nestled beneath an old tree. Sam kept expecting to see the towering figure of the Hulk, as she'd taken to calling her captor, but she liked the feeling of safety Dylan gave her. It was a feeling she hadn't known for a very long time.

"Are you up to talking?" He stirred sugar into his coffee.

"Yes." She'd expected him to wait until they were home. "And I'm sorry I've been so—you know. It was the shock."

"It's okay. How about you tell me what happened?"

"That's just it, I don't really know." She blew across the top of her coffee and inhaled deeply.

"From the beginning," he suggested. "One day you were working on cars, the next you'd vanished."

She nodded, but it seemed a lifetime ago. "One morning, and it was the same as any other morning, I had breakfast and then—I don't know."

"Do you remember leaving your father's house? Or walking across the field at the back of the house?"

"No. I remember having breakfast. After that, it's a blank."

"The police found a scarf that they thought belonged to you," he said. "It was in the field at the back of your father's house."

"Really?" It was strangely reassuring to know that

people had been looking for her. "I lost that the day before."

"Ah."

"What does that mean, 'Ah'?"

"Nothing, carry on. What else can you remember?"

"I had breakfast," she said, "and the next thing I knew, I was being bundled out of a van and into a house in Glasgow."

"Glasgow?"

"Yeah. I was locked in a room on the third floor of an old house. I only knew it was Glasgow because I recognised the bridge, the Clyde Arc. There was a programme on TV about it, and I remember someone saying that locals call it the Squinty Bridge because of the way it crosses the river at an angle."

She could tell Dylan had never heard of the bridge.

"How long were you in Glasgow?" he asked.

"About a month. At first, he was good to me—"

"Sullivan?"

"I never heard his name. He was a big bloke, very strong, and I used to think of him as the Hulk. Anyway, at first he looked after me quite well. I was a prisoner, yes, but I had my own bathroom. He even brought me some books. The food was crap, nothing hot, but he said I'd only be there for a couple of weeks at the most and then I'd go home."

Things hadn't been too bad. She'd believed she was being taught a lesson, thought someone wanted to make some money out of it. She'd known her dad would pay any ransom demand, and she'd thought it only a matter of time.

"A couple of weeks turned into a month," she said. "There must have been a mix-up with the ransom. I don't know."

"Ransom? You believe Sullivan—the Hulk—kidnapped you?"

"He must have, mustn't he?"

Dylan shrugged at that. "Carry on."

"He became more and more angry. After about six weeks, he dragged me out of that room, bundled me into the back of a horsebox and took me to Orkney. Except I didn't know it was Orkney until I heard him on the phone to someone. I was in a house by the sea."

"The one I found you in yesterday?"

"No. Something happened. We only arrived at that one the afternoon before you turned up."

"Where were you before then?"

"It was quite a modern place, but it had a hateful cellar that was wet and cold. Everything smelled damp. It was right on the shore. And on a different island. I'm fairly certain it was Westray." She only knew that because she'd seen an Ordnance Survey map of the island and there was a mark on it that she thought matched the sweep of the coastline she could see from one of the windows. "At first, I was locked in a room that had a view of the sea. On the rare occasions he had company, I was gagged, tied up and put in the cellar. After a couple of weeks though, I spent all my time in that cellar."

She could smell it now. The floor had been damp, soggy earth.

"Okay. So you were taken from your home and arrived in Glasgow. Had you been drugged? Knocked out? What?"

She wasn't sure. "You know that feeling you get when they give you anaesthetic in hospital? Like you have to tell them you're still wide awake and then you realise you're too weak to move or speak? It was like that. I suppose I was drugged." She bit into her muffin. "I woke up properly when he was getting me out of the van."

"And you never heard any names mentioned?"

"No. I heard nothing when I was in Glasgow. When I got to that cottage, the one that I think was on Westray, people sometimes visited. I heard them talking, but I couldn't make out the words. I never heard anyone use his name."

The fear refused to leave her, as did the smell of that cellar.

"Three days before you found me," she said, "something happened. I heard stuff and I know two things. One, it had something to do with Alan Roderick. He's my mum's husband. Sorry, you'll know that. And two—" this she hardly dared to believe "—he's dead. Alan Roderick is dead."

Dylan wasn't surprised by this news. "Yes. Murdered, to be precise. What made you think it was connected to him?"

"The other night, I heard him—the Hulk, as I called him—talking to someone. There was a huge panic on because someone was dead and they had to, and I quote, 'get the girls out.' I didn't know which girls he was talking about, whether I was one of them or not. I wasn't though, because he started talking about Glasgow. He said the filth—that's the police—would be crawling all over Glasgow." She stopped. "What's funny?"

"Nothing really. I used to be filth myself."

"You were a policeman?" He didn't look like one.

"Yes. I was booted off the force. Sorry, carry on."

"It was only later that I realised they were talking about Alan Roderick. They didn't mention him by name, but said he'd dropped the two girls off in Glasgow as arranged but had been murdered. They mentioned a lorry, then they mentioned Taylor's, where he worked. They said the filth would be crawling all over his lorry. I knew it was him."

She took a sip of coffee. "It was the same night they talked about me. Called me a liability and said I was surplus to requirements. He—the Hulk—well, the way he spoke, I think he was being paid to keep me. No, I don't think it, I'm sure of it."

"Ah." There was a wealth of understanding in that word. "Yes, you could be right."

"It was Alan, wasn't it? He was paying the Hulk to keep me out of the way. When they were talking about me, they said they hadn't bargained on keeping me for so long, that it hadn't been part of the deal, and that really, they could—" she swallowed hard "—dispose of me."

Dylan didn't comment, but she sensed the anger in him.

"The next day, the two foreign girls joined me in that bloody cellar. And then, the three of us were packed away in that horsebox and taken to that other place—where you found us."

A sparrow danced at her feet, looking for crumbs, and she broke a small piece of muffin and scattered crumbs for the bird.

"What happened to Alan Roderick?" she asked. "Who killed him?"

Dylan shrugged. "I don't know."

She had the feeling he was lying.

"Your boyfriend was arrested," he said, "but they let him go. Apparently, Jack was snooping around the house."

At mention of Jack's name a whole gamut of emotions caught her. He was still spoken of as her boyfriend. He was snooping round Alan's house so he must still care about her.

"Why was he arrested? And why was he snooping?"

Dylan made a steeple of his fingers and rested his chin on them. "I was hoping you could tell me."

"Me? I've no idea."

Three teenagers sat at a nearby table, but Dylan paid them no heed. "Why did you think Alan Roderick was involved? Was it something to do with the message you left on Jack's answer machine? Do you remember leaving a message?"

She remembered the message. "I'd been trying to find out if James Carlton—he's my boss, *was* my boss—was fiddling the books. He wasn't. At least, I don't think he was. But when I phoned Jack, I'd just walked Lydia and Emma home from school."

The thought of Alan Roderick still sickened her. She was glad he was dead. Glad that he'd never touch those girls, or any other girls again.

"It was something Lydia said," she said. "I think—no, I'm sure of it. He was abusing my sisters. Sexually."

She saw Dylan wince.

"I didn't know what to do," she said. "I had to leave the girls with him and Mum on the Thursday. I had no choice. But it was okay because I knew they'd be safe while Mum was there. I didn't know what to do, who to talk to. I couldn't keep it to myself though."

"You confronted Alan Roderick?" Dylan was frowning as if he didn't understand.

"Not exactly. He knew when I dropped the girls off at the house that I was as angry as fuck with him. He raced after me when I left the house, but I kept running. I couldn't bear to even look at him let alone talk to him."

He was dead, she reminded herself. He'd never hurt Lydia and Emma again.

"Later, though—well, I had to tell him what I knew. I phoned him that night on his mobile. He was at a club, Indie Street. I said I was going to the police in the morning. I told him what Lydia had said and he just laughed at me. He said I knew nothing. I did, though, didn't I? It's obvious. The next day, I was—kidnapped."

"Hmm."

"What's that supposed to mean?"

"I don't know." He gave her that half-smile of his.

She'd pushed her muffin aside but, damn it, she wasn't letting a pervert like Alan Roderick spoil her enjoyment of the first muffin she'd eaten for ages. "Well, I'm glad he's dead. What Mum ever saw in him, I don't know."

"Was he—? I mean, did he ever try anything on with you?"

"What? Oh, my fucking—no!"

"I just wondered if that was why you went to live with your father."

"No. God, if that bastard had laid a finger on me, or tried to, I would have killed him." She washed the thought away with the last of her coffee. "No, I didn't like living in the same house as him because he's a— was a pain in the arse. But it was Mum and me really. We seemed to be fighting day in, day out. I was four-teen and thought I should be able to do as I liked. All the other girls were seeing boys and going to dances. She thought I was too young. I left because I thought Dad would give me more freedom." She wasn't sure he had though. In a different way, his fussing had been worse. "Is Mum all right?"

"She's fine. She has a flat in town and they're stay-ing there at the moment. But yes, they're all fine."

She'd missed her mother desperately, more than she would have believed. They'd spent so much time ar-guing but Sam would have given anything to be able to spar with her, to fight and make up.

She knew the flat. It was small, pokey. She couldn't imagine them living in it.

"How did you know where I was?" she asked.

"I didn't." He spoke calmly, but his lips were a thin, angry line. "I met someone who recognised my photo of Alan Roderick. He told me he'd seen him with a man called Sullivan, a man who owned properties on Westray and Hoy, and who towed a horsebox. If I hadn't met that man, I would have been back in England on Wednesday."

She shuddered. "But how did you find us at the cottage?"

"I was looking for horseboxes, and having no luck, so I walked up to see the Old Man of Hoy. I got lost. I was hoping someone at the cottage could put me back on the right track. But then I spotted the horsebox. I was having a good look round when I found your locket. I recognised it from your photos. It was then that I knew I should break into the cottage."

The muffin turned to dust in her mouth. "So if you *hadn't* got lost—"

"Quite."

She would still be there. Or she would have been pushed over the cliffs. It was impossible to say what would have happened, but she suspected that she and the two foreign girls had been destined to meet their end at those tall cliffs.

"It's over now," he said, and he smiled.

"Yeah. I kept hoping the police would find me or—"

"They would have. Eventually."

She didn't believe him. "How's my dad?"

"He's okay." Another smile that was meant to re-assure. "And Rusty."

Rusty was waiting for her. It was thinking of him and imagining burying her face against his warm body that had kept her sane.

"And Jack?" She'd tried not to think about Jack and she refused to think of the baby she'd lost—

"He's okay too. He's been arrested more times than I've had clean shirts but, yes, he's good."

"What else has he been arrested for?" Another question she didn't like to ask.

"When you vanished. Apparently the neighbours heard you fighting."

"Oh, for—"

"And then when Alan Roderick was murdered."

"But they know he's innocent now, don't they?"

"Yes. Yes, he's fine."

"Is he—I mean, do you know if he's got a girlfriend or—"

Dylan smiled at that. "You'll get a warm welcome from Jack."

She felt herself sag with relief. Alan was dead and everyone else was waiting for her.

"With this hair?" She had to joke to hide the lump that had jammed in her throat.

"With any hair."

"It'll grow." That bastard had shaved it off and dyed it. Why he'd done that she had no idea. It wasn't as if she ever saw anyone.

"Of course it will." He drained his coffee cup. "He said—Jack said you were pregnant. Is that true? Was it a false alarm?"

"I don't know." She put up a hand to prevent him

from saying anything else. "And I don't want to talk about it."

"Okay." He stood up. "Come on, let's hit the road. Are you driving or am I?"

She grinned. "I'll fight you for the keys."

FORTY-TWO

SAM HUNT was a pretty amazing young woman. Given all she'd been through, Dylan thought her incredibly brave.

She was a damn good driver too. She drove like someone who knew how precious the Morgan was, how the gear lever should be coaxed into action, how the engine revs should be made to purr like a satisfied tiger.

Bev—Dylan offered up a silent apology, but Bev forced her car into gear and braked or accelerated too fast for comfort. That was when she wasn't checking her hair in the rearview mirror, applying makeup or fumbling for a toffee.

"God, it's been forever since I drove a car." Sam was keeping the Morgan to a steady seventy miles per hour. "I've got a Porsche, you know." That familiar frown marred her features. "At least, I *had* a Porsche."

"It's in your father's garage."

She smiled at that and put a little more pressure on the accelerator.

She was more relaxed—until they drew level with the sign for Dawson's Clough. Two tears ran down her face and she brushed them away with an impatient hand.

"Take a left here," he said.

"But it's straight on for Dad's."

"We're going to your mother's." He would stand for no argument on that score.

"Can't we see Dad first? All Mum will do is tell me my hair looks a mess."

"Then she'll be right, won't she?"

A reluctant laugh sprang from her lips.

"Your mother loves you very much," he said.

"If you say so. And then we'll go to Dad's?"

"Just watch the paintwork."

When they arrived at Marion Roderick's, she'd just got home and answered the door while taking off her jacket.

"Dylan, hi. I've—" Her gaze travelled past him to Sam and she gave a tight little cry. She stepped forward, touched Sam's arm as if she didn't trust her own sight, and then almost squeezed the breath from the poor girl. "Oh, my God. Sam!"

Dylan managed to usher them inside, away from the neighbours' line of sight, but they didn't let each other go. They simply stood in the hallway, arms clinging, tears racing down their faces, sobs racking their bodies.

"I thought I'd never see you again!" Marion crushed Sam's body.

"So did I." Sam tried to dry her eyes but fresh tears fell and Marion had to wipe them away.

"What have you done to your hair?" Marion asked, and Sam half laughed and half choked.

"What did I tell you, Dylan?"

Marion couldn't take her eyes off her daughter. "What happened, Sam? Why did you go? Where have you been?" She lifted her daughter's chin. "Why didn't you call me? Just to let me know you were safe? And Dylan said—thought—you might have been pregnant?"

Sam grasped her mother's hand and led her into the small sitting room. "I don't know if I was pregnant, or if the test gave me the wrong result. Two weeks after—after I took the test, I started bleeding heavily. I think I might have lost it. My periods have been like clockwork since." She drew in a shaky breath. "I don't know, but I must have lost it, mustn't I? Anyway, I don't want to talk about it yet."

"But surely you've seen a doctor? Sam, you have, haven't you? My God, what's been happening? Where have you been…?"

Dylan could allow them a little privacy. He owed them that much before he shattered their newfound happiness.

He crossed to the kitchen where a bottle of whisky sat invitingly on the counter. He felt sure Marion wouldn't mind if he helped himself. Unable to find a glass, he poured a good measure into a blue and white mug and took a swig.

Sam's sisters arrived and yet more mayhem followed.

Dylan poured himself another drink and sipped it slowly while listening to the noise coming from the adjoining room.

Marion came into the kitchen, reached for his hand

and squeezed it. "Thank you. I can't make sense of anything, but Sam's back with us. Nothing else matters, does it? She's trying to persuade Lydia and Emma to go and play outside. Then we'll be able to talk. Dylan, I really can't thank you enough."

"I did nothing." He could put it off no longer. "Will you do something for me? Call Rob and ask him to come over? Don't mention Sam."

Her smile was bright with tears. "It'll be such a surprise for him."

"It certainly will."

Her call was quick and to the point, but she failed to keep the excitement from her voice. Dylan wondered if Hunt suspected anything.

When she ended the call, Marion drummed long, slender fingers on the worktop. "You probably haven't heard about Alan. The police took away his computer and found some—" She broke off, unable to continue for a moment. "Images of children," she managed at last.

"Oh, Marion." Dylan hated the loss of anyone's life but, in Alan Roderick's case, he was prepared to make an exception. "I think Sam knew—" He stopped. How could he tell Marion that her own children may have suffered at his hands?

She tugged on his arm. "Sam knew? About Lydia and Emma?"

"Oh, God." Everything dropped into place. "So did you, didn't you?"

She looked away.

"Marion? You knew, didn't you? That's why you did what you did."

She dropped his hand and walked to stare out the window. "I came out of the library one night and some—thug threatened me at knifepoint. He wanted money. Said Alan owed him money. A thousand pounds. Alan paid—or rather he didn't pay—that man to frighten you off. Do you know where Alan's money came from? Selling those images. Probably worse."

There was no probably about it. Add smuggling in young girls from Eastern Europe for the sex trade among other things.

"I suppose he thought that, while you were looking for Sam," she said, "you'd find out what he was up to. I don't know. Anyway, he—this thug said I had to get the money and meet him the following night. I planned to confront Alan. I wanted to know exactly why he didn't want you looking into Sam's disappearance. I—" She was shaking, and her teeth were chattering. Dylan struggled to catch her words. "I went home unexpectedly and—and found Alan with Lydia."

She spun round, her face frighteningly pale. "So, yes, that's why I did what I did. And I'll tell you something else. I'd do it again if I had to."

"I'm so sorry." Dylan wished the words didn't sound so inadequate.

"You were cheap, Dylan." Marion couldn't seem to stop talking. "It was a thousand pounds to rough you up a bit but, if you took no notice, it was going to cost a lot more."

"So you paid him off? And then paid him to visit your home while you and the children were at the swimming pool?"

She nodded, her gaze on her feet. "I paid him. He paid someone else."

She lifted her face, but her eyes didn't meet his. She examined her shaking hands. "What will you do about it, Dylan?"

A few years ago, he would have known exactly what to do. That was before he'd lost all faith in the country's judicial system. What would be achieved by seeing Marion behind bars?

"What *can* I do?" he asked. "You were at the swimming pool, remember?"

She threw her arms around his waist and squeezed him. "Thank you."

Before he could comment, the doorbell rang.

How Dylan wished there was an easier way of doing this.

FORTY-THREE

Hunt had obviously dressed up and splashed on some cologne, presumably for Marion's benefit.

"Marion, sweetheart, this is—" He broke off as he spotted Dylan and didn't even try to hide his disappointment. "Oh, good to see you, Dylan. I didn't realise you were here."

"I've come to give you my final account."

The sound of her father's voice brought Sam dashing through from the bedroom. She stopped short and every last vestige of colour drained from Hunt's face. Dylan half-expected him to keel over.

"Dad!" Sam ran forward, hesitated for a fraction of a second, probably because his shocked reaction made her uncertain, then wrapped her arms tight around him. "I knew you'd keep looking for me. I knew you'd never give up."

Hunt, unsurprisingly, was incapable of speech.

In the end, it was Marion who gave a high-pitched, false laugh. "You could say something, Rob."

Hunt, it seemed, couldn't.

"Dylan's found Sam," Marion said. "Say something, for God's sake."

"The thing is, Marion—" Dylan *really* wished

there was an easier way to say this. "I didn't find her. Sam was never lost."

Sam lifted her head. "What are you talking about?"

This would break her heart, but she had to know the truth.

"One phone call from your father, Sam, and you could have been home."

"What?" Marion's voice was spiked with icy shock.

Two pairs of eyes looked at Dylan as if he'd suddenly become fluent in Arabic. The other pair, Hunt's, were the eyes of a dead man.

"I thought it odd, Rob," Dylan said, "that you'd employed me when you sounded sure I wouldn't find her. I know you employed me on Marion's suggestion, at her insistence even, but your lack of faith—especially considering the money you were paying me—seemed very strange."

"What are you talking about?" Sam asked again.

"When I phoned you yesterday, Marion," Dylan said, "I asked you about a man called Sullivan. You said you knew of a Matthew Sullivan, and that he was a friend of Alan's."

"Yes." She dragged the word out.

"No," Hunt cried.

"You also told me that Rob couldn't possibly have known him." He switched his attention to Hunt. "You never knew that, did you, Rob? You had no idea that you and Alan shared a mutual friend."

"It's not true!"

"I asked Frank—ex-D.C.I. Willoughby—to check out Sullivan." Dylan wasn't giving Hunt a chance to speak. "He still has friends on the force, thank God, and they checked army records. The police can be very efficient, you know. You and Sullivan—or should I say Mattie?—go back a long way, don't you?"

"What are you talking about?" Sam stepped away from her father and shook an accusing finger at Dylan.

Instead of answering her, Dylan kept his attention on Hunt. "When did you meet up with Mattie again, Rob? That's his name, isn't it? Matthew Sullivan?"

"He—he was in Dawson's Clough on business. But—"

"Business with Alan Roderick."

"No!" Hunt's denial came with all the force of a bullet.

"Yes. You didn't know that? You didn't know they were—"

"You're lying!"

"I'm sorry, Sam, but I'm afraid I'm not. Your father's ex-army pal owns a property in Glasgow and two on remote islands in Orkney. Your father had you taken away—"

"What?" Marion reeled back as if her ex-husband was a ticking bomb.

"Yes." Dylan was struggling to keep the fury from his voice. "It was those postcards, Rob. I saw two from Scrabster and I was told they arrived regularly. I also knew Alan drove his lorry up there. I thought there must be a connection between the two of you, that you were involved in something together, but I was damned if I could figure out what. As soon as I found Sam in Orkney, I knew you were behind it. The postcards—one thanking you for the gift."

Hunt gripped the back of a chair as if his life depended on it.

"Rob, no." Marion's voice was a whisper. She tugged on Hunt's arm. "Please tell me this isn't true."

"And then," Dylan said, "when Sam told me about the panic caused by Roderick's murder, and how a couple of foreign girls had arrived—"

"Rob?" Marion's hand continued to tug on her ex-husband's arm.

"Roderick's job, as far as I can gather, was to smuggle young girls in from Hungary or Romania," Dylan said. "They ended up at a sex business in Glasgow. Sullivan ran the place. From a safe distance, of course."

"No," Hunt said, shaking his head.

If Dylan hadn't been so angry, so furiously angry, he would have laughed. The irony of Hunt sharing an acquaintance with Alan Roderick, a man he'd always hated with a passion, amused him.

"No doubt you paid your chum Mattie handsomely for keeping your daughter," Dylan said.

"She had to be hidden—the police, you know—but I had to make sure she was well cared for, didn't I?"

Dylan couldn't stand the whining sound of Hunt's voice. "Well cared for? She was chained like a wild animal."

"No. Sam, tell him. It wasn't like that, was it, sweetheart?"

"You?" Sam pummelled her father's chest as she

screamed at him. "It was you? You paid him to keep me there? He was going to have me killed. He said I could be disposed of and he'd still get the money. He said he hadn't expected to have to keep me for so long."

"No, Sam!"

"Yes!" She screamed the word at him.

"Rob, why?" Marion was disbelieving. Appalled.

"I did it for you, Marion. For us. For all of us." Hunt's voice was pleading now. Sickening. "I thought you'd come back to me. It was going to bring us together again."

"What?" Dylan was possibly more shocked than anyone.

Fool that he was, he hadn't considered that as a possibility. Truth be told, he'd had no idea *why* Hunt wanted Sam out of the way, but he'd assumed it had been to keep her away from Jack Fleming.

But no. Hunt had done this terrible thing believing it would win back his wife.

"Oh, Christ!" The Partridges' marriage had been glued back together when their daughter, Fiona, was lost to them. Dylan had seen the reports in the local paper, had seen the photos of the reunited parents holding hands and describing how the ordeal had brought them back together. He should have known.

No, he shouldn't. Who but a madman would do such a wicked thing?

"It wasn't meant to go on for so long." Hunt's voice broke on a sob. "A month, that's all. But you wouldn't listen, Marion. You wouldn't come home." He grabbed Marion's hands in his. "I did it for you, sweetheart."

"Dear God." There was no colour in Marion's face. "You kept suggesting we go to Barcelona to look for her. You even said we should visit London and Paris—and all the while, you could have brought her home."

"You total bastard," Sam said. "You're mad, you know that, don't you? Stark, staring, fucking mad."

Marion freed herself from his grip and pulled Sam into her arms.

Hunt dropped to his knees, his hands covering his face, and cried like a baby.

"You selfish, thoughtless, lying—" Dylan hauled him to his feet and pushed him up against the wall. "You robbed Sam of ten months of her life. You put your own daughter's life in danger."

Before he did something he might regret, Dylan let him go. Hunt dropped to the floor like a sack of flour.

"I'm out of here." Dylan needed to get away from the madness that was Hunt. "I have a lot of explaining to do to the men in blue. I need to make a statement—tell them why I abandoned two foreigners in a hospital and how I needed to get Sam back home for her own safety."

Dylan walked out of the flat and hoped he never had to see Rob Hunt again.

FORTY-FOUR

DYLAN had been staring at the rolling departures board for half an hour. It didn't change. Their plane was still showing as delayed by two hours.

Across the hall, his mother and his son were standing in the shop doorway, amusing themselves by trying on hats.

Dylan wished he could amuse himself, but he hated airports at the best of times. He loathed them when long delays were involved.

"I won't understand you if I live to be a hundred," Bev said.

"Sorry? How do you mean?"

"Alan Roderick." She sipped at the coffee they'd bought to pass some time. "If there's a mystery, you have to worry away at it until you learn the truth. Yet Roderick is murdered and the not knowing who did it doesn't seem to bother you at all."

"Any one of a hundred people could be responsible." He trusted Bev, knew she wouldn't say a word to anyone, but there were times when things were best left alone. There was no point telling her all he knew about Roderick's killer. "He's no loss to the world. If he hadn't been killed, the good old British taxpayer would be spending a fortune to keep him locked up for years."

"Hmm. It's still unlike you." She shuddered. "Just imagine being married to a man like that. It makes my skin crawl."

"As I said, he's no loss to the world."

There were no excuses for a man like Roderick. By all accounts, he'd come from a good family. His father was a teacher, his mother a nurse. He was an only child, and reports said he was a lonely child. That was no excuse though.

He'd played truant when a schoolboy, then joined the army where he'd been involved in every scam going. He'd been attracted to drugs—and young children. From abusing children, he'd progressed to selling indecent images. That had led to a meeting with Mattie Sullivan and, between them, they'd worked out a way to bring in young girls from Romania. Sullivan had soon employed others.

Thankfully, the police had arrested Sullivan and he was now in custody where he belonged. A man by the name of George Cottle, who'd been living in Romania for almost ten years, had also been arrested. It was he who found the young girls and promised them riches aplenty in Britain before seeing them loaded onto Roderick's lorry.

"The man who was running the brothels," Bev said. "Sullivan. How did he meet up with Rob Hunt?"

"They were old army acquaintances, but hadn't kept in touch. It was a chance meeting when Sullivan was in Dawson's Clough to see Alan Roderick. Hunt had read in the local newspapers about the young girl, Fiona Partridge, who'd gone missing and how it had brought her parents together. Over a drink, he mentioned it to Sullivan. Of course, Sullivan saw a means of making a lot of money and he came up with the idea of keeping Sam hidden for a while, just until Marion came to her senses and returned to Hunt. At least, that's what Hunt is claiming."

"What will happen to him?"

"Hunt? I don't know. He's seeing a psychiatrist at the moment."

"That poor kid."

Dylan smiled at that. "Sam will be fine."

She'd phoned Dylan last week to tell him two things. One, she and Jack were engaged and he was to expect a wedding invitation. Two, she had somehow, and Dylan still couldn't imagine how, managed to get her old job back.

"I begged, pleaded and grovelled," she'd told him. "Oh, and I'd pinched a couple of his files so I returned those and promised never, ever to suspect him of wrongdoing again."

"And he gave you your job back?" Dylan had asked in amazement.

"Eventually, yeah. I can be quite charming when I try, you know."

Dylan could believe that, but he was still amazed that James Carlton was allowing her back. He wasn't convinced that Carlton was as innocent as he claimed, but there was no proof of any shady deals or dodgy insurance claims. It wasn't his problem. If Carlton was guilty of anything, Sam would soon be on his case. The knowledge made him smile.

"And he's as mad as hell at you," Sam had said. "Fancy telling him you were a TV producer, Dylan. How crap is that? Still, he fell for it. He's really pissed off to learn that he won't be on the telly after all…"

Dylan looked up at the departures board. Their plane was still listed as delayed. Almost every other plane flying out of Heathrow was on schedule. It had to be an omen.

"Poor Sam never left home that day," Bev murmured. "Fancy her own father telling everyone that she'd left the house and vanished." She frowned. "Who drugged her? Her dad or someone else?"

"According to Hunt, it was Sullivan. He did the deed, put her in his van and carried her off to Glasgow."

"You did well, Dylan. I'm so proud of you."

"I got lucky."

If it wasn't for a poor sense of direction, if he hadn't got himself lost and ended up at that cottage, if he hadn't seen the horsebox and, more important, found that locket—

He'd got lucky. If he hadn't, Sam would still be there. Or she would be dead.

He didn't want to think about it.

But all's well that ends well, he reminded himself. Sam was back where she belonged and Dylan had been paid in full. It was lucky he'd insisted on a large payment in advance followed by weekly instalments. As he hadn't liked to present a bill to a man he'd found guilty, he'd been prepared to write off the relatively small amount he was still owed. Marion, however, had insisted on seeing and paying his final account.

"Anyway," he said, "you can talk. I can't understand you either. Why have you turned down that job offer?"

He'd seen how excited Bev was about it. She'd accepted their offer and he'd been pleased for her. True, he hadn't known what the hell they were going to do when she was working in Blackburn, but he'd been fairly pleased for her. Then, on a whim, she'd told them she had to turn it down.

"We could have worked something out," he said. "You could have stayed in Blackburn during the week or something, just until we sorted things out."

That's what they were supposed to be doing, sorting things out. She'd decided that, so long as they didn't kill each other on this holiday—and Dylan thought it far more likely this holiday would kill them—then they would get back together and concentrate on being a family again.

"The job wasn't for me." She was looking everywhere but at Dylan.

"You said it was made for you. It was a head's job—everything you wanted."

"Yes, but—" She broke off.

"But what?"

All around them, people rushed to catch their planes. The lucky devils were heading for Spain, Italy, Portugal, New York and every other destination known to man. Except one.

"Bev? But what?"

"Something came up," she said.

"Like what?"

"I'll tell you after the holiday."

"What? Oh, no, you won't. I'll spend the entire time worrying."

She shrugged at that, but she looked nervous. Very nervous.

"Should I worry?" he asked.

Her expression was a mixture of *yes* and *maybe,* and his imagination surged into overdrive.

"Tell me," he said. "Seriously, Bev. Me worrying to death while riding a sodding camel will not be a pretty sight."

She tried to smile at that.

"Well?" His imagination had already taken him to every oncology centre in the country and robbed Luke of his mother.

She took a deep breath and leaned back from him. "I'm pregnant."

Those words went round and round Dylan's brain but still didn't make sense. "What?"

"You're going to be a father. That night you stayed—remember? I was drunk—remember?"

"Hey, Dad, look what I've got."

Feeling as if he'd gone ten rounds with Mike Tyson, Dylan turned to see a shiny mobile phone case Luke was holding.

"Very nice. Yes, that's great, Luke."

"Bev, they've got that perfume you like."

Dylan watched as Bev, eager to escape, followed his mother and Luke back to the shop.

He sat at their table while, all around him, people bought drinks and magazines, checked their watches, stared at the departures boards.

Pregnant.

Luke was eleven. They'd tried for another child for years, had both endured dozens of tests and examinations, and had been told that it was very unlikely Bev would conceive again. They'd accepted it. Not happily, but they'd accepted it. That was years ago. Luke was eleven for God's sake.

Announcements telling people not to smoke and reminding them to keep hand luggage with them at all times drifted over the PA system.

He finished his coffee and looked toward the shop. Bev was standing there watching him. She was chewing her bottom lip. He recognised that expression. It was the same one she'd worn when she'd had to explain how she'd driven her car into the back of his Morgan.

The memory made him smile and, spotting it, her shoulders sagged with relief.

He wandered over to her.

"Does she know?" he asked, nodding to the back of his shop where his mother and Luke were inspecting scarves.

"No. It's just me, you and the doctor who thought he was doing a routine test for diabetes. It's a bit of a shock, isn't it?" She grimaced at the understatement.

"Just a bit."

"What will we do, Dylan?"

"Oh, from memory, I expect we'll go without sleep and wander around like zombies in a house that smells of baby sick for a couple of years."

"Yeah." Her smile was dreamy, as if he'd just promised her the sun, the moon and the stars. "We'll get by, won't we?"

"Of course we will. So long as we survive those sodding camels."

* * * * *

REQUEST YOUR FREE BOOKS!

2 FREE NOVELS
PLUS 2 FREE GIFTS!

MYSTERY **W🌐RLDWIDE LIBRARY** ®
™

Your Partner in Crime